THE PROPOSITION

Fifteen thousand dollars. Carolyn dropped into a nearby chair. Michael had charmed her family, turned the tables on her so-called rules, and the point he was trying to make was crystal clear: she was not above being bought for fifteen thousand dollars. And he was right. It was she, Carolyn, who would be seen as the petty one if she didn't agree to a date with this bodacious, rich jock, all for the sake of charity.

Alli came to stand over her sister. "It's not that you don't want to go out with Michael. I think you're scared." She stepped back and crossed her arms. "Look at her, Steph. I think he handled that brain of hers without much effort, and she's scared that he might be every bit as smart as she is."

Stephanie sat behind the desk and twirled the check between her fingers. "Yeah, you have to admit, Alli, our sister's a snob who doesn't think a guy who plays football is good enough for her."

"That is not true." Carolyn sat up, knowing they were baiting her but shamed by the realization that they might not be totally wrong.

"All right. When you have dinner at his table tonight, prove it," Alli said. "Be civil to him."

"And when he brings up the date," Stephanie added, "go for it."

Carolyn had known what was coming. Her gaze flew from one sister to the other, and from the look in their eyes, there was no way out of this predicament.

Others books by Shirley Harrison

PICTURE PERFECT
UNDER A BLUE MOON
DANGEROUS FORTUNE

Published by BET/Arabesque Books

THE
PROPOSITION

Shirley Harrison

BET Publications LLC
http://www.bet.com
http://www.arabesquebooks.com

To my mother, Minnie Reeves

ACKNOWLEDGMENTS

Thank you to my sister, Sharon, for sharing with me an incident that happened to her during Super Bowl week. It seems that while she was banking she had an interesting encounter with a professional athlete. As we laughed about his proposal, little did she suspect that it would become the basis for this novel.

And here, Sharon, is the rest of the story. . . .

Prologue

It was a gray, bleak Atlanta landscape that met Carolyn Hardy's unhappy squint as she departed the warmth of her car to enter the cruel January cold.

The huge sign, which overlooked the contemporary bank building and adjoining parking lot, not only proclaimed the date and hour, but confirmed what Carolyn's shiver was already telling her—that the noonday temperature continued to hover below freezing for the third consecutive day. And despite the bank's maintenance staff's best efforts to clear up the remains of the unexpected snow from days before, pockets of ice continued to cling to the ground.

Carolyn pulled her coat tight against the freezing breeze, her cheeks and ungloved hands smarting at the slap of the crackling air. Clad in unrelieved layers of black, from her slacks and sweater to her leather swing coat, she cautiously treaded between the piles of slush and ice, the toes of her sleek boots carefully testing the path that led to the safety of the bank's front door.

Lunchtime banking was not Carolyn's favorite activity, especially when it occurred a few days before a big sports weekend with the city overrun with out-of-town visitors, and when she had too many transactions for drive-through convenience. To make matters worse, she had to return to her client's project site within the hour and review an engineering glitch. That meant she'd be having lunch with dinner once again. As her hand found its way into her coat pocket, she felt her trusty cell phone, never far away, nestled there.

The guard at the door tipped his hat while he held the door open for her. She rushed through, nodding an acknowledgement as she surveyed the room, pleased that it wasn't as crowded as she had expected. Why, she could even fill out her deposit slips beforehand, she thought sarcastically, as she headed for the nearest counter.

The inquisitive glances thrown her way by the other bank patrons went unnoticed by Carolyn, as did a lot of things that occurred around her. She was generally single-minded when it came to tasks and went about each one with the same intensity. So when the doors behind her swung open again, she didn't look up from her writing to notice the tall, physically powerful man who entered. Nor did she notice that the branch manager, who had been standing outside a glassed office, now hurried to greet this new customer who was quickly capturing the curiosity of patrons and employees, alike.

Michael Hennessey let the doors swing closed behind him as his gaze darted around the room to chase the source of his lusty interest. Minutes earlier, as he'd parked his car, Michael had been intrigued by what he could only describe as a thing of beauty as she floated on long legs across the icy parking lot. He had watched as she'd come in here, his own destination; but where was she now?

As he stood there, Michael accepted the disbelieving stares, and then the momentary blank looks of the scattered bank patrons before their telling grins signaled that recognition had set in. In fact, he was quite used to being gawked at—it came with fame and fortune.

The dark-suited man in the crisp white shirt who hurried toward Michael was most likely a bank manager. Michael smiled because he was used to this drill, too. The fawning manager, realizing that Michael was the wealthy customer referred by the Ritz-Carlton's concierge, would do his job well.

Michael stepped farther into the bank and scanned the room again, but this time he applied more scrutiny, his raised hand effectively stalling the anxious manager's welcome speech. It was a given that all eyes in the bank had been refocused on Michael . . . with the pointed exception being the interesting pair that belonged to the woman writing at the counter across the room and straight ahead.

Michael's heart leapt as he took a deep breath. It was her, all right. He would recognize her healthy limbs anywhere. Michael cocked his thick brows as he leisurely appraised the woman bent over the table, her hip jutting out saucily, totally unaware of his stare. Smelling a victory, he smiled and tossed his keys in the air, catching them up as confidently as if they were a football, and strode toward her in his own inimitable and assured strut. She glanced up for a second, only to return to her task, unconcerned and seemingly unaffected.

That was not the case for Michael. She was absolutely the most beautiful thing he had ever set his eyes on, and he had to have her. So what if she hadn't recognized him, was Michael's slightly disappointed thought; but now, closer to her, it was clear that his first impression of her had been right on the mark.

She didn't display the flashy kind of video beauty that was at his beck and call twenty-four/seven. From what he could tell, hers was more subdued . . . natural, he decided. Clear brown eyes, flawless skin—he didn't think she wore much more than lipstick—and classily dressed, from head to foot, in black. Nothing shabby about her . . . she looked sharply professional, right down to her square leather bag resting on the counter. *Damn, heart, be still.*

As he closed in on her, she shifted against the table.

Her coat—the belt trailed innocently from its loop to the floor—was draped open just enough to reveal long legs encased in more black. Damn. Michael experienced a rush from the onset of his lust, and drew in a hard breath, letting it out with an audible sigh. She was sexy to a fault, and he had to have her. He would meet her, get her name, number . . . whatever. If she turned out to be half as good as she looked, he wouldn't ever let her get away.

He reached the counter just as the object of his desire replaced the chained courtesy pen in its holder.

While Carolyn looked over her deposit slips one last time for good measure, she absently returned the pen to its slot before she spun about to get in the teller line. Suddenly something appeared directly in front of her. She tried pulling up, but tripped on her coat belt instead, and stumbled head first into what she now knew was some taller person's chest. Her deposit slips and papers slipped from her fingers to the floor.

Before she knew it, big hands reached inside her coat and caught her by the waist to keep her balanced.

"Excuse me." Carolyn managed to mutter the words as she backed away from the solid male wall. She looked up into a broad smile framed within a ruggedly handsome face. Her breath caught in her throat as she tried to take this big man in with one sweeping glance—his turtleneck sweater swathed an enormous neck and chest before it tapered to disappear inside a trim waistline—while he stooped to pick up her bank papers. Carolyn absently tucked her hair behind her ear as she, literally, tried to find her breath again.

"You dropped these." His deep voice was like pleasant thunder as he raised himself to his full height again.

How nice of him. Carolyn sighed the pleasant thought and looked straight up into his face to tell him so, only to find his eyes resting on her chest in a frank assessment. Carolyn could now see the large diamond stud that sparkled from his earlobe and frowned as she realized the dream man of thirty seconds ago was only an overgrown schoolboy with rampant testosterone.

She snatched her papers from his fingers amid the snickering that could be heard from the other bank patrons.

"Thank you," she said icily, and quickly moved around him to enter the teller line, expecting him to follow and try some lame line to get her name and number. But surprisingly, he remained where he stood, and simply winked when she darted a glance his way. He turned to join a man who waited nearby, who ushered him into an office.

"Humph," Carolyn snorted aloud. What was that about, she wondered? She looked toward the office the stranger had entered, and was embarrassed when her eyes locked with his. Mortified, she jerked her head back around and stared straight ahead.

"Honey, I think he's sweet on you."

Carolyn turned to the low voice at her shoulder and saw an older white-haired woman. "Pardon?"

"That young man with you at the counter. Don't you know who he is?"

At Carolyn's blank stare, the older woman filled her in. "That's Michael Hennessey, the football player."

When Carolyn frowned, the woman added, "He's the one in those TV commercials for that sports drink." The woman glanced toward the office where the subject of their discussion could be seen through the glass wall as he talked with the bank manager. "You know, he's probably in town for the Super Bowl weekend. And lucky you," she giggled, "he's single."

Carolyn swallowed her rising disdain as she thanked the woman for the unsolicited information. Suffering the curious glances of a few, she turned back to her place in line, thinking she had been right after all. The man was an overgrown jock. Carolyn inched forward with the line and glanced at her watch with an impatient sigh. In ten minutes, however, the incident was forgotten as she reached the teller window and completed her banking.

As Carolyn pushed through the bank doors and bravely faced the blast of cold air, her thoughts returned to the client's project site. At the same time, the cell phone in her pocket sounded its familiar tone. She fished it from her pocket, noted the caller at a glance, and switched into her problem-solving mode.

But no sooner had she taken a few cautious steps across the icy ground than she realized someone had taken up stride alongside her.

"Well, what do you know," a familiar deep voice said. "The beautiful lady in black."

It was the man with the roving eyes from inside the bank.

"I promise I'll be there in fifteen minutes," she said into the phone. "Just sit tight." Carolyn gave Michael a sidelong glance before she stuck the cell phone into her coat pocket, disconcerted by the unusual race of her pulse. "Did you find more of my papers on the floor?"

"Nothing like that. I just wanted to see you, that's all. Maybe enjoy a little conversation—over dinner?"

"We met inside, and you didn't seem to want to talk there." She darted a frown his way. "What you did mostly was stare at my chest."

The tall man chuckled lightly, but persisted. "What can I say. You're a beautiful woman. Maybe I could still have that conversation over dinner . . . say, tonight?"

Both his proximity and his words kept Carolyn's pulse pumping, the frosty air barely noticeable this time around. "Are you trying to pick me up in the bank parking lot?"

"I'm doing my best," he said, laughing. "By the way, I'm Michael Hennessey. I'm a visitor for the rest of the week."

Carolyn fought his charm. After all, athletes weren't her style. They were too earthy, with too few inhibitions. And this one was too self-assured by a mile. Seeing her car just ahead, she closed her fingers around the key ring in her pocket and pointed the remote signal to release the door locks.

"Aren't you going to ask if I'm really Michael Hennessey?"

"You don't know who you are?" she asked good-naturedly.

"What I meant was . . ." His chuckle was a deep rumble as he realized she was making fun of him. "Okay, so you aren't into sports; I can live with that."

"A lady in the bank told me who you are, so I already know you're some sort of football player."

He mouthed her last words incredulously before he shook his head and let out another chuckle. "I'll thank you to know I'm not just some player. I'm one hell of a wide receiver."

"Of course. You should always be the best that you can be."

Michael groaned in good humor. "I see I've got my work cut out for me. You don't have anything against ball-players, do you?" he asked earnestly. "And you're not wearing rings, so I'm guessing you're not married. You could at least tell me your name."

"I have two rules, Mr. Hennessey—"

"Michael," he interrupted. "And, you have rules?"

Carolyn nodded. "First, I don't go out with men unless I know them. I don't know you. Second, going out has to be worth my while, too, something I want to do as much as you."

She had reached her car, but before she could pull the door latch, Michael reached around and opened it for her. After she slid neatly behind the wheel, he continued to hold the door open.

"Right now I'm late for my work project." Carolyn smiled patiently. "You seem like a nice person, and if I had more time, I'm sure we might have been able to—"

"I want to see you again," Michael cut in brusquely. "I'm attending a few celebrity affairs this week; some business, some strictly pleasure." He leaned down so he could see her face. "Why don't you attend them all with me? In return, I'll make sure you have a good time, at no expense to you, of course. I can even set up an account at your store of choice for expenses."

Carolyn's brow shot up. "You're propositioning me . . . ?"

"To be my date around town, yeah . . . and for the rest of the week. This way, there's something in it for you, and we get to know each other. We can end it Sunday with the Super Bowl."

Carolyn was mildly incensed at his gall. Did he really expect her to take money from him, a stranger in town who needed a convenient date and God knows what else?

"Who knows? If we hit it off, maybe you'll want to go on with me to the Player's Bowl . . . in Hawaii." He grinned proudly. "What do you say to that?"

She turned the key in the ignition, and the engine purred to life. "I have to go," was what Carolyn said, and she tried to close the door that he still held open.

"Will you think about the weekend and we can talk about the rest?" he asked in a rush. "I'm staying at the Ritz-Carlton. Ask for Mr. H, and the desk will connect you to my suite." His eyes were steady and insistent as they held hers. "You still haven't told me your name."

She shook her head. "Obviously, this is not our time, so some things are best left unspoken." Carolyn pulled at her door, and this time Michael let it go.

Shifting the gear smoothly out of park, she drove off, her eyes darting to the handsome figure of a man displayed in her rear view mirror. It was a shame that he'd turned out to be so predictably male. That predictability was the main reason she seldom dated. Anyway, she had much to do and accomplish in her career. Not dating helped to keep her focused. Another glance at the image in the mirror, though, made her wonder out loud, "Oh, but what if . . . ?"

Michael watched until her car turned into the traffic and disappeared. He had to change her mind. Maybe if he sweetened the deal and made it really worth her while. He reached in his pocket and pulled out the slip of paper from the manager's desk that contained her scribbled name and address. Carolyn Hardy. The syllables, easily memorized from her deposit slip, now rolled off his tongue.

He could tell she was a woman who enjoyed fine things. A grin began to stretch his face: He'd entice her with an offer she couldn't refuse. And she'd call him, too, her rules be damned, because he was going to use the never-fail gift that worked every time. After all, she was a woman.

He looked up into the gray sky as the cold air settled around him. Super Bowls weren't meant to be enjoyed in this kind of weather. Palm trees and beaches, that was more his style. He zipped his leather jacket and returned to complete his business in the bank.

Carolyn unzipped her boots and left them inside the door of her downtown loft apartment. She was glad that the day was over—one more day and the weekend could settle in. Wiggling her toes, she dropped her keys, purse, and the project's spec reports on the nearby counter—tonight's homework. She picked up a small remote and with a touch, soft music filled the air.

Relaxed by the harmony, Carolyn moved deeper into the apartment. City lights illuminated the large, segmented Victorian windows that lit her way as she crossed through living spaces defined with paintings and triptych dividers to the window seat. Kneeling on the cushioned chair, she looked out onto the early evening streets below that had begun to fill with out-of-town sports revelers. There would be no overtime worries this weekend for Carolyn. Her male-dominated office considered Super Bowl weekend a sacrosanct tradition.

She dropped down onto the cushion and closed tired eyes, only to have her peace disrupted by an insistent ring. Groaning at the interruption, she blindly reached for the phone, grabbing it off a nearby table.

"Miss Carolyn Hardy?" a precise woman's voice inquired.

"Yes," she answered the strange voice, her eyes still closed. "And who is this?"

"I'm Nina Swift, sales manager with Saks Fifth Avenue, Buckhead. I'm calling to finalize the arrangements for your shopping visit in our store."

Carolyn's eyes opened. "What?"

"You are one lucky lady, Miss Hardy, if I may say so myself. Of course, we'll have a car sent over for you, and you will have at your service the undivided attention of a superb personal shopper. So, can I arrange a car for you, say, tomorrow morning at nine?"

Carolyn had frowned throughout the woman's spiel, and now sat up from the window seat. "I . . . you have the wrong person. I have no idea what it is you're talking about."

"I'm referring to your shopping gift, Miss Hardy. The fifteen thousand dollar gift."

Carolyn's mouth dropped. "What are you talking about?" Either a joke was being played on her by someone—most likely her sister Alli—or they did indeed have the wrong person.

"Oh dear." The woman's voice rose several octaves. "You really don't know about it, do you? I'm sorry, Miss Hardy. Our staff was to have informed you earlier of your gift."

Carolyn rubbed her temple in confusion. "Miss, um, Swift, I can assure you, you've made the mistake, which explains why I was never informed. I'm sure you'll find the right—"

"Oh, we don't make mistakes of this size, Miss Hardy." The woman talked fast and the shuffle of paper could be heard. "I have it right here. Let's see, the gift was arranged just this afternoon by Mr. Michael Hennessey."

At the sound of that name, Carolyn's hackles rose straight up. "Did you say Michael Hennessey?"

"Yes. It's written right here on your confirmation package." Miss Swift seemed to have regained her poise.

He had some nerve. Carolyn jumped up from the couch, her heart hammering against her chest. "Did he include an explanation?"

"Well, those kinds of details aren't usually written in a confirmation, Miss Hardy." She let out a light chuckle. "We, ah, presume the recipient will know the answer to that."

"Why, that arrogant . . ." Carolyn blew out a hard breath before she could speak again. "You've got that right. I know very well what this is for. And you can tell Mr. Hennessey that he can take his gift, if he wants to call it that, and shove it where the sun don't shine."

"Oh, dear, this is highly unusual," the flustered sales manager gushed. "We don't get requests to take back gifts of this sort. In fact, I don't think I know how to do that."

"Well, I do." Carolyn dropped the phone back into the cradle, livid that the persistent, insufferable jock actually thought he could buy her. Fifteen thousand dollars? He had to be crazy. What was it he had said when she left him today? He was staying at the Ritz-Carlton, and she should ask for Mr. H.

"Man, let's blow this room. The sun's been down for two whole hours, and we still hanging 'round the crib."

Roland Anderson, known as Rollie to his boys, played the familiar complaint to an unsympathetic ear.

Michael sat in the dimly lit living room of the spacious suite on the upper floor of the luxury hotel. The curtains were drawn back and he could view the sparkling nightscape of city lights from the balcony.

He was tired and detached after the long season, and didn't really want to carouse again tonight, but Michael knew his friend would continue to complain until he relented and accompanied him to the clubs. The rest of the posse was downstairs, waiting. He looked up as Rollie crossed the room to replace the CD in the stereo. His friend was dressed in his usual flash with a matching brim pulled low over his eyes.

Michael looked away to his watch, and then to the silent phone beside him before he sighed deeply. Surely Carolyn had been contacted by now. So why hadn't she called?

"Man, that chick you met ain't worth giving up the day, is she?" Rollie turned from the stereo. "Hell, I can round up a couple more for a lot less than what you put out for that one."

"Hey, just chill, okay?"

"You the man." The downbeat from the happening sounds played to Rollie's funky mood, and he gyrated through the living room and out onto the balcony, in sync with the staccato beats.

Michael shook his head at his friend's foolishness. "Hey, why don't you go on?" he suggested. "Take the car and pick up the others. I'll meet up with you later."

The next second, the phone rang and Michael quickly answered it.

"Mr. Hennessey," a richly urbane voice responded, "a Miss Carolyn Hardy is on the line for you. Shall I put her through, sir?"

Michael's relief was incalculable, and his heart thumped as he sat up straight. "Sure." He gestured to Rollie to cut the music and wiped his hand across his mouth, surprised at this attack of nerves at the prospect of talking with her again.

Rollie laughed out loud at his friend's relief.

Smiling, Michael cupped his hand over the mouthpiece. "Go on, get out of here, you fool." As he watched Rollie cut off the stereo and leave the room, he lifted the phone to his ear in time to hear her voice.

"Hello?" She was hesitant. "I'm trying to reach Mr. H."

Michael savored the smooth, deep quality in her voice for a moment before he answered. "Carolyn? This is Michael."

"How did you get my name?" Her serene tones had turned curt. "I imagine you also know my address, since you've given out my phone number."

Warning bells sounded in Michael's head. "Well, um, it wasn't too difficult. It was on your deposit slip. You sound upset."

"Oh, you think I'm just upset? Who do you think you are, invading my privacy this way? How dare you?"

Michael was taken aback by her quickly spewed angry questions. "Wait a minute. What did I do?"

"At first," she stated calmly, "I thought your unique come-on for an extended date was simply presumptuous on your part."

Michael looked at the phone. What in hell was she talking about? He returned it to his ear. "So, what's the problem with it now?"

"I'm not for sale, that's the problem," she bellowed through the phone. "What makes you think that your offer of money is going to make me want to go out with you even more? Have you lost what little brain you have?"

"What?" Michael sputtered. "I didn't want you to worry about expenses, that's all. I thought you'd like to have a little money to buy a few things for when we go out. You know, a trinket or two. Woman, you need to lighten up. You don't seem to know it, but you're being treated nice. What's wrong with that?"

"What's wrong is you insulted me, you lout. Do you think I'm dumb? What else am I supposed to do for fifteen thousand dollars? Sleep with you?"

"Hey, that's your decision, not mine."

"You still don't get it, do you? I was right all along. You're nothing but a misguided jock who's proof that a fool and his money are soon parted."

Michael's eyes narrowed at her words. "Hey, now wait a minute, you're the one slinging insults."

She laughed in his ear. "I don't believe you'd recognize an insult if it bit you on your butt."

Angry, Michael stalked across the room with the phone. "You should've counted yourself lucky. I could have found more willing women for a whole lot less, but I thought you were special, so I didn't care. Hell, it was to have a good time for four days. I never shelled out this much before."

Carolyn's gasp was loud through the phone. "Would you listen to yourself? I don't believe it; it's all about you. Everything they say in the news about you spoiled, rich athletes is true. You're a bunch of self-centered egotists. Just stay clear of me and don't you dare call me again."

"Oh, don't worry, I won't," he fired back in retaliation, not sure when this train had begun to derail. "And by the sounds you make, nobody else is going to be calling you, either. You know, you sure as hell turned out to be one uptight . . . let me give you a clue . . . it rhymes with witch—"

A click resounded in Michael's ear. Livid that she'd hung up on him, he slammed the "off" button and threw the phone across the room.

"Hey, Bro', be careful. I take it the new chick's not

joining us tonight?" Rollie had stuck his head in the door-way, grinning from ear to ear.

"Damn, I don't know what happened, man." Michael rubbed his face, confused by her attitude, and returned to his chair. He shook his head in sincere puzzlement. "The shopping trip always floats 'em in. You know that. So what the hell happened this time?"

Rollie strolled toward his friend. "The way I see it, man, you don't want to get mixed up with some chick who don't want to take the time to understand you and your special needs. Hey, my girl's cousins are downstairs, and they are lookin' good and ready to party." He slapped Michael across the shoulder. "Come on, let's get out of here and have some fun."

Michael mumbled an agreement, but in his mind's eye, he couldn't forget his encounter earlier that day with the most beautiful woman he'd ever seen.

One

. . . *Two Years Later, Present Day*

"Alli, the answer is still no. I'll attend your winter carnival benefit, but I won't be auctioned off like some eager bachelorette." Carolyn turned out of the foyer and started up the east wing staircase of her family's home on her way to her mother's suite.

"Puh-leeze." Alexandra Hardy, called Alli by nearly everyone who knew her, made a valiant plea as her petite figure bounded up the stairs at her sister's heels. Being the baby girl in the family, Alli could wheedle anything out of her older sisters and brother. But extracting this particular favor from her obstinate middle sister would not be easy.

"Anyway," Alli countered at Carolyn's back, "you know it's not *my* benefit. It's supposed to kick off Stephanie's magazine's anniversary." Stephanie Hardy Rogers was the oldest Hardy sibling and publisher of *EthniCulture* magazine, one of the holdings of their well-respected, family-owned business, Hardy Enterprises.

"It was your idea to include this dating game in the program, though."

"Only because we needed something to liven things up," Alli explained with a wave of her arms that sent her bracelets clinking in a frenzy. "Did you see some of that stuff in Steph's original lineup? Old rich people giving speeches between hors d'oeuvres. Boring."

When Carolyn reached the landing, she looked over her shoulder at her sister's petulant frown before she continued down the hall. "Anything and everyone over thirty is boring to you, child."

"You're only five years my senior, so don't patronize me. Anyway, it's not like you'll be missing out on a hot date tomorrow night."

"Listen to you." Carolyn shot the words back over her shoulder. "And, you're wanting a favor from me." She noted her sister's frustration as Alli ran her hand through the short, jet-black fly-away curls that covered her head.

"We've already printed up the pictures and stats on a slew of good-looking bachelors, Caro, but I didn't get enough unattached women to confirm. That's why I need your help."

They reached Mrs. Hardy's suite, and Carolyn rapped against the partly opened sitting room door.

"Come on in. Are the two of you arguing in the hall?" Elizabeth Hardy sat in the corner of a stuffed and tufted love seat with her feet resting atop a wide ottoman and a brocade-covered journal open on her lap.

Still a handsome woman as she neared sixty, she had a slight build like Alli and wore her dark hair, with liberal sprinkles of gray, in a short, tapered cut. She placed her pen across the journal page to save her spot before she looked up at her daughters.

"All right, what's the problem?" she inquired.

"I came by the house to pay you a visit, that's all," Carolyn explained as she bent to place a kiss on her mother's upturned cheek. "That's when I was ambushed by Alli." She cocked her brow at Alli, who leaned against the wall with her arms folded. They were near polar opposites in personality, and she knew her vivacious younger sister wasn't going to take the criticism without an explanation.

"I'm short on bachelorettes for the carnival tomorrow night, and all I want her to do is volunteer herself as a date in the auction. It's all for charity, for heaven's sake. I've been asking her all week, mom, but she flat out refuses to help me."

"Why not?" Mrs. Hardy's eyes rested on Carolyn. "She really wants this benefit to be a success—what with Justin out of town, it's all been left in her hands."

"For the first time since I started interning for him at the office," Alli said, "he's let me develop one of my own ideas for a benefit and given me control."

Carolyn sighed at the mention of her brother, Justin Hardy, CEO and president of the family business. They were as close as a sister and brother could be, and he would be the first to understand her reticence. It was too bad that he was away and couldn't stick up for her decision.

"I don't want to be paraded in front of a roomful of people like a slab of meat." Carolyn punctuated her words. "It's degrading."

"For goodness sake," Alli said, her eyes stretched wide in response to her sister's words. "It's not like that at all. You should lighten up and not be so stodgy. Plus, you don't have to *parade* across the runway." A twinkle played in her eyes. "Just come out from behind the curtains, and take a few of your regal steps while you're wearing something very nice . . ." She strode seductively across the floor to demonstrate. "Then you give your name and occupation, that's all. And at the signal from the emcee, the bidding begins." She stopped her vamping to plead again. "It'll be fun for one night and it's for a good cause."

Carolyn couldn't help it, and found herself laughing with her mother at Alli's show.

"I agree with Alli," Mrs. Hardy said. "Do it for fun."

Carolyn looked skeptical. "But what if I'm won by some boorish guy I don't even know? I don't want to be forced to go out with someone like that."

Encouraged that her sister's resolve was weakening, Alli seized the opportunity. "If that's all you're worried about, don't be. The winning bidder agrees not to renege on their charity bid, regardless of whether the parties agree to arrange a future date or not." She frowned. "But you do have to sit with your winning bidder through dinner and the remainder of the program. Now, that's not asking too much for charity, is it?"

"Go on, help your sister out," Mrs. Hardy urged her older daughter. "She's really worked hard on this benefit."

One look at Alli's pleading face, coupled with a view of her mother's kind one, and Carolyn let out a defeated breath. "Oh, I don't know. This is such short notice, Alli. And I don't have any fun formal stuff to wear—"

"Oh, don't worry about that. I've got just the number. In fact, it was made for you."

Carolyn wasn't convinced. "Alli, you're four inches shorter than me. Besides, I don't wear *anything* in your closet."

"No, no, even you'd like this dress—it's a designer original I had planned to have altered because it drags on the floor on me. Caro, puh-leeze," she drawled again. "If you do the auction, you can keep it."

Carolyn turned to her mother, caught her growing smile, and knew she had lost. "Okay, I'll look at this dress, and if I can wear it, maybe I'll do the auction." When her sister squealed in delight and hugged her, Carolyn added, "But, I swear, Alli Hardy, if I wind up regretting this, you'll never hear the end of it."

"Aw, you're just afraid nobody will bid on you except Edward," Alli teased.

Carolyn frowned. "Oh, dear, I didn't think of that possibility." Edward Nelson was both the Hardy family's personal attorney and a member of Hardy Enterprises' legal staff. He had been smitten with Carolyn for as long as any of them could remember, even though the affection was not returned. "But maybe I can turn it into a plus," she commented enigmatically.

Alli grabbed Carolyn's hand and pulled her toward the door.

"Mama, we'll be right back." To Carolyn, she said, "Come on, let me show you the dress. You're going to love it."

"We've put good numbers on the table for the Atlanta Wildcats' general manager to mull over, but it's a given they'll bite for a four-year no-cut deal. The Wildcats want you badly, and they know a lot of other teams do, too."

Jeffrey Kingston, Michael's agent and mentor, took a breath as he quickly flipped to another page in the thick packet of papers stacked on the table between them.

The two men sat across from each other in the spacious solarium of Michael's sprawling new home. Their voices were muted by the calming gurgle from the waterfall garden set in the center of the floor below a huge skylight.

"Study these incentives, Michael. I've put the usual things in here . . . number of receptions, yards made, selection to the Player's Bowl, and so on. Let me know if there's anything in there you don't want, like, or understand."

Michael reached for the pages before he looked up at the man who had been at his side since that very first professional contract was negotiated nine years before, when Michael was fresh out of college and the number two draft pick.

"You think they'll agree to a contract that's sweeter than any other one obtained by a wide receiver?"

Jeffrey smiled. "Before you even add in your incentives, it's a major record-breaker, Michael. You've proven you deserve it, year after year, and they know it."

Michael joined his agent in a jubilant smile. "I guess I can squeeze in four more years of peak performance before I'm set out to pasture."

Michael hunched over the table and perused the items noted on page after page. "It looks pretty much in order," he said after a while. "I'll read it more carefully later." It was a rule Jeffrey had hammered into him over the years—read every line of a contract.

"Good." Jeffrey settled back on the sofa and stretched his arm across the back. "Take the time to get familiar with the deal, especially the areas I've highlighted, like the signing bonus structure. After all, you're the one who'll have to perform those feats on the field."

Michael smoothed his palm across his hair before he leaned back, too. "You know, I'm looking forward to this time off before spring camp."

"The last two years have really been rough, I know, but you survived, and the best is probably yet to come. On and off the field." Jeffrey drew in a deep breath and looked Michael squarely in the eye. "I spent a lot of time talking with your mother over the years. We would be about the same age now if she were still alive, and I want to tell you, Michael, she'd be proud of you and the changes you've made with the direction of your life."

"Thanks." Michael's throat had tightened at the mention of his mother, and now he swallowed hard. "And even though I know it, I don't think I'll ever get tired of hearing it."

"So, tell me, how's it going for you in your new town?"

Michael sat up and clasped his hands. "You know, I didn't think I'd like living down south full time when I've only lived up in the northeast; but, hey, I think it's going to work out."

"You made a wise decision to come here," Jeffrey

agreed. "I lived here a few years after I graduated from Auburn—Atlanta is one of the few places that offers both city lights and country-living charm." He raised a brow at Michael. "Maybe you'll finally meet that special some-body and settle down." He nodded at the idea. "There's no time like the present."

"I'm not thinking about that," Michael said with a laugh. "I have a whole lot on my plate as it is right about now."

"Your free-agency is a fact, Michael, so don't look back, and know that the Wildcats are anxious to bring you aboard and show you off . . . once the contract is signed, of course."

They talked of other things, business and personal, while Jeffrey re-packed his briefcase. Soon, they stood and shook hands as they said goodbye.

"Enjoy these next few months of free time," Jeffrey suggested. "I'll be back here before spring training camp starts. We'll meet with the team's general manager to fi-nalize a contract, and then we'll let them announce it to the press. Meanwhile, you know mum's the word to the media about details of our discussion with the team."

Michael was used to the drill. "That goes without say-ing."

Jeffrey gave him a friendly slap on the back. "Person-ally, I'm glad you're starting over in a new city, away from the sad memories." He looked at Michael. "The bad influences, too. But leeches tend to find blood. It's their life food, so you be careful."

"Don't worry about me. I've always been straight with you."

"I know that."

"And I can still handle the pressure."

"I have no doubt." Jeffrey paused a moment. "You should be seen around the city, get involved in the local charities, especially ones that the Wildcats support. Before long, you'll have the sports writers and the people buzzing about your residence here and demanding that the team sign you up, too."

"Yeah, I've already been getting some calls. A few of the Wildcats I know who live here want me to appear at some of their charity functions. I've even got a few invitations for the weekend I'm thinking about honoring."

"Good, good." Jeffrey hefted his briefcase into his hand.

"Mr. Pitts will get you to the airport." Michael looked toward the doorway. "He's around here somewhere."

As if on cue, a gray-haired gentleman who looked to be in his late fifties appeared in the room, neatly dressed in slacks, shirt, and a dark jacket.

"I've already brought the car around, Mr. Hennessey. I figured Mr. Kingston would be ready soon."

Michael shook his head and grinned. "Jeffrey, I've asked Mr. Pitts to call me Michael at least twice a day since he and his wife took over the household when I moved in.

Mr. Pitts' eyes twinkled above his smile. "And like I've said, Mr. Hennessey, I will when you call me Eldridge."

"So you see," Michael laughed, "we're at an impasse, here."

Jeffrey shook hands with Eldridge. "It's nice to meet you, sir. I think you're just what the doctor ordered for this young man's household."

"We're quite happy with things, too," Eldridge replied.

Michael watched the two men depart the room together. He walked over to the window and continued to watch them pass through the side garden and gate until they were out of sight as they headed for the front driveway.

Heaving a deep sigh, Michael quickly walked in the opposite direction across the room and out into the hallway. He came upon a set of imposing double doors that he pushed open to reveal a well-stocked library, most of its volumes acquired from the previous owners.

He made his way to the massive desk that commanded the middle of the room, and shuffled through a stack of invitations until he found the one that had aroused his curiosity upon its arrival two weeks before. Just as he had then, he wondered if he'd happened upon a coincidence or a stroke of fate. However it turned out, Jeffrey was right. He had to set down roots and sell himself in a new town, and that meant getting out and handling public perceptions. He decided he'd start by honoring this particular invitation for tomorrow. It would be interesting to see what the night would hold.

TWO

The grand ballroom at the Marquis Plaza Hotel was alive with energy, excitement, and a cross-section of Atlanta's influential community, young and old. Because the affair was intended to raise money for charity and celebrate the success of Stephanie's magazine, they held the purse on both counts.

Carolyn did not retire to her seat at the family's reserved tables, nor did she mix with the specially invited guests over cocktails. She preferred to hang out backstage instead, behind the runway set up for the auction, where she kept reminding herself of the reason she had sold out her standards, repeating it like a mantra: *This is for a good cause; I'm doing this for a good cause.*

The glittering event was being covered by the local media, thanks, in part, to the high-profile audience. Carolyn had arrived for the affair alone, and kept behind the scenes where she watched Alli work out the last-minute kinks in the entertainment lineup, a job she seemed to handle quite efficiently in her strapless, sequined gown. Carolyn smiled at the "in your face" color. Only Alli could pull off fuchsia.

As cheers went up now and again on the other side of the curtain, Carolyn finally asked Alli what was happening.

"Throughout the evening, our emcee will introduce special guests seated in the audience," Alli replied, not looking up from her clipboard as they walked. "I don't suppose you've met him yet. He's that new anchor on channel four, Blake something or other. If you ask me, he looks better on TV."

Carolyn smiled as she glanced around the cavernous space. She recognized magazine staffers, all in evening attire. They hurried back and forth, ensuring that the event proceeded in seamless fashion. When she didn't see any of the other singles to be auctioned, she wondered why.

She caught up with Alli again. "I thought the auction would be at the beginning of the evening."

Alli stopped and turned to her sister. "Are you still nervous about it? We moved it back a bit for balance, but it's next, just before dinner." She surveyed her sister up and down as though for the first time.

"What?" Carolyn asked suspiciously.

"You, Caro. You look dynamite. That dress was made for someone tall like you, girl."

The multi-colored harlequin print gown, a Randolph Duke design, was made of silk charmeuse with an accordion-pleated skirt that kissed the floor, accentuating Carolyn's long limbs when she moved. The halter top was held up with a gold neck ring. With her hair loose and flowing to her shoulders, Carolyn's entire carriage gave her the look of a woman comfortable with fashion.

Of course, that was nowhere near how Carolyn actually felt, and she smoothed her clammy hands down the sides of what she agreed was an absolute dream of an evening gown—though certainly not what she would ever have found in her own closet. Her own wardrobe consisted of basic black and other solid colors that fit into her business lifestyle.

"I'm really not worried about the bidding," Carolyn

said. "I've already covered the possibilities on that with Edward."

"Edward?" Alli's clipboard slid to her chest. "You've made it your adult life's ambition to avoid Edward, so what would you plan with him?"

"Well, I prefer the devil I know to the devil I don't, so he's going to bid a respectable price for me, and I won't be beholden to anyone for dinner here or a date later on." Her mouth pulled into a self-satisfied smile.

"That's not the point of the auction, Caro," Alli argued, "and who knows, you might have met someone who could inject some fun in that straight-as-an-arrow life of yours." She went back to her clipboard list.

"You're just mad because I figured a way around this debacle waiting to happen, that's all."

Alli propped her hand on her sequined hip. "Everyone knows you and Justin are the brains in the family, but you saw what happened to him. Davina came along and knocked his superior thinking down a peg or two and he fell for her hook, line, and sinker."

Carolyn knew that to be true. Davina Spenser was an artist who had swept into their brother's life, and a couple more committed to or made for each other couldn't be found. But what did that have to do with her? She said as much to her sister.

"Just watch," Alli continued. "One day the same thing is going to happen to you, and your brain won't be the only organ to get you through it. You may have to rely on your heart for a change."

"Listen to you, the love maven," Carolyn laughed. "You go out with someone new every month."

"That's my point. At least I go out," Alli retorted.

"Well, my fairy tale won't happen tonight, because I'll be home in my bed, alone, way before my car turns into a pumpkin at midnight."

The tuxedoed emcee came bounding from around the

curtained stage to join them, a wide grin locked across his face.

"Everything's set for the auction, and our livestock is champing at the bit to be let out," he joked, as his attention strayed to Carolyn, who stood behind Alli. He raised his brows in appreciation. "Well, hello there," he said, straightening his collar. "Don't tell me—you're one of our bachelorettes, right?"

A frown formed on Carolyn's brow as she replied to the unctuous host. "Do I look like I'm champing—"

Alli quickly interrupted and smoothly made introductions, stumbling over Blake Christopher's last name until he jogged her memory.

"Carolyn was just asking about the other participants, Blake. I thought they were supposed to be back here?"

"We decided to put them in the next room, so we could instruct and prep everybody at once," Blake answered.

Carolyn's frown deepened. "Instruct and prep? What's difficult about going through a curtain?—"

"Don't you think you should get in there anyway?" Alli interjected. With a plastic smile on her face, she took Blake by the arm and walked away, busily discussing the program.

Carolyn sighed and walked toward the assigned room, wishing the whole thing were over. Soon it would be, and she'd be forever indebted to Edward for helping her out. She'd worry about that later, though. For now, she opened the door and joined what she considered to be the other victims.

Michael plopped an hors d'oeuvre in his mouth as he witnessed the high-spirited bidding among a group of squealing ladies for the tuxedo-clad Wildcat linebacker, Jemahl Thompson, who strutted up the runway.

During cocktails before the start of the black-tie affair, Michael had learned he'd share the same table with Jemahl and four others: Reginald Hall, a local bank president and his wife, Valerie; and Deirdre Gordon, the regional publicist for one of Michael's endorsement companies, and her husband, Frank. After introductions had been exchanged, the group had meshed well, with Michael and Jemahl supplying autographs for the married couples' kids. Soon after, Jemahl had been whisked backstage by an attractive woman floating in bright sequins.

Another host of cheers went up over the live band's rollicking music as Jemahl's hulking form turned and paraded up the runway one more time in an open play for higher bids, a rose in his big hand looking sorely out of place.

Amused by his friend's showmanship, Michael shook his head, glad that he had been spared the opportunity to perform. When he had resided in New Jersey, Michael had appeared at hundreds of these benefits and, like Jemahl, had relished in those good times. With an inward cringe, he acknowledged that he had also been wilder in those days, a few years younger . . . and way dumb, if the truth be known.

White ping-pong paddles with large black numbers emblazoned across their width bobbed in the air, thrust upwards by hopeful women who wanted the big guy for a date. Each bob represented a hundred dollar incremental bid that the emcee both recognized and exploited, raising Jemahl's sale price to a thousand dollars.

"Michael, why aren't you up there? How did they miss out on asking you to do this?"

The question came from the bank president's wife, Valerie. Michael picked up the white paddle that carried his seat number from the table. He smiled at the number thirty-two; it was the same number he wore on the field.

"By the looks of things, I'm chalking it up to good luck."

The men nodded in agreement as they all laughed.

"I was told you recently arrived in town," Deirdre said. Michael nodded. "Only a few months now."

"It's all in the news that you're a free agent these days, and looking for a new team. Have you thought about joining our Wildcats?" Reginald's brows rose in curiosity as he lifted his glass to his lips.

"Sold!" boomed the emcee's voice.

The attention at Michael's table reverted to the stage.

At the same time, a cheer went up and an excited woman jumped to her feet, waving her paddle wildly in the air. "Yes, yes," she yelled out.

"Bidder number one hundred seventy-two gets the date for the price of twelve hundred dollars, and all of it going to a worthwhile cause. Congratulations." Blake Christopher's voice resonated through the loudspeakers and across the room as the cameras on the sidelines recorded the entire spectacle.

The house lights had come up and the attendant escorted the winning bidder from her table and through a side door, presumably to claim her prize, while the audience anted up for the next installment of fun.

"So far, everyone who's been auctioned has raised at least a thousand dollars," Valerie said. "That's great."

"Who's next?" Reginald looked from the darkened stage to his program.

Michael had leaned back in his seat to leisurely scan the vibrant room—interested in the far-off possibility that a curious coincidence of names had suggested—just as the house lights dimmed for the next auction.

"The stage is lit," Deirdre observed. "It's a woman this time; isn't that a fabulous dress she's wearing?"

"Mmm . . . Absolutely gorgeous," Valerie agreed. "Look at the way it flows."

"Yeah, I can see," Reginald commented, before he received a playful punch in the ribs from his wife.

The room's interest was once again being drawn to the

stage; Michael, aware that his attention had drifted from the goings-on there, reluctantly interrupted his hopeful search of the room and turned his gaze toward the bright runway to watch the fun. A woman had stepped away from the curtain amid the band's steady, pulsating percussions. For a moment, she shielded her eyes from the blinding stage lights. She appeared to be waiting for her cue to take to the runway.

Carolyn's thoughts were decidedly ungracious. When was that jerk of an emcee going to start the intro? It felt as though she'd been standing at the curtain for an eternity while he pumped the crowd with a toothy grin.

"All right, gentlemen, this is a treat. I met our next lovely bachelorette backstage, and she is a beauty," Blake spouted. "In fact, she's a member of Atlanta's own illustrious Hardy clan, sponsors of tonight's benefit. Would you please put your hands together for . . ." Blake dragged out the name to elicit the maximum dramatic effect. "Miss Carolyn Hardy."

Carolyn swallowed her disdain for the emcee, and forced a smile as she made the short walk to the microphone at the opposite end of the stage. Underneath, she suffered a level of exposure she never wanted to repeat.

With the clearing of her throat her only outward sign of discomfort, Carolyn introduced herself and then shared her occupation.

"I'm a senior engineer with Geary & Geary Engineers of Atlanta." She stepped back from the microphone, trying to find a familiar face in the audience beyond the hot klieg lights, but met only the white, blinding glare from the lamps. Not quite sure what would happen next as Blake opened the bidding with three hundred dollars, Carolyn was fatalistic—her drama should be over in the next few minutes.

* * *

Michael's drama had steadily escalated. It had started at the mention of her name and continued to build the moment her low voice swept over the audience. He sat up in his chair: the coincidence in names he had wondered about since he'd seen the invitation was now a reality. As though he were in the thrall of a dream, he dared not speak lest the fantasy fade and wake him.

Straining forward in his chair, oblivious to the auction itself, Michael tried to make out Carolyn's every feature as she stood there, caught in the bright light, his recollection in overdrive to make sure that it was she and not a dream. Her hair flowed and her long limbs swayed with a self-assured gait against the softly draped material as she came around the mike stand and took the obligatory walk across the stage.

Michael exhaled in a rush. She wasn't a fantasy, and her beauty was just as he'd remembered; but most importantly, she was unattached, the unknown fact that had kept his curiosity about her in check when he'd returned to her town.

Blake pulled the bids from the air at a quick pace, and called them out. "Bam—we're already at twelve hundred . . . do I hear thirteen?" He pointed to a paddle. "We're at fourteen." He pointed at another. "Fifteen." Blake looked around the room. "Fifteen, going once . . ."

The ultimate words brought Michael back into the present, and his heart lurched at this possibly lost opportunity.

"Going twice—"

"Two thousand," Michael blurted out. A roar of laughing approval and claps from the audience followed his words.

"Raise your paddle, raise your paddle," Valerie urged, and Michael vigorously complied.

"Well, now, this is getting interesting," Blake called out from the podium as he looked to Carolyn. "Do we hear another bid?"

"Twenty-two hundred." The shout behind a raised paddle came from the front corner table.

"Twenty-five," Michael countered without a pause, his competitive nature roused.

"Atta, boy." Deirdre's husband, Frank, slapped Michael's shoulder. "I say, if you're serious about something, go for it all the way."

Michael smiled. "That's exactly what I intend to do." The evening was suddenly fun, and he couldn't wait to see Carolyn's face when she recognized her bidder. He raised his brows at the devilish thought, and her last words echoed in his head. She'd see who had the last laugh.

"Ah, twenty-eight," the front table bidder announced.

The crowd was now a part of the bidding war between Michael and the front table, the room egging on each bidder, in turn, to take the lead.

Meanwhile, Carolyn had come to center stage, dumbstruck by what was happening, and listened as Blake played it for all it was worth. She tried, to no avail, to peer into the audience and identify the other bidder who had started this escalation game with Edward—one which Edward had foolishly become mired in and could possibly lose.

"Thirty-five hundred." The voice from the middle table thrust the paddle skyward.

What? This was ridiculous. Who would spend that much for a date—and with her? Carolyn looked to Blake as he stepped from behind his podium to join her.

"Carolyn, you've got some real admirers out there tonight, but their bids will go toward a great cause, right audience?" As the crowd cheered and clapped, Blake shamelessly urged them on.

"All right, come on, do I hear a higher bid? Any other

takers? Carolyn, do you want to say anything? How about another walk up the runway?"

Carolyn blanched at the idea, but managed a smile at the front table where she knew her family and Edward were seated. "No, but I sure am ready for this to be over with."

The audience laughed at her candor.

"All right, then, thirty-five hundred dollars from bidder number thirty-two, going once . . ."

"Fo-four thousand," Edward stumbled over the words from the front table.

What? Carolyn couldn't believe her ears. Why didn't someone at her family's table stop him, for Christ's sake?

"Whoa, this is getting big time." Blake played to the noisy audience even as he preened for the news cameras. "And, it's great. But, hey, we can go higher. What do you say, audience?"

Carolyn closed her eyes for a moment, and held her breath in hopes that the unknown bidder would give up. It wasn't to be.

"Seventy-five hundred dollars." The stranger shouted loud enough to stop the room for a full few seconds, before it erupted with a din of unintelligible babble mixed with applause.

"All right," Blake shouted above the rising noise. "That's the bid of a man who wants to make a statement. Going once . . ."

This had all become unreal for Carolyn. Blake left her side for the edge of the stage and searched the audience for a return bid, but no vocal orders came, no other paddles bobbed.

"Going twice . . ."

Carolyn had long lost hope that Edward would rescue her.

The crowd unanimously yelled the word "Sold!" as they broke into spontaneous applause and cheers. Blake, however, had rushed to his podium and now fumbled with his sheets to find the owner of the number thirty-two bidding paddle.

"You're right," the emcee boomed through his mike. "A date with Carolyn Hardy is sold for seventy-five hundred dollars, a record sale so far, to bidder number thirty-two."

Carolyn looked from Blake to the audience, but she still couldn't make out the persistent bidder, so she turned to exit the stage, knowing she'd meet him shortly, anyway.

"And our bidder is none other than Mr. Michael Hennessey."

A surprised "whoop" went up from the crowd at the name.

Carolyn was crossing the dark runway as the name streaked through her mind and, literally, stopped her in her tracks.

Discomfited, she vaguely remembered a similar name associated with fame and money. She turned to look back at the audience in the vicinity of the stranger's voice. The stage lights were doused and she could see, but there was only the back of a tuxedoed figure being escorted from the area. He was on his way to meet her, his purchased date.

A distant memory jarred loose and flitted across her mind's eye, catching her breath in her throat. "No, it can't be," Carolyn muttered to herself. Her hand flew to her heart as she drew in a deep breath.

It couldn't possibly be that same person from so long ago—it couldn't be. She shook her head in disbelief. Or could it?

Three

"Wow, girl, is it true what they're saying?"

"I heard Michael Hennessey himself was trying to bid on you."

"Trying?" another woman gossiped, "I heard he practically closed down the bids with a hunk of money."

Carolyn silently wound her way through the throng that had gathered at the entryway backstage, the curious questions and comments thrown her way proof that the improbable debacle she had predicted had actually happened. Boy, did Alli owe her big time for this spectacle. Carolyn avoided public displays, and she'd just been part of a big one.

When she was free of the crowd, she saw her sister, Stephanie, motion to her from a door up ahead.

"Carolyn, in here," she said. "Alli's bringing the bidder around so the two of you can meet."

When she joined Stephanie at the door, she whispered, "Do you want to tell me what just happened out there? Edward was at your table. He was supposed to make a reasonable bid and get it closed. Instead, he made a fool of himself."

"You set Edward up to bid for you?" her sister asked. "Shame on you." Her playful brown eyes lit up with delight as they entered the room. "Well, I guess somebody else wanted you a lot more than good old Edward did. You heard who your bidder was, didn't you?"

Slightly annoyed at her sister's lack of empathy, Carolyn answered, "I—I'm not sure."

Two other couples and the attendant who had been in the room were leaving just as Alli appeared in the door, a wide smile on her face.

"He's here now," Stephanie said.

"Look at who I have with me. Your date, Carolyn, and he's . . . well, he's Michael Hennessey," Alli gushed, "the football player from the New Jersey Knights."

"Formerly with the Knights," a deep voice corrected Alli from behind the door.

Carolyn craned her neck to watch him fill the entrance and then follow Alli into the room. Resplendent in a tuxedo that was superbly tailored to his large frame, he was a study in confidence.

Carolyn was instantly transported back to the wintry day at the bank. He was as she remembered him, sucking up the room's energy with his presence just as he had then, as though he were some giant vacuum. He still possessed the handsomely squared jaw and the flashing smile. And then she remembered that outrageous offer that had proven he was only a pathetic jock. Carolyn's eyes narrowed as they finally made contact with his.

"I see you're still making absurd propositions with your money, Mr. Hennessey. I'm surprised you're trying to use it to buy an uptight, ah, witch."

"Carolyn," Stephanie jerked her eyes around to her sister. "What are you saying?"

"So you remember me." Michael stepped closer. "Maybe you forgot your own dating rules. I mean, look at you, leaving yourself open to get purchased by a misguided jock," he countered. His eyes didn't waver from hers as he came further into the room.

"Now just a minute, you two—you know each other, don't you?" Alli's gazed flowed between them.

"Yes." They answered in sync.

"How?" Alli asked.

"When?" Stephanie joined in.

"A long time ago," Michael said. "In fact, we made a big impression on each other."

"What is it with you? Have you been trying to find me or something?" Carolyn tried to steady her voice, but seeing him again, and under these circumstances, was unsettling.

"It wasn't planned that I'd be here tonight," she continued, "so how did you know I'd be in the auction?"

Michael smiled easily. "I didn't."

"You mean you just started bidding on me out of the blue?"

He nodded. "You do seem to be able to put a high price on your time, and I couldn't pass up the opportunity to see if I could meet it this go-round, that's all."

Exasperated, Carolyn scowled at his reference to their last meeting.

Alli folded her arms. "Carolyn, old girl," she said, "you've been holding out on your sisters."

"Well, since you two know each other, that should make things simpler," Stephanie said. "A date between old friends is nice."

"I'm game." Michael reached inside his jacket and pulled out a discreetly folded checkbook.

"If you'll come over here," Stephanie said, directing him to a desk and chair, "we can take care of the business part of this arrangement."

Carolyn swallowed hard as she helplessly watched the two of them go about their business, not liking one bit the idea that Michael would get exactly what he'd wanted before and at his price, but at the expense of her standards. Why, he hadn't learned a lesson at all, and it wasn't right.

"There's no way I'm going out with him," she exclaimed to Alli, "and you can just can the dinner tonight, as well."

"Carolyn, you can't renege now," Alli argued. "You promised me you'd abide by the rules, and at least honor the dinner part."

Stephanie turned to them from the desk, and Michael followed suit, the pen to write the check still poised in his hand.

"You don't understand," Carolyn tried to explain. "I hadn't planned on him being in the audience and bidding on me."

Michael set the pen down. "Since when did life follow your plan?" Folding his arms, he casually leaned against the desk.

Carolyn whirled in Michael's direction. "Don't you dare preach to me. You still haven't learned that money won't buy everything." She saw the flinch of his eye before he pushed off the desk. Had she touched a nerve?

"I know that better than you think." He came to a stop squarely in front of Carolyn. "In this case, though, my predilection for parting with my money can buy a lot of kids a safe place to have fun while they learn. So what if I eat dinner with a woman who doesn't see the good in it? It's only one night, and I'm doing my part because, in the end, it's all for charity." He looked down at her, his brow cocked above his steady smile. "What about your part?"

At a loss for words, Carolyn pulled in a huff of breath, properly chastised.

"He's right, you know," Stephanie said. "If you won't abide by the rules, Mr. Hennessey doesn't have to stand by his bid, either."

A knock came at the door, and an attendant stuck her head into the room. Alli rushed to the door and directed the attendant and the latest auctioned couple to the next room. "We're not finished in here," she explained, before she closed the door again.

Carolyn realized she was creating all sorts of problems—not to mention a back-up—with her vacillating. "Damn you," she said, and looked up at Michael, who continued to stand before her. She crossed her arms and tried to speak for his ears only.

"You didn't have to embarrass me publicly like you did, and in front of everyone with that outlandish bid."

"Embarrass?" Alli walked up and joined them. "You got the highest bid tonight, girl. That's an honor."

"You don't think you're worth it?" Michael challenged. His eyes swept over her body, from head to foot. "In that case, maybe I did go overboard, even for charity."

She stiffened at his jibe. "Don't you see, you're a public figure, and the news people got the whole thing on film. We'll probably be all over the news this weekend as their comic relief story."

Another thought occurred to Carolyn and she looked to Stephanie, who leaned against the desk, her arms crossed. "I just thought about something. What'll they say in my office on Monday if it's on the news, huh? I'll become a joke."

Michael shook his head, and looked to Carolyn's sisters for answers. "What is she talking about?"

"She works in one of those staid, corporate offices where they have Muzak pumped in for fun, and the good-looking women are usually reserved for jumping out of cakes."

"I see," Michael said. He looked back at Carolyn and grinned. "I should have known."

"Laugh if you want, but I've worked hard the last five years building a reputation with my firm as a serious career woman. Stephanie's a publisher. She knows how rough it can be for women to be taken seriously."

"Carolyn, the auction wasn't that bad." Stephanie left

the desk and joined them. "Your reaction is way out of proportion."

"But don't you see? In one night, he's destroyed my credibility by making me the center of some silly dating game. Do you know how hard it is to regain respect in a business dominated by men?"

Carolyn had yet to crack a smile and Michael realized she believed her serious ranting. As he listened to the three sisters argue their points, he could see that Carolyn was as high-strung as she'd been on that phone two years before. Even so, Michael couldn't deny that she was still as luscious a fruit as he'd ever wanted to pluck. Swallowing the thoughts that fed his rising desire, he vowed not to blow this opportunity. He would make Carolyn honor this date, if for no other reason than to teach that hoity-toity little butt of hers a lesson. He interrupted the women.

"Hey, if you want to leave tonight without a lot of fuss, and with your business reputation intact, then don't have a fit in front of everybody and mess up the charity angle," he suggested.

Alli giggled. "He's right, Carolyn, stop having a fit."

"And if anyone asks," he continued, "tell them it was a planned rivalry between three friends, and it was all done for charity." He raised his brows. "That is, unless the other bidder is upset about losing and will say differently."

"Oh, that was Edward, the family's business attorney. He's all right," Alli offered.

Though Michael frowned at the knowledge, his voice carried a tease. "So that's what this is all about? You wanted him to win the bid?"

"Of course, I did . . . I mean, no, he just knows the family, that's all. I didn't want to go out with either of you," Carolyn quickly explained.

Michael turned and strode to the desk where the pen and his checkbook had been left. He looked back at the women, Alli and Stephanie flanking Carolyn. They were a good-looking, close-knit family, and probably had no idea how lucky they were to have each other.

"Do we get on with this?" he asked. "I believe I'm ready for that dinner."

"Carolyn, you are going to honor your promise, right?" Alli looked up at her sister before she squeezed her arm.

"Of course, she is," Stephanie intervened, and caught up Carolyn's other arm. "No Hardy ever balked on a deal, and you won't be the first."

Carolyn bit down on her lip to halt an escape of words.

"Good." Michael sat at the desk and wrote the check as the three women looked on. When he finished, he tore it from the book and left it on the table next to the pen. As he pocketed his checkbook, his long strides brought him back to the women. He stopped in front of Carolyn.

She felt a poke in her sides from both sisters, urging her to say something appropriate before he left the room. Carolyn drew in her breath and looked past his broad shoulders to his classically chiseled features. Okay, so what if he had a generous mouth, dark eyes . . . she frowned at the unbidden thoughts and blinked away the possibilities.

"Mr. Hennessey, for the sake of the charity, of course I'll join you at your table for dinner tonight." She tried to make the forced words less wooden. "As for the date, I'd like to think on it a little longer."

His glance darted to include all the women. "Please, call me Michael." He returned his attention to Carolyn. "By the way, you'll find the check I left is double my original bid."

"What?" Stephanie and Alli's voices rose a chorus.

Carolyn's brows narrowed at this new twist. What was he trying to pull?

"The check is good if both of us decide to have that date after all. For charity, of course."

Suspicion weaved through Carolyn's brain. She watched him leave the room and pull the door closed.

Alli's shriek sounded from the desk. "It's a check for fifteen thousand dollars." She waved it in the air. "We're going to easily make our goal tonight, Stephanie, and I'm a success."

"Only if Carolyn does her part, remember?" Eager to see the check, Stephanie moved to Alli's side as quickly as her gown would allow.

Fifteen thousand dollars. Carolyn dropped into a nearby chair. Michael had charmed her family, turned the tables on her so-called rules, and the point he was trying to make was crystal clear: she was not above being bought for fifteen thousand dollars. And he was right. It was she, Carolyn, who would be seen as the petty one if she didn't agree to a date with this bodacious and rich sports jock, all for the sake of charity.

Alli came to stand over her sister. "It's not that you don't want to go out with Michael. I think you're scared." She stepped back and crossed her arms. "Look at her, Steph. I think he handled that brain of hers without much effort and she's scared that he might be every bit as smart as she is."

Stephanie sat behind the desk and twirled the check between her fingers. "Yeah, you have to admit, Alli, our sister's a snob, and doesn't think a guy who plays football is good enough for her."

"That is not true." Carolyn sat up, knowing they were baiting her, but she was shamed by the realization that they might not be totally wrong.

"All right, when you have dinner at his table tonight, prove it," Alli said. "Be civil to him."

"And when he brings up the date," Stephanie added, "go for it."

Carolyn had known what was coming. Her gaze flew from one sister to the other, and from the look in their eyes, there was no way out of this predicament.

Four

Carolyn picked at the roast beef. She had been seated at Michael's side since the start of dinner, and surprisingly enough, not one insult had been exchanged. The reason could have been that they had spent the time fielding curious questions from the other two couples, not to mention the steady interruptions from people who came by to greet Michael now that it was open knowledge he was in attendance. It was almost with regret that Carolyn realized they had barely exchanged words at all.

"I was pretty surprised to hear you were a member of the Hardy family that put on this event."

Michael's low words had been whispered near her bare shoulder and pulled Carolyn from her reverie. She turned to his voice and found his face close to hers, the smell of sandalwood a pleasant diversion.

"I'm surprised you haven't made it your business to know everything about me."

He chuckled at the haughty words. "Now I know what's been missing from dinner. Your spice." He pushed his plate back before he rested his forearm there, turning slightly so that she was fully in his view. "Tell me, did you think about me much over the last two years?"

The air seemed chillier, and Carolyn shivered under his gaze. "You're missing your earring."

Michael touched his lobe. "Only on special occasions. You're not wearing your cell phone."

Carolyn shifted in her chair. "Alli took it. She was afraid it would go off in my pocket while I was on stage." They locked eyes before they both broke into a relieved smile.

"Are you going to tell me how you found me here tonight?"

"Like I said before, it was by accident. I'm here at the invitation of my endorsement deal with—"

"Those ads on television," Carolyn interrupted, "where you outleap the leopard."

"So, you have been following my career, huh?" he teased.

She raised her brow cynically. "Who believes that stuff?"

Michael let out a low chuckle. "It's entertainment, that's all, and not meant to be taken seriously. Except for you, I suspect no one does."

She snorted. "You'd be surprised at the number of children who do." Silence followed her words and their attention returned to the table.

"Your family owns the Hardy Art Galleries. Do you paint?"

"No, I just sit on various boards." When she glanced at him, his look had turned puzzled, so she explained. "Ours is a family-owned fine arts business."

"That's right. Your brother, Justin, took over the company last year," Reginald joined in from his seat across the table. "He diversified the company quite nicely into publishing and artistic management."

"I remember now," Frank Gordon responded. "He also got involved with an artist over those lost paintings and some kind of fine arts forgery ring."

Valerie Hall set her wineglass down. "It was all over the papers about them when it happened last year. And after all they went through, the two of them ended up together."

"Yes, and they're very happy." Carolyn looked at Michael. "Her name is Davina Spenser, and she's the real artist in the family."

"Oh, I think that is so romantic," Deirdre said. "Nothing tests relationships like a sinking ship."

Frank Gordon groaned. "You compare everything to *Titanic*."

While the others laughed, Michael turned back to Carolyn. "Interesting family of yours. You'll have to tell me about them, and I'll have to visit the gallery to see if anything there interests me."

"You'll love it, Michael. It's just off from downtown," Valerie said, and proceeded to tell him about the place.

The chatty woman had saved Carolyn from having to extend a personal invitation. She felt no guilt on that point; on balance, she had at least been courteous and civil. She turned back to the table as waiters swooped in to clear things away.

While Michael continued to talk with the others, Carolyn took the time to dart a few sidelong glances in his direction. For a football player, he wasn't at all what she'd expected. Yes, he was tall and broad chested—muscular is what it was probably called; but surprisingly, he possessed fewer rough edges and had more manners than she'd expected. Two years ago it hadn't taken him long to live up to the stereotype that was always in the news; he had shown his colors quite quickly, back then.

She looked at him again, but this time her gaze took on an unkindly glint. The man had probably slept with more women than he could count, forget knowing their names. She'd heard about the kind of fast life pro athletes lived. He was like a rock star—the groupies probably waited at the hotels to throw themselves at him. So why did he show up here and bid on her? Maybe it was all for the sake of public appearances. Good grief—he did, after all, come with his publicist. A sigh of regret slipped out. Too bad he was self-centered, materialistic . . . she shook off the direction of her roaming thoughts.

"Are you cold? Here—you can take my jacket." Michael solicitously began to shrug out of his coat.

"No, no." Carolyn stopped him with a firm hand to his arm and pushed away from the table. "I think I will step outside for a minute to clear my head, though."

He leaned in and spoke close to her ear. "Sounds like a good idea. I'll go with you."

Carolyn had no time to react before he was up from his chair and pulling hers out.

"Excuse us a moment," he said to the others as he took Carolyn's hand. After he helped her from the table, he led her across the ballroom to the nearest exit.

The multi-level garden terrace was empty when Michael drew Carolyn with him through the elevated flower beds arrayed with colorful, giant bromeliads and other tropical flora.

"Is this better?" he asked, and slowly released Carolyn's hand. They walked side by side.

"More air is circulating, though I don't believe it's any warmer out here than it was inside."

"In that case, my coat's still available."

The small talk had subsided into silence when Michael abruptly stopped and turned to face Carolyn. She tilted her head in curiosity, not sure of his intent, and Michael was struck once again with the full impact of her singular beauty. Taken separately the parts were common enough; but what a picture the pieces made when put together.

Her mouth was too wide and full for a classic pout, and her eyes too large and brown to be "happening," and she didn't wear a hairstyle; rather, her hair, dark and thick as it brushed her shoulders, seemed as carefree as she was uptight. He was intrigued by that. Having met her sisters, he wondered what had made her so vulnerable. It was a puzzle that could more than keep him occupied and focused for the time being. He would take the bull by the horns and tell her what was on his mind.

"Carolyn, I realize I didn't make a good first impression that day at the bank." It pleased him to see the beginnings of a smile form on her face. "In fact, I pretty much shot myself in the foot."

"You didn't fare much better when we talked on the phone."

He chuckled. "Okay, so I shot myself in the foot twice. One day, maybe you'll let me try and explain what was going on in my head."

"We'll see."

"Deal." They continued their stroll through the terrace. "Anyway, even though our first meeting lasted all of fifteen minutes, it sort of stuck with me over the years. So, when I got to Atlanta, I actually thought about you, wondered if you were still the 'attitude queen' or whether you might even be happily married."

"Were you surprised to learn that I still have what you'd call an attitude? With the way you burst back into my life, can you blame me?"

"Maybe not; but this is all nothing more than healthy curiosity about you. I was thrown for a loop when I saw you on that stage. I'm no stalker, and I won't even press you about the date if it's not what you want." He stopped Carolyn with a touch to her arm. "All I want to do is wipe out that earlier impression you have of me. That's it. You know, things change, and people change over time."

"Well, you did show up again, throwing your money around." When he opened his mouth to speak, she raised her hand to stop his interjection. "I know, I know. This time it was for a good cause." Carolyn propped her hands on her hips. "I guess I'll help you remain a man of your word."

"You want to do the date thing after all?"

"Yes. I do have a condition, though."

Michael groaned loudly. "Why didn't I expect that?"

"This is about *my* comfort level, so we'll have dinner, but with my family next Sunday."

Michael watched as her eyes seemed to glow with pride from this last minute reprieve she'd brokered for herself. "Oh, you think I'll refuse, don't you?" He grinned as he said, "It's a deal if you add my condition."

"What?" Carolyn asked, and rested her hand on her hip. "This could go on all night."

"It's only fair since this was supposed to be a date of my choosing. I'm sure your sisters would understand."

"All right," Carolyn acquiesced. "What's your condition?"

"That we go on a second date where I get to choose the location."

"I don't see where that's fair," Carolyn argued.

"Then let your family decide if we go on a second one."

"You've already won over Alli and Stephanie with the size of your checkbook."

"All right, the family vote will have to be unanimous. Deal?"

Carolyn crossed her arms a moment, and Michael could see that she was already figuring a way to ultimately outsmart him. He smiled at her "never say never" attitude.

"You seem pretty sure of yourself, but you have a deal, Michael."

When she thrust her hand out, he caught it up in his for a hearty shake. "That's the first time you've used my given name, and I like it."

"Let's see how the next dinner turns out," she warned, "before we talk about what we like."

Michael chuckled as he took her arm, tucked it inside the crook of his, and escorted her back toward the main ballroom for the remainder of the evening's event, liking how things had fared thus far.

A few hours later, Michael arrived home and quietly let himself into the settled household. As he made his way up the stairs, he was beckoned by the lights in the wing that remained bright.

When he reached the landing, he could see that the settee in the anteroom of the double suite ahead was occupied. Mrs. Pitts, his housekeeper and Eldridge's wife, sat there under a lighted wall sconce. Her head was bowed, and her hands moved in intricate patterns as the needles they held darted up and down in the length of yarn.

He kept his voice low as he made his way to her side. "Mrs. Pitts, it's after midnight. Why haven't you gone to bed?"

She looked up at Michael's words and dropped the knitting in her lap. "Oh, you're home. Now that you're here, I will go."

Michael immediately looked toward the two bedroom doors on opposite walls at her back. "Is everything okay? Was there a problem? Is she asleep?"

She nodded. "She was restless all evening, and I told her no matter what time you came home, you'd stop in."

Smiling, Michael went to the bedroom door on Mrs. Pitts's left.

Mrs. Pitts joined him in a smile as she gathered up her knitting bag. "She recorded a new song today, but if she wakes when you go in there, don't you dare let her perform at this time of night. Tomorrow is soon enough."

She stood to leave. "I think you spoil her entirely too much." She tilted her head and smiled gently at Michael. "But then again, I understand why." She walked past him to the stairs. "Goodnight, Michael."

"Goodnight, Mrs. Pitts."

He opened the bedroom door and walked in. The night lamp's pale radiance in the pink and white decorated room gave an ethereal cast to all it touched. He walked to the head of the canopied bed where Halina was curled on her side beneath a soft pink comforter.

Michael dropped to one knee and placed a kiss on her forehead.

She immediately flipped onto her back, her eyes fluttering for a few seconds before they opened on their own accord and recognition set in.

"Daddy." In a flash, she sat up and threw her arms around Michael's neck. "Did you have a good time at your party?"

"The best," Michael said, and ruffled her pony tailed hair. "But aren't you supposed to be sleep."

She nodded her head as a yawn escaped her mouth. "I wanted to hear about the party, and play my new song for you."

"It's after midnight."

"I'm not sleepy anymore." She reached behind her pillow and pulled out her familiar gray and pink cassette music recorder with its dangling microphone attachment.

Michael smiled at her seven-year-old logic, kissed her cheek, and then coaxed her back under the covers. "Tomorrow is soon enough for all that. And I promise I'll tell you all about the party, too."

"I won't forget," she said, her eyes already closed in sleep.

"I know," Michael smiled as he quietly left the room.

After he closed her door, he walked across the anteroom to the opposite door. Opening it, he stuck his head inside and in the murky shadows saw eleven-year-old Adam's long limbs stretched across the unturned bed, comfortably relaxed in sleep. A deejay's voice spoke in a low volume from a boom box that was resting on the computer table which was draped with a carelessly flung shirt. Michael smiled at the familiar disarray and closed the door.

Now that he had at least two dates tied down with Carolyn Hardy, and his family was safe in bed, all was pretty much right with the world. He pulled the collar loose around his neck as he turned toward the staircase to retire to his own suite.

Five

The graph that materialized on the TI-85 screen in front of Carolyn made no sense. She nibbled at her lip as she re-entered values in the calculator for the third time in the hope that this sequence would finally match one of her results. Just as she pressed the "enter" key, the phone rang from the corner of her desk.

The undule quiet of the Saturday office magnified the harsh, impatient ring. Her attention didn't waver from her equations as she punched the speaker button and spoke her name, absentmindedly awaiting a response.

"It's Michael Hennessey. Did I catch you at a bad time? When you work on Saturday, though, that makes it bad all around, don't you think?"

Carolyn jerked her head around at the sound of the familiar voice and stared stupidly at the phone.

"How did you get my work number?" she blurted out in surprise.

"I called your family's art gallery and spoke with your sister—"

"That would be Alli," Carolyn interrupted with a sigh. Reaching across the papers on her desk, she picked up the receiver and brought it to her ear. "I'm sure you didn't have to charm her too much to get my number."

Michael's deep chuckle echoed through the phone.

"Don't be too hard on her—it's your fault I had to ask her."

"My fault?" Carolyn echoed.

"She gave me your number because I needed your parents' address. You didn't forget about dinner tomorrow, did you?"

"Of course not." How could she? Her sisters had constantly reminded her of the promise. If the truth be known, it had been foremost in her thoughts most of the week, anyway.

"If you'd like, I could pick you up at your place and then we could ride there together."

Carolyn's head snapped up before she quickly squelched that notion. "No, that's not necessary. I'll, uh, give you the directions, and we can meet there." She preferred to maintain her privacy—at least with respect to her residence. That was why she'd suggested the family home for dinner in the first place.

Carolyn gave him the address and basic directions, already deciding that, though she could be civil to him, he was a complication she'd be glad to dispose of. She was looking forward to things returning to normal, and they would, after this weekend, because she had no intention of seeing him again after tomorrow.

"I should have no problems finding it." After a pause, he said, "So, what time should I show up?"

"Five o'clock."

"Alli thought it was earlier."

"Pardon?"

Michael's chuckle rumbled through the phone as he realized she wasn't listening. "Nothing important. I'll see you tomorrow."

The recipient of Carolyn's divided attention, Michael opted to ring off rather than extend the call with small talk. She was mildly curious about why he didn't draw out the call after going through the effort to locate her;

but she knew she hadn't given him much of a reason to continue. If he couldn't deal with her, then that was his problem. It was common knowledge to those who knew Carolyn that she had no time for men who couldn't hold their own in her company. She was a strong woman and made no apologies for it. She reached across the desk to replace the phone in the cradle, her brows knitted in thought.

The week had sped by much faster than she had wanted, but in any case, she had never intended to give this dinner any serious thought. To do so would have awarded it significance, something she was avoiding. She shook her head clear of the entire fog that was Michael Hennessey. She certainly had no interest in football players, certainly not in this player in particular. No, she had much loftier goals.

Carolyn returned her attention to the calculator and digested the answer it had produced prior to the call. Once again, the solution was off. She picked up her pencil and returned to her notes, her head cleared of men and dinners as she tackled her short term goal: solve this probability problem.

Michael, too, was in deep thought as he looked at the phone on the library desk. Carolyn was something else, but he sensed there was a lot more to her, if he could somehow melt that shell of ice.

He'd just come in from the basketball court with Adam and a few of his friends. Michael looked down at the gym shorts and sneakers he wore and saw a parent trying to bond with his kid, doing the best he could do with the limited knowledge he had. But when Carolyn looked at him, he knew she still saw that bejeweled, fast-living, money-spending football player, and Michael had only himself to blame for that impression.

Michael rubbed a knot out of his neck, a slick glaze of perspiration still there from the basketball workout. True, he hadn't forgotten how to have fun, but that had been tempered by the responsibility of raising two kids. He would make her see the changes. He still had two opportunities ahead of him.

A knock came from outside the open library door, and Michael looked up. Mrs. Pitts stood there with another portable phone pressed to her chest.

"Mrs. Pitts, are you looking for me?" Michael pushed off the desk and walked across the room to meet her at the door.

"This call came in for you on the second line, Michael." The housekeeper's explanation was almost apologetic. "You must have been on the phone at the time."

He reached for the phone she handed him. "Who is it?"

"It's a Mr. Rollie Anderson, and he said I should make it my business to find you because you wouldn't want to miss his call."

Recognition immediately streaked through Michael, and he drew in a deep breath. "Thank you. I'll take it in here, Mrs. Pitts." He saw that she had something draped across her arm. A towel. She handed it to him.

"I've already corralled Adam and his friends to clean up, but you got away."

He smiled. "You take good care of us, Mrs. Pitts. Thanks. Oh, and don't worry about the caller. He's just an old friend," he explained as he closed the library door.

He turned his attention to the phone. "All right," he said, mimicking anger, "what's the idea of giving those kinds of orders to my housekeeper?"

"Michael, you big old bastard, long time no see," the caller said with a hacking laugh.

"What's going on with you, man?" Michael asked his longtime friend from the old neighborhood. "You're still on the inside, right? Did they set a trial date yet for the robbery charge?"

A gleeful laugh erupted from the phone. "That's why I'm calling, man. I'm free." He laughed again. "I told you they'd have to drop the charges."

"No kidding?" Michael asked, astonished, and dropped into the chair at the desk. "When did all this happen?"

"You know this jackass of a District Attorney up here has it in for me. Get this, he calls me his cat with nine lives. Ain't that some stuff." He laughed again. "I got the last laugh, though. Spell it—insufficient evidence and no witnesses. My attorney says they're doing the paperwork, and I should be out of this damn lockup in twenty-four hours."

Michael swallowed his surprise and expressed delight instead at this unexpected turn of events. "So what're you planning on doing now? Think, Rollie. Think. Why don't you just settle down with Glenda like a normal husband and quit that street stuff."

"Nah, man, now you know as well as I do there ain't nothin' normal about some of us, including me and you. My tail's been coolin' in this can and now I am ready to breakout and par-ty." He accented each word in special street style. "Enough about me, though. I heard you left town and that you're getting ready to break out with the Wildcats in Atlanta."

"I couldn't see you before I left. And you know I can't talk about deals in the making, man. Anyway, I needed a break from the old stuff. So here I am."

"Hey, maybe I'll just mosey on South myself. I know a few guys down that way. You know the two of us always been a thing together, man. I can introduce you to some folks down there."

"No, Rollie. I don't need any of that. You just get your life together and thank the Lord you were able to get off this time. Armed robbery is serious stuff."

"Yeah, man. I know. Like I told you before, I got hooked up with some worthless boys, and I was an innocent. I didn't know what they were doin'. And listen, I appreciate you taking care of the attorney fees for me."

"And in return, you promised me you'd get back with Glenda and fly right, though, didn't you?"

"I know. But I'm paying you back this time, man. My brother-in-law helped Glenda handle the detailing business while I was out of circulation. But everybody's cool, I'm getting my game together again, and it's gonna be like old times."

Michael hoped not. Rollie had been in and out of jail fighting six felony charges for the last eighteen months. It was during that same period that Michael's life had also undergone change and made a 180 degree turn. He couldn't afford to go back to the old times, but he couldn't turn his back on Rollie, either. In the old days, when neither of them had any money, Rollie never turned his back on him.

"Listen, when you get out, give me a call and let me know what you're doing. What I suggest you do is get your business going again and take care of your wife and daughter."

"Yeah, yeah," Rollie laughed. "I'll be in touch."

After they exchanged goodbyes, Michael shook his head as he cut off the phone. Rollie had at least nine lives, all right. Ever since elementary school, no matter what the problem, his friend always seemed to land on his feet.

Michael heard the library door open, and turned just as it was pushed wider by little Halina, who dropped an overnight bag as she came toward him at a gallop. He dropped the cell phone onto the desk and stooped to meet her, his arms open wide.

"Whoaaa . . ." Michael laughed as she launched herself into his arms. He scooped her up before he playfully stumbled backwards and onto the leather couch. "What are you today, a strong safety?" he teased.

"No," she laughed. "Can't you tell? I'm a linebacker."

Michael looked over her head and saw that Mrs. Pitts lingered near the door. "So, how did your first sleep-over go?"

Halina sat up on Michael's lap. "It was okay, I guess," she said earnestly. Her eyes suddenly brightened. "We had a talent show, and I sang. I taped it for you."

"Good for you," Michael said.

"Still, I missed you and Adam."

He grinned at her innocent loss of memory. Insisting she was a big girl, she hadn't wanted Michael and Adam to drop her off or pick her up. Instead, Mr. Pitts had done the honors. "Maybe we'll be around next time," he said, and chucked her under the chin. "When you have one at our house."

"I can?" Her eyes grew wide and she jumped off his lap and rushed back to Mrs. Pitts at the door. "Daddy says I can have a sleep over, too, just like Marie did."

"So I heard," Mrs. Pitts said. "Why don't you run along and unpack your bag. I'll be up in a minute to help, okay?"

"Okay." Halina grabbed her overnight tote from the floor and bounded from the room with a yell. "Bye, daddy!"

"Bye, baby." Michael sat up on the sofa and looked up at Mrs. Pitts. "So, how did it really go?"

"Eldridge says she seemed fine when he picked her up. Mrs. Thornton, Marie's mother, called and also said she did well. It was natural that she was a little quiet and standoffish at first, but she soon warmed to the other girls. Best of all, she didn't have any nightmares or bed-wetting incidents."

"That's good news." Michael nodded and clasped his hands. "Really good. She's doing better with our move here than I expected." He looked up at Mrs. Pitts. "You have been remarkable with both of the kids. I don't know how to thank you for that."

"They're good children, Michael."

"I'm figuring the therapist will want a report on Halina's progress. I'll have to make sure he's aware of how she's doing."

They could hear a ball bouncing on the parquet hallway floor, the *thwack* growing louder as it neared the library door. Michael smiled as he dropped back on the sofa and patiently waited for Mrs. Pitts to lay down the law.

"When I get hold of him . . ." Mrs. Pitts stepped into the hall just as tall and gangly Adam appeared. The housekeeper expertly caught the basketball on an up bounce and took it away from him.

"How many times do I have to tell you? No ball playing in the house, Adam."

"Sorry, I forgot." His grin confirmed that he knew he was wrong, and he sheepishly joined Michael on the sofa.

The housekeeper propped the ball on her hip. "I think I'll just hold onto this until you go outside again," she said before she left them.

Michael gazed over at Adam. "You gotta follow house rules, sport, and not give her a hard time. She even makes me follow them."

"Yeah, I know."

"We don't want her and Mr. Pitts pulling out on us, not after we're getting used to each other."

"She's okay. Halina likes her, too. Not like that neat freak we had in Jersey." They both laughed at the reminder of one of the housekeepers from hell that they'd survived. "So, when are you coming back outside for the rematch, old man?"

"I thought you could use the break." Michael reached over and squeezed Adam's head as he protested. "Anyway, you got your other three partners out there to go to the hoops with you."

"I saw Mr. Pitts drive up with Halina." He darted a guarded look at Michael. "Did she like being away from home last night?"

The reason for Adam's presence was now clear. Protective of his sister, he was interested in how she'd fared on her second sleep over. Michael smiled into intense dark eyes that gave off a mirror image of Adam's mother.

"It went well. I gave her the go ahead to plan one of her own."

Adam let out a sigh of relief. "Hey, cool." He jumped up from the sofa. "Now, about our rematch—the fellas are waiting in the kitchen."

Michael followed suit. "I'm right behind you.

Six

"So, how did a smart woman like yourself get roped into a date this way?" Douglas Bradley, a close Hardy family friend, set his glass on the table near his arm chair so he could give Carolyn his undivided attention.

Carolyn rested her head against the back of the sofa. "From the way things have turned out, I'm not *that* smart," she grunted.

They sat across from each other in the quietly elegant salon of Elizabeth Hardy's home as they waited for Michael, Stephanie, and her husband, William, to arrive for dinner.

Douglas chuckled at Carolyn's self-pity, his salt and pepper brows arched in chastisement. "Now you're feeling sorry for yourself. This isn't the Carolyn I know at all."

"Well," she said, crossing her arms tightly, "this Carolyn might wring Alli's neck before the evening is over."

"Oh, so it's Alli, huh? Is she instigator this time, or just meddler?"

"You know Alli. She can manage either label whenever she deems it appropriate, and I'm afraid she's going to have a field day at dinner."

"Hmm . . . you're not pleased we're having Michael Hennessey join us?" He shifted forward in his chair. "I understand from Stephanie and Alli that he's quite the charmer with the ladies." As he looked at Carolyn, a broad smile grew on his face. "But, you're obviously unimpressed."

Carolyn returned Douglas's gaze and saw in his eyes a gleam of sympathy for her particular situation. Like Carolyn's mother, Douglas was a widower. He had been the close friend and business partner of Jacob Hardy, her father, right up until Jacob's unexpected death last year, and he still remained a good friend to her mother, and a frequent visitor with the family.

"Maybe something is wrong with me, then." Carolyn shifted restlessly on the sofa. "I'm not a poor loser, and I'm fine with today because it's only a dinner, but I'm still angry at being manipulated into doing something I really wanted no part of."

"What makes you think you're being manipulated?"

She sat up. "You know my sisters, Mr. Bradley. I know they're using this as a matchmaking exercise. So, of course, I have to fight them."

"You're fighting this arrangement because your sisters want you to have dinner with Michael Hennessey."

"Exactly."

"That little favor you did for Alli has taken on a life of its own that you can't control. I think this all boils down to the fact that you don't like not being in control."

"Maybe," she repeated, and considered his take on her reaction to Michael.

Douglas motioned to Carolyn's cell phone resting on the coffee table in front of them.

"How's that job of yours going these days? You're never too far from it with that thing. Are you about to make partner?"

Carolyn laughed. "Heavens, no. I've only just made team leader and now senior engineer."

"With the hours your mother tells me you put in, you could make partner by the time you're thirty."

"Well, that all depends," she said.

"On what? Your hard work?"

"No—on whether I can first become a man, and then, by another miracle, change my race." She made a face at her facetious comment. "It's why I'm so clear on my choices. I have to keep on top of things, or I could slide backward."

"I don't understand, Carolyn. If you know there's a glass ceiling limiting your flight, why don't you just get out of that room, create your own building where the sky's the limit and, while you're at it, don't forget to enjoy life." Douglas tilted his head sagely. "It's what your father and Justin did."

Carolyn swallowed hard. That was the same advice Justin had offered. If she insisted on working as hard as she did, then leave the firm and branch out on her own. How could she tell them that fear stopped her cold every time? She was ashamed, but the thought of not having a safety net in the event of failure had the power to make her hyperventilate. Carolyn wanted to make her own success, but she didn't think she wanted it enough to put her faith in her own ability to the test. She pushed the private, daunting thought from her head, replacing it with her usual façade of strength.

"Well, I could be that one employee G & G will be forced to acknowledge in the long run. I could be the one to change things."

"You know, the corporate status quo can be a pretty intractable force."

"That I can deal with. What I'll need help on is getting through dinner without wringing little Alli's neck."

"Wring my neck? Why?" Alli breezed into view and plopped onto the sofa next to Carolyn, setting off what sounded like an assembly of bells. She gave Carolyn a close inspection.

"Well, you're looking fetching today in that cream-colored suit. I figured you'd show up in your de rigueur black and scare the poor man off for good." She sniffed the air. "What are we having for dinner? Smells good, like chicken."

"Mrs. Taylor prepared rosemary chicken, to be exact," Carolyn answered as she returned Alli's scrutiny in kind, not in the least thrown off by her sister's divergent and rapid fire sentences. "And you showed up today wearing what? Bells on your toes?"

"Nice, aren't they?" Alli stuck her foot out and there were, indeed, tiny golden bells sewn across the front of the slipper-like jade-colored shoes that matched Alli's silk blouse and slacks.

"Dinner is ready, and Stephanie and William just arrived." Mrs. Hardy had come to the salon door to make the announcement. "As soon as Carolyn's guest arrives, we can eat." She looked over at Carolyn on the sofa. "Have you heard anything from him?"

"Yeah, why hasn't Michael arrived?" Alli asked Carolyn. "You did give the man the right directions, didn't you?"

"Of course, I did," Carolyn said. She looked at her watch and frowned at the four o'clock hour, the standing time for their Sunday dinners, and felt a belated twinge of guilt. She saw her earlier action for what it was: an immature attempt to avoid dinner with Michael.

She darted a guilty look toward the salon door her mother had vacated, and then turned to Douglas. "Maybe he was held up unexpectedly by something or the other."

Douglas made no comment, but cleared his throat. "Tell me, Alli, how did you manage to get Carolyn mixed up in your dating game, anyway?"

Alli nudged her sister in the side. "I'm sure you've heard Caro's version, but mine is much better, and I'm dying to tell it," she said.

Settling back into his chair, Douglas said, "I'm betting we've got the time."

Michael glanced at the clock in his car as he drove through the gates that led him to the circular drive in front of the two-story house with the distinct look of a castle. He was ten minutes early so he wouldn't be late, but not appear overly anxious, either. After all, he was Carolyn's date, not the family's choice of a dinner guest, so he needed to make a good impression.

He parked the car, and after unfolding his long frame from the two-seater, he fished out flowers, wine, and a boxed dessert from the passenger side, then took the bricked walkway up to the double-door entrance. The doorbell had barely rung before it was flung open by Carolyn.

Michael had not yet grown accustomed to her special beauty, and before he could find his tongue to express his pleasure, she shot a quick glance behind her and stepped onto the covered porch beside him, pulling the door shut.

"Listen," she said in a low voice. "Dinner has been ready for an hour, and Mrs. Taylor, my mom's cook, is livid and on the warpath." She quickly shot another glance at the door behind her. "Mama insisted we wait for you, and now Stephanie says she may have to leave soon for a meeting."

Michael narrowed his gaze. "What did you do?"

She sighed. "I played a little joke on you yesterday, and it seems to have backfired in my face. I'm sorry; but you can't tell them I caused all this."

So. She had tried to sabotage his visit. Michael was amused by the mixed message of her apology and the sheer panic in her eyes that he might reveal what she had done to the family.

"Why don't we both save face and just say you estimated the wrong time for dinner?" he suggested.

"No, that won't work. We have a standard Sunday dinner time, and it's always four o'clock."

The front door pushed open to the sound of bells. "Carolyn, is it Michael? Mom wants to know." Alli stuck her head around the door. When she saw Michael, a smile broke out on her face as she joined them on the porch.

"Michael, we were beginning to worry about you. Carolyn, why are you hogging the man out here in the cold?"

"He's, um . . ." Carolyn looked at Michael.

"I, uh, was telling Carolyn about my flat tire—I didn't know the number here to let her know I'd be about an hour late. So, here I am," he said. "Late."

Alli's gaze strayed to the sleek, silver sports car parked near the other vehicles before she looked back at Michael. "Well, I must say, you don't look any worse for the wear." She looped her arm through his. "Come on in and let's eat. I'll take this wine for you."

Michael gave Carolyn a conspiratorial glance before he allowed Alli to draw him into the foyer, with Carolyn bringing up the rear.

The foyer was a long and wide hallway with a staircase on the right set off by a spectacular chandelier suspended from the second-floor ceiling. Michael slowed as he passed by the remarkable paintings that hung on the walls, and waited for Carolyn.

"This is fantastic," he said, looking up and then around.

"It is, isn't it?" Carolyn agreed distractedly.

"Everyone's waiting in the salon up ahead," Alli said, turning into a doorway midway down the hall.

They entered behind Alli just as she announced to everyone that Michael had arrived.

"Mom, he brought this nice bottle of wine for dinner."

Carolyn introduced Michael to everyone before he launched into an apology to the group for arriving late.

He presented Mrs. Hardy with the dessert in the white cardboard box.

Elizabeth smiled at Michael as she peeked inside. "Thank you. We can't fault you for having to deal with a flat tire now, can we?"

Michael unfurled the tissue from the flowers he held and revealed a bouquet of still-lively carnations. "If you could make sure your cook, Mrs. Taylor, gets these, I'd appreciate it. Tell her I'm sorry for holding up her dinner."

Mrs. Hardy turned to the door. "You can come with me right now and tell her yourself. It's a lovely gesture and she'd love to hear it. Everyone else, to the dining room."

Michael looked over at Carolyn, and could see by the look she gave him in return that she knew the flowers—her favorites, according to Alli—had been for her. It was just as well that they'd been used this way. Right about now, he figured she didn't think she deserved them, anyway.

"You don't have much free time before your spring training camp starts, I'll bet," Douglas said to Michael at the table.

"Don't I know it," Michael answered over the chicken's flavorful aroma. "I'll start some off-season conditioning in a few more weeks."

"What are you, six-three, two-hundred thirty?" William asked.

"That's about right," Michael said.

He grunted. "Pretty tall for a wide receiver."

"I never did hear the details of how you and Carolyn first met," Mrs. Hardy said.

"That's right," Alli began, "On the night of the auction, I remember the two of you saying you already knew each other." She darted a smile at Carolyn. "So, where did you go to meet up with a well-known football player?"

Carolyn was not amused by Alli's comment and looked at Michael before she answered. "The bank."

"The bank?" Alli asked, disappointment in her voice. "You met at the bank?"

"About two years ago," Michael explained as he smiled. "I was in town for the Super Bowl, and offered to take Carolyn."

"And I, of course, declined," she added brightly.

"Of course," Alli agreed. "Do you even know what that is?"

Michael chuckled and looked at Carolyn. "At the time, I don't know that she did."

"I know what the Super Bowl is," she said in good humor. "I work in an office filled with men, so I'm not that bad on sports." She looked at Michael. "He's still upset that I didn't know who the heck he was."

They all laughed as Michael joined in at his own expense. "She's right, she's right."

"Do you have family in this area?" Stephanie asked.

"No," Michael answered. "Family for me is pretty small. My mother died during my second year in the league."

"I'm sorry to hear that," Mrs. Hardy said.

"Our dad died last year," Alli volunteered soberly. "A heart attack."

At that moment, Carolyn's cell phone rang. "Excuse me," she said, and lifted it from her lap to see the caller's name. "I've got to take this." Already, she was pushing her chair back from the table. "I have to speak with a few people so I'll talk in the library—I'll try not to be too long." She was already talking into the phone before she exited the room.

Elizabeth watched her daughter leave the room before

she spoke. "I wish she would take a day off from that project she's leading. It's Sunday, for heaven's sake."

"She'll learn to slow down in her own time," Douglas said.

"I worry about her," Mrs. Hardy continued. "She's too intense."

"Be happy that she's only received one call so far." Alli turned to Michael. "Usually, they start in on her early, and she doesn't even get around to eating."

"Enough complaints about Carolyn," Mrs. Hardy warned. "We have to remember Michael is Carolyn's guest, and she wouldn't want these comments about her uttered carelessly."

"So, she has all the markings of a workaholic, huh?" Michael looked around the table for agreements.

"Dyed in the wool, like her brother," William said.

"Hey, now, in defense of Justin," Douglas argued, "he plays hard at business and pleasure, and he knows how to keep the two separate."

"Don't worry about Carolyn, Mama." Stephanie set her glass down as she explained her point. "She's got a lot riding on her reputation and expertise right now. I was the same way, though Carolyn is much more focused than I ever was."

"That's because you had me around to help." William leaned over and playfully nudged his wife.

"Not to mention your two kids," Alli added.

"I don't know if all that was a help or hindrance," Stephanie replied, and joined in with the chuckles from across the table.

As Michael listened to the family's small talk, it brought on a bit of nostalgia for his own family dinner table. He remembered how his mother worried over the slightest problem she perceived he was facing—from the football field to street life. Surprisingly for him, Mrs. Hardy worried in much the same way.

"When she takes the time to explore life outside of the office, she'll come around," Mrs. Hardy was saying. "But she just won't take that time."

"Maybe I can help," Michael said.

"You think so? How?" Douglas asked.

"Well, I've got time on my hands right now. And because I'm new in town, maybe I can encourage her to spend time with me and show me around, that sort of thing."

"You don't know our Carolyn," Stephanie said. "It won't work."

Alli nodded in agreement. "She'll never agree to it."

"She will if it's her idea," Michael said.

"How do you do that?" Alli wanted to know.

"Give the man a moment to speak his piece," Mrs. Hardy said to everyone around the table.

Michael explained his arrangement with Carolyn whereby the family would decide if they should have a second date. "When she brings it up, and everyone agrees we should go out again, it's a start."

"He's right, it'll work," Alli said.

Mrs. Hardy looked at Michael. "Even without the suggestion, I think I would have agreed that you and Carolyn deserve a second date, and away from us."

"Thank you, Mrs. Hardy," Michael said. "I'd very much like another date with your daughter."

She gently wagged her finger at him. "A word of warning, though, Michael. My daughter is no Milquetoast." She looked down the table. "None of them are, and I raised them that way. So, while we may hand you an opening with Carolyn, remember, it'll be up to you to continue the journey from there."

"I think I'm up to the task." He grinned and picked up his wineglass.

Douglas joined him by raising his glass, too. "We

should all make a toast." He raised his glass as did the others. "To a smooth journey."

"And strong libations. You're going to need it with Carolyn," Alli warned.

"Cheers." Douglas's bass rose above the chorus from around the table. He nodded to Michael as everyone sipped from their glasses.

"I enjoyed dinner, Carolyn. Thanks for inviting me. Your family was great about everything." Michael had stopped inside the foyer as he prepared to leave.

Carolyn stood alongside him, her arms crossed over her chest. "Yeah, they were pretty enthusiastic about you, too, so their vote for another date shouldn't have come as a surprise." She turned to him. "After arranging for you to arrive late, and getting Mrs. Taylor and Stephanie upset, it serves me right."

Michael put on an astonished expression. "You're not angry about another date with me?"

"Well, I wouldn't go that far."

"Where will we meet? Your place or mine?"

Carolyn couldn't help but smile at his eagerness. "Let's try yours for a start." She dropped her hands and reached out to open the door. "Goodbye, Michael."

"Until next time."

It took only a moment, and he was gone. Carolyn closed the door and leaned against it.

She closed her eyes, still not used to the idea that Michael would be around for another week. She wasn't sure how much she embraced the idea, either.

"So, did he steal a kiss?"

Carolyn's eyes flew open at Alli's voice and she pushed away from the door. "Of course not. I just met the man last week."

"Uh-uh," a disappointed Alli corrected her sister. "The

two of you have been simmering for two years. Things should be nice and tender right about now, so I'm surprised he didn't try anything."

Carolyn shook her head at her sister's caustic humor. "I'm not. And I admit I was wrong about one thing: he's far from being a stupid jock."

Seven

"It sounds a lot like fate that you ran into her twice in two years, and both times were purely coincidental." Mrs. Pitts slathered chocolate icing on a layer cake as she stood at the kitchen counter with Michael.

His hip was braced against the counter and his arms casually crossed as they chatted. "That remains to be seen. Carolyn's the kind of woman who would chase fate off with its tail tucked."

"She's no nonsense, huh?" Mrs. Pitts laughed. "Well, I know you're a good man, but a girl can't be too careful these days. Her idea to meet you here before dinner was wise on her part, so don't give her any flack for that. By the way, where is she? It's already past nine."

Michael smiled. "Our dinner reservations are not until ten."

"Why so late?"

He shrugged. "She's a busy engineer and loves every minute of it."

"This is a change. The man cooling his heels while waiting for the woman to show up." She shook her head. "Didn't happen like that in my day. Of course," she winked at Michael, "maybe it should have."

"So, tell me, do I pass muster?" He stood away from

the counter and held his arms wide, smiling for her approval.

Mrs. Pitts pushed the cake aside and surveyed Michael with critical eyes. They roamed over his turtleneck, coupled with the well-cut suit, as though she were a proud mother. The dark leather boots completed the look.

"You look like a man anxious to impress a woman," she finally answered. "I get the feeling tonight is special."

He leaned against the counter again. "A lot is riding on me just spending some time with her with no distractions, so we can get to know each other. If tonight doesn't go as planned, I may have to pull a rabbit out of a hat to get her to see me again."

"It'll be fine," Mrs. Pitts said, returning to the cake. "She's probably as anxious about tonight as you are."

He squinted doubtfully. "You think so?"

"Sure. If she didn't care a thing about tonight and wanted to put you off, she'd show up wearing a gunnysack or something." She nodded her head sagely. "Take my word, she'll show up as a knockout and you'll see she wants to impress you, too."

As if on cue, the chime for the front door sounded.

"She's here," Michael said, and with long, purposeful strides, headed for the door.

"Good luck."

Michael slowed to look back over his shoulder. "Thanks."

Carolyn turned from the doorbell and slowly looked around the wide portico of the secluded house, and then out and beyond the floodlights that bathed the house in a pale glow. From what she had seen as she steered up the winding drive, this majestic brick in-town residence had a lot of acreage attached to the main property, a scarce commodity within the city limits these days.

She wondered if his reasons for buying in the city mirrored hers. The city offered more resources that fit her business life than a cozy spread buried in a suburban gated community could. She had opted for a loft apartment downtown that suited her perfectly. Learning Michael's address had renewed her interest in him as well as posed a conundrum: Which was the real Michael—the offensive one from two years ago, or this new and seemingly improved one he kept lobbing her way?

She heard a click from somewhere on the other side of the door, and suspected she was being viewed. Seconds later, the door opened.

"Carolyn." Michael greeted her and pushed the door wide open. "Please, come in."

"Thank you," she answered and stepped onto the shiny parquet floor in the softly lit foyer.

"Any problems finding the house?" he asked.

"No, I've been in this area of Blackland Road before."

Michael closed the door after Carolyn cleared the entryway. "Our reservations are at ten. We can leave as soon as I get my coat."

As he showed her through the foyer, his pleasant scent—the clean aroma of sandalwood—assailed Carolyn's nostrils.

"You don't mind that we're eating late?" Carolyn asked. "I couldn't get away any earlier."

"No, I'm fine with it."

"I tend to be a night owl, myself."

"Working?" Michael inquired.

"Usually," she answered with a glance toward him. "My schedule is mercurial; breakfast is brunch, lunch is late afternoon, and dinner is whenever I get home at night, which is usually long after seven."

"That's no way for you to live."

"It's become second nature. I sometimes forget it's not the norm."

Michael had led her into the living room. She had presumed a contemporary setting would be more to his taste—a bachelor's pad complete with glass and sharp angles. Instead, the room was surprisingly traditional, with comfortable, upholstered pieces, soft wall colors, and a masterful, raised hearth fireplace that commanded the far wall.

As Carolyn turned from observing the room, she realized she was the subject of Michael's undivided attention. She watched as his eyes, in obvious appreciation, took in her dress.

Carolyn looked down at her open coat which revealed her two-piece wool knit outfit that reached her knees, completed with silk hose and heels. "Did I dress appropriately for the restaurant you chose?" she asked.

"You look . . . very nice tonight," Michael said.

She eyed him just as he was eyeing her. "And so do you."

Two years ago—no, two weeks ago, even, Carolyn's response to his interest would have been quite different: she'd have left him in a huff. Now, he was already becoming so familiar that the experience of basking in the warmth that his eyes generated wasn't altogether unpleasant. In fact, Carolyn was hard-pressed to remove herself from it.

He smiled, as though he recognized her dilemma. "I'll get my coat." He turned on his heels and left through another door.

Looking after him, she sighed and crossed her arms. What had happened to the levelheaded woman who didn't have time for this kind of thing? Had she forgotten so quickly that this was Michael Hennessey, the man she didn't want to let off the hook? She bit down on her lip, unsure just what it was that she was supposed to do. *Let the evening unfold,* she told herself, *and see what it holds.*

Carolyn meandered across the large, well-appointed

room, and looked for some sign of the real Michael. No bronzed football on a pedestal? No giant posters of himself for all to honor upon entering? Michael's footsteps signaled his return to the room.

"Your home decor is quite beautiful. Inviting, too," she said to him. "Your choices?"

"Just the furnishings," he said as he joined her in the center of the room. "In time, I'll put my own stamp on everything. For now, I'm still deciding on some things."

"That's what I did with my loft." She looked around the room again. "I let it grow on me a bit before I started furnishing it."

"Do you like to decorate? Maybe you could loan me your talents."

"Me? Heaven's no," she laughed. "I was always better at designing an efficient garden walk than picking out window treatments to match the wallpaper."

"Which means we should stick with the professionals." He smiled down on her. "We did agree that I would drive tonight, right?"

"I don't think the question ever came up," she said.

"Then we'll make it official." He arched one eyebrow at her, as though he anticipated her refusal. "I'll drive."

"Okay." Carolyn's smile grew as Michael continued to stare. "What?" she asked innocently.

"No argument? No dealmaking? Are you sure you're not coming down with something?" He leaned toward her and laid his hand against her forehead. "You seem pretty normal . . ." He dropped his hand and looked down at her. ". . . More beautiful, too, when you smile."

She looked away. "It's way past nine. We should probably go."

As Michael accompanied Carolyn across the room toward the foyer, a small, clear voice spoke up from behind them.

"Are you leaving now?"

Carolyn stopped and turned with Michael. She saw a little girl standing on the other side of the living room. Dressed in footed pajamas, her hair was gathered up in two ponytails and she clutched what Carolyn recognized as an Addie doll by the hair.

"Halina, what are you doing out of bed?" Michael left Carolyn's side and walked back to the child as she rubbed her eyes.

"I woke up," the little girl replied, "so I tried to find you, and I heard you down here."

Michael tossed his coat onto the sofa and stooped beside her, concern in his voice. "You had another nightmare?"

"I dunno." She rubbed her eyes again. "Maybe."

Carolyn had watched the interaction between Michael and the child with interest, and the possibilities piled up. Was she a visiting relative . . . or his child? If the latter were true, why hadn't he mentioned it, and where was the mother? Was he divorced? She had never considered that possibility. Or, for heaven's sake, even worse, was he separated? Maybe the mother was just a former girlfriend . . . suppose she lived in the house? Questions swirled through her head as they multiplied, unanswered.

Michael smiled, turning his head until Carolyn was in his view. When he motioned for her to join him and the child, she did.

"Do you think you might feel better if I introduce my dinner guest before we leave?" he asked Halina.

She dropped her hand as she raised her large, liquid gaze to Carolyn. "Okay."

Michael stood and made the formal introduction. "This is Carolyn Hardy."

Carolyn smiled at the little girl before she glanced toward Michael, anticipating his explanation.

"Carolyn, meet Halina, my daughter."

Carolyn reacted with a slight flicker of her brow, though

her smile widened as she leaned forward and shook Halina's hand. She *was* his child after all, which meant there was a mother somewhere, as well.

"It's nice meeting you, Halina. You have a beautiful name."

Halina had stepped forward to grasp Carolyn's hand. "Thank you," she said, stepping back. Her attention had already returned to Michael as she craned her neck to look at him. "Will you be gone a very long time?"

He bent down to her level. "No matter what time I return, I promise I'll come by your room and check on you. Now, come on and let me take you up there before Mrs. Pitts gets wind of the fact that you're running around past your bedtime."

"I'll take her up if you want me to."

A youthful voice had floated in from the interior hall, and Carolyn looked toward the door, surprised as a jeans-clad boy sauntered into the room. A sports cap was pulled low over his dark hair as he fiddled with the controls on the logo-emblazoned headphones looped around his neck. Another child?

"Come on, Halina," the young boy said.

"No," she spouted loudly. "I want Daddy to take me."

Michael breathed out a sigh as he scooped Halina into his arms. "I'll put her to bed." He looked around at Carolyn, his face apologetic. "Adam, I'd like you to meet Carolyn Hardy."

"I already know she's the chick you're taking out. You told us about her, remember?"

Carolyn lifted her eyebrows at the label.

"Watch your mouth," Michael warned him.

"That's okay." Carolyn tried to turn off the questions as she nodded toward Adam. "Hello."

"Michael—" An older woman with a salt-and-pepper Afro came in from the hallway. "I thought you and Miss Hardy had left."

Carolyn drew in another confused breath and decided not to hazard a guess about this new person and simply wait for yet another introduction.

"Why is Halina out of bed?" the woman asked. "And what's everybody doing in here?"

"She woke up and came downstairs looking for us," Adam said.

"Mrs. Pitts, you might as well meet Carolyn, too. Everybody else has," Michael said, and turned to Carolyn. "Mrs. Pitts and her husband usually manage to keep both the people and things in order around here."

The older woman lifted a corner of the apron she wore tied around her waist, and wiped her hands. "We don't seem to be doing an especially good job tonight, though," she said, grinning good-naturedly. "Good evening, Miss Hardy. The only one left for you to meet is Eldridge, my husband, but he's probably out in the garage."

"Well, since Michael has kept silent about his family I have to admit, it has been both interesting and unexpected meeting all of you," Carolyn said.

Michael gave Carolyn a beseeching look. "I promise we'll be on our way as soon as I put Halina to bed."

"As for you . . ." Michael returned his attention to Halina with a fatherly squeeze. "It's upstairs and off to sleep." He quickly strode through the door with the giggling child.

Carolyn stood by as Mrs. Pitts attempted to regain some control over the house by directing Adam back to the study. When he left, she turned her interest to Carolyn.

"Miss Hardy—"

"Carolyn, please."

She smiled, and it suited her concerned face. "All right, Carolyn. Can I get anything for you before Michael returns? Why don't you take off your coat?"

"That's probably a good idea," she said, not sure how long Michael would be, and having grown warm from the extra layer. She shrugged from the coat with Mrs. Pitts's help, and then handed it to her.

"Michael didn't expect all of this interruption. I know for a fact that he was quite looking forward to your evening." Mrs. Pitts spoke as she went over to the chair and placed Carolyn's coat with Michael's. "And you're such a lovely young lady—everything he described. I'm sure he's going to hurry right back so you can make your reservation on time."

Her words brought a flush to Carolyn's face. So, he had discussed her with the housekeeper? She didn't know whether to be flattered or put off, though it was nice to know that he had described her in glowing terms.

Mrs. Pitts had returned to Carolyn's side. "I know, why don't you let me get you something from the kitchen . . . tea, coffee?"

"I promise," Carolyn shook her head and smiled at the woman's persuasive hospitality. "I'm fine. I'll just look around and admire this beautiful room until he returns."

"In that case, feel free to explore the others, as well. The solarium, my favorite, is down at the end of the hall," she advised. She then announced that she'd be in the kitchen if needed, and left Carolyn alone.

A clock somewhere on the main floor chimed the quarter hour. In fifteen minutes, she and Michael would be late for dinner. The onus this night would be on Michael—much like the anxiety she suffered at their last dinner, when she'd been caught by her own abysmal lie.

She walked about the room and found herself in front of a set of French doors. She peeked through them, surprised that a terrace lay on the other side. She suspected these doors offered a spectacular view in the springtime. Her curiosity roused, she took Mrs. Pitts's advice. Venturing out of the living room, she strolled into the hall and turned right.

Moving along the hallway, she paused when she came

upon a double set of doors that stood ajar. She peeked through into a library, a massive room with an equally massive desk in its center. Pulling the doors closed, she moved on. Farther down, the hall ended at the doorway of what she fathomed to be the solarium Mrs. Pitts spoke of.

The doorbell rang.

Carolyn jerked at the sound of the bells and looked behind her, expecting Mrs. Pitts to appear. When no one materialized, she retraced her steps and returned to the living room where she looked through to the foyer. An older man stood at the open door and talked with an unseen visitor. She suspected she was having her first glimpse of Mr. Pitts.

Mr. Pitts spoke to the visitor in low tones, and Carolyn kept to the far wall in the living room so as not to invade on that privacy. When the person finally moved into the house from the porch, Carolyn heard Mr. Pitts's words before she saw him.

"If you'll wait in here, sir, I'll get Mr. Hennessey for you."

"A'right, you do that," the visitor drawled loudly. "But, don't forget I told you he knows me."

Mr. Pitts walked across the living room to find Michael for this man.

"Good evening, Miss Hardy," he said in passing.

Carolyn muttered a response to his back and then turned back to the visitor. He was a man of more than average height who was dressed in a pointed-collar shirt paired with a dark, rust-colored suit. His hat was perched cockily over his forehead. He looked as though he were about to step onto a stage. She smothered a laugh—manners had taught her tact and emotional control. Instead, she simply looked away. But it was too late, the man saw her interest and started walking toward her.

"Well, well, well . . ." He clasped his hands behind his

back and smiled, revealing short straight teeth beneath a thin, light mustache. "Hello there."

Carolyn sized him up immediately and didn't respond. Earrings adorned both lobes and though Carolyn couldn't see them, she suspected he was the type who'd have a few tattoos languishing somewhere beneath his clothes.

"My boy must be keeping you a secret."

Carolyn frowned and opened her mouth to speak as footfalls sounded from the hallway. Michael had returned. Both she and the stranger shifted their focus to the door.

Michael looked past Carolyn to the stranger behind her. "Rollie?"

Carolyn followed Michael's astonished gaze back to the preening man.

"Nothin' but the real thing, my man." Rollie whisked past Carolyn and gave Michael a bear hug, all the while laughing out loud. "I'm back in town to put some flavor in your life."

Eight

"Rollie, what are you doing here?" Michael stepped back and looked across his friend's shoulder into Carolyn's perplexed face. He had the uneasy sensation that his best-laid plans for a private evening were turning to dust, and abruptly turned back to Rollie.

"When did you get into town?" he asked. "You didn't tell me you were coming here tonight when we talked on the phone."

"Hey, man, what can I say?" Rollie held his hands wide and smiled. "I haven't seen you in over a year, and I'm here now. You want me to leave?"

"I'm serious." Michael probed for a deeper reason. He knew his friend better than anyone else, and something was up. Hell, the last time they talked a few days before, Rollie was supposed to be getting his business back on track. And out of the blue, he shows up here? Yeah, it was a given that Rollie was up to something. "What's with you, showing up like this?"

Rollie rubbed his chin as his gaze dropped to Carolyn. "I can see why you don't want to be disturbed, Bro'." He turned back to Michael. "You want to introduce me to your lady, man?"

Michael held his frustration in check at the direction the evening was taking, and looked to Carolyn.

"I know," she said, and took the couple of steps that brought her to his side. Clasping her hands behind her back, she arched her brow. "You'd like me to meet your friend, right?"

He sucked in an audible breath. "Yeah, his name is Rollie Anderson, and I've known him since grade school." In a possessive gesture he had not previously displayed, Michael curved his hand to her back and they turned as one to greet his friend. "Rollie, this is Carolyn Hardy,"

"I am pleased to meet you, and that ain't no lie," Rollie chuckled, exaggerating each drawn-out syllable.

When Rollie stepped toward Carolyn, Michael moved to cut him off. "We were just leaving the house for dinner."

"Yeah, I see, but I need to talk to you a minute." Rollie motioned with his head toward another room.

Michael glanced at his watch, aware that their reservations were in serious jeopardy.

Rollie drew his brows together. "It's important, man. It won't take long."

"Sure, sure," Michael said absently as he once again turned to Carolyn, trying to read in her face whether she'd accept another delay to their evening.

"Go ahead," she said to Michael before she turned away and walked back to the sofa. "I'll wait here for you."

"Come on." Michael barked the order at Rollie, his long strides taking him through the door as his friend fell into step behind him.

Michael pulled the library doors closed behind Rollie. Alone with his friend, he let out an expletive. "I know you, Rollie, so what the hell's going on? And what made you show up tonight of all nights, and with no warning?"

"Aw, you're just mad 'cause you think I messed up your stuff," Rollie joked. He made a beeline across the room for what he had already figured out was the bar. He lifted the hidden front latch of the bow-front bar that sat nestled in the corner. Opening the doors, he drew out a bottle of bourbon; selecting a tumbler, he held them both aloft as he turned back to Michael.

"A toast to both of us, man. I am so glad to be out of that damn stinking jail cell."

Michael crossed his arms and strode over to lean against the wide desk, shaking his head at his friend of so many years. He had seen and put up with a lot of bad behavior from Rollie, but always with the understanding and promise that his friend would do better next time. Unfortunately, next time never seemed to arrive for Rollie.

"Okay, you want to tell me what's so important that you showed up unexpectedly and spoiled my evening?"

Rollie threw a shot of the bourbon down his throat, then stretched his face in a delicious grimace. "Damn, I almost forgot. You always did keep the good stuff." He poured another shot into the glass before he set the bottle on top of the bar and joined Michael in the middle of the room.

"Get on with it, man," Michael urged.

"A'right, a'right, I'll tell you. I knew some guys driving down to Atlanta, so I caught a ride. They're the ones I told you about from down this way, remember?" At Michael's nod, he continued. "Anyway, when we got to their hotel, I took a cab over here."

Michael shook his head and let out a relieved smile. "So, you need cash?" He reached into his back pocket as he talked. "You didn't leave the cabdriver at the front gate waiting to get paid, did you?"

"Nah, I went on and paid him," Rollie said, shaking his hand to stay Michael's wallet. "But he wouldn't drive on your private road, so I had to walk up that long-assed driveway of yours in the cold." Rollie took a swallow from his glass. "I don't think he believed I was visiting a friend."

Michael laughed. "Man, I'm about the only one you have left. You have screwed my evening and I've about run out of patience."

Rollie looked around the room. "By the way, I think I liked your crib in Jersey better than this one," he chuckled. "Now, that place was made for partying. But, this . . ." He gestured in a circle around the room, "Hell, this is a house." He looked up at Michael as though astonished by the fact. "A real damn house, and I'm in a library, with books and stuff. You got more books in here than the prison library."

"Come on off that. You know Adam and Halina are with me. I couldn't raise them in the old place. Anyway, the change coming here is doing all of us good."

"Yeah," Rollie agreed. "I almost forgot. Things are different these days." He took another swig from the glass. "So, am I welcome around here?"

Troubled by his own hesitation at the obvious request, Michael moved away from the desk and pushed his hands into his pockets. "You don't need cab fare, but you need a place to stay, is that it?"

"Just for a few days while I check out some business going down around these parts, that's all."

Michael knew all too well what that meant and realized his relief had been premature. He frowned at the telltale words; his friend was about to break another promise. It was too late to make the dinner date, and Rollie's problem was more serious than he had first thought.

"Wait here," Michael said, and returned to the library doors. He stuck his head out and called Mrs. Pitts. When she quickly appeared at the door, Michael explained the problem and gave her a set of instructions for an alternative plan. With one problem solved, Michael closed the library doors and turned to his friend, the other problem.

"You're telling me you showed up in town to take care of some business? Damn it, Rollie, you said you were making things up to Glenda and working on getting your life back in order, not getting back into crap guaranteed to make trouble, or even land you in jail again."

Rollie set his glass down, anxious to explain things. "Glenda's still mad as hell. And those charges got dropped."

"Through sheer luck, that's all. These 'dudes' you know. Where'd you meet them? In jail?" When his friend didn't respond, Michael slammed his fist on the desk with another expletive. "Why don't you give up on this stuff?"

"Easy for you to say," Rollie huffed right back. "You got something."

"That was low, man, and you know it. I'm right here for you, and I always have been, right from the beginning."

Rollie sighed as he rubbed his head, seemingly frustrated by Michael's comments. "Okay, I know. But you tell me, how do I refuse an opportunity to turn twenty G's into a three hundred percent profit?" His eyes brightened at Michael's attention. "You see, this dude—"

"Man, where is your head? And where are you getting twenty thousand dollars from?"

Rollie paced away from Michael before he turned. "That's why I wanted to talk with you. You see, if you make me this loan, I can pay you back from the profits."

"Profits from what, Rollie?" Michael tried not to preach, but he couldn't help it. "I'm not messing with any illegal stuff, and without even knowing your man's deal, it smells bad. My answer is the same as it's been before when you find these deals; and you sure as hell should know by now not to ask me to put up the money."

"Damn, damn." Rollie paced back to the bar and poured himself another drink. "I know twenty thou don't mean that much to you, man. You keep chump change like that in your safe. Why, I've seen you drop that in a Jersey casino while the night's still young."

"Yeah," Michael agreed, and walked away from his friend. He felt some surprise at Rollie's jaded description. It mirrored the same sorry opinion that Carolyn had formed about him. But Michael recognized their views as the price he had to pay for leading a self-gratifying existence for so long without considering the consequences.

He turned back to Rollie. "That was then. I told you before, things have changed since you've been gone, man. I've cleaned up my act. A lot. Part of it was because I had to; but, then again, I was getting tired of the crazy stuff, too."

"Yeah." Rollie glanced over at Michael, and with a shake of his head, dropped to the sofa. "I guess all the women, liquor, and partying you can handle every night can get boring. I'll believe it when I see it, man."

"I haven't changed my thinking about getting involved in the illegal stuff, like drugs. It's not my thing, and it never was, and if you were anybody else, I'd kick your narrow ass out the door for even asking me to get involved."

Rollie laughed. "Yeah, I know, and you would, too. You always did try to keep my nose clean, keep me on the straight and narrow, like when you got my business started, and when you helped me get a place set up while Glenda was pregnant." He tilted the tumbler to his mouth and swallowed hard. "You even got me a good attorney this time around, too. I guess it wasn't his fault the judge wouldn't grant bail."

"No, it was your fault for previously jumping bail on some other charges," Michael pointed out. They both shared a laugh before Michael continued in a more serious tone. "Rollie, you're my man, always have been and always will be. You can ask me for just about anything, but not this. Not the bad stuff."

"I know, I know." He looked over at Michael. "Remember how your agent, Jeffrey, took me aside one time and tried to explain things to me?" He laughed at the memory. "It was so funny, this big old tall, blond white man talking to me like he was my daddy, and saying you're high-profile, and it was my responsibility as your low-profile friend to stay clean and keep you out of the media. Afterwards, he was sweating and stuff, scared to death I was gonna jump him or something."

"Jeffrey's all right; he has been in the business a long time. He knows any whiff of scandal and the media will be on it like a dog on red meat. I'd be crucified. But I don't worry 'cause my heart's not in that stuff, anyway."

"Yeah, I know." Rollie set his empty glass on the table. "So, I can still hang out a few days? I left my bag outside. That butler of yours acted like he didn't want to let me in."

"That was Mr. Pitts. I'm fine with you crashing around here for a while—we have lots of space. I'll ask Mrs. Pitts to put you in a room. But you've got to keep it together, Rollie. I have kids running around this time."

"I'm cool with everything, I swear." Rollie crossed his arms as he settled into the sofa. "So, what's going on with you and that good-looking honey in there? She didn't seem too happy about me showing up."

Michael shook his head at his friend. "Carolyn. She's off limits, you hear?"

Rollie raised his hand in defense. "I hear ya. Are things serious between you two? You didn't tell her about me, how we go way back?"

"Hey, I was just as shocked as she was to see you standing there." Michael walked over to the bar and, after selecting a glass, poured himself a splash of the brandy as he listened to a quarter hour chime from the clock in the back hall. An hour had passed since he had stood in the kitchen with Mrs. Pitts and talked with such anticipation and enthusiasm about the evening ahead.

"You know, I've been trying to make some headway with this woman for about two years." He raised the glass to his lips. His swallowed gulp produced a welcome burn at the back of his throat.

"Two years?" Rollie inquired.

Michael turned to his friend as he swallowed again and nodded. "Remember the Super Bowl weekend we spent in Atlanta, and the woman I tried to get to go out with me?"

Rollie's eyes stretched in amazement as the memory set in. "The uptight chick you argued with on the phone?"

"That's her."

"Nah, man. Say it ain't so. Where did you see her again?"

"A couple of weeks ago I bought her at an auction."

"You what?"

Chuckling, Michael relayed the circumstances of his reunion with Carolyn to a curious Rollie.

"You have to be the luckiest S.O.B. around," Rollie declared. "I can't believe she's giving you the time of day after the way she wore you out."

"Well, that may still be the case, with the way this evening is shaping up." He looked at his watch. "I'm going to find her so I can explain the change of plans. You, meanwhile, wait in here, and I'll let you know what's up."

Rollie raised his glass once more. "Me and Mr. Bourbon can renew our acquaintance in the meantime."

After ten minutes in the living room, Carolyn had gotten tired of waiting, and resumed her walk through the house. Surprisingly, she wasn't upset with Michael for running into a string of interruptions that delayed their dinner. In fact, she suspected he was more upset than she was. His friend seemed a colorful enough character—just what Carolyn had envisioned Michael to be. *Had* envisioned? She was, once again, surprised at her revisionist thinking when it came to Michael, and wondered when her view of him had begun to stabilize, and then change for the better.

She passed the library where she heard Michael's raised voice, his words indistinct, in conversation with his friend. She moved farther along and ended up in the solarium, a beautiful room of pale greens and creams, filled with flowers set around the room and at the walls. The centerpiece, a simulated waterfall circled by plants, rose from the middle of the floor.

"Hi."

Carolyn whirled at the voice behind her. It was Adam, the young man she had met earlier. The headphones were still draped around his neck, and a tablet of some sort was tucked under his arm. She returned his greeting.

"You haven't left for dinner yet?" he asked as he came up to her.

"No, Michael had an unexpected visitor."

Adam's eyes rolled. "That's Rollie; he's kind of flaky, you know. Mrs. Pitts told me he was here."

Carolyn smiled at Adam's youthful honesty. "I've met a few people like that in my time."

"Well, we get to meet them more often than most people," he said as he dropped his gangly frame onto the back of the sofa. "Mrs. Pitts says that's because Michael is famous and attracts them." He seemed to realize the implication of what he'd said, and tried to explain.

"Oh, I don't mean you. You seem pretty normal, and I can tell Michael likes you." He darted a glance at Carolyn. "He told us all about you."

"Really?" Carolyn crossed her arms, intrigued that he called his father by his given name.

Adam nodded as he straightened from the sofa. "I was going to the kitchen for ice cream. Since you haven't eaten yet, do you want some, too?"

Carolyn's hesitation was brief. "Sounds like a great idea, Adam. I'd love to."

She fell in step with Adam as he led her out of the solarium and into the kitchen, her thoughts running to the obvious irony of her eating with her date's heretofore unknown son. What other surprises did the evening have in store?

Nine

When Michael returned to the living room to get Carolyn, she was nowhere in sight. His mood sank as he realized she had left. It was exactly the thing she would do at the first chance, he thought angrily. As he crossed the room to the foyer to see if her car was still in the drive, he spied her coat on the sofa next to his, and savored the lurch in his chest. So, she hadn't gone after all. Suddenly, things were looking up again. Turning, he went to find her.

He ran into Mrs. Pitts in the hall. "Have you seen Carolyn?"

"No," she answered. "I told her earlier that she could have a look around the house if she wanted. I also called the restaurant, and the chef was glad to prepare three dinners to be catered. He promised he'd have them delivered within the hour."

Michael sighed in relief. "Good, good."

"What are you doing about that friend of yours? Eldridge says he left a bag on the front step."

He quirked his brow at the disapproval he heard in her voice. "I need you to prepare a room for him. His name is Rollie Anderson and he's in the library right now. I'll explain later, but he'll be visiting for a few days."

"All right," she said hesitantly. "I'll get it done right

away if you say so." She quickly stepped away, disappearing down the hallway.

Michael turned his attention back to finding Carolyn. Convinced she wouldn't be on the terraces in the cold or in the living quarters upstairs, he made a quick search of one side of the first level. When he crossed to search the other side, he heard two voices as he neared the kitchen. There, the voices' owners were seated at the wide counter.

Adam was hunched over, deep in conversation with Carolyn. She sat comfortably on a high-backed barstool, her legs crossed as she ate a spoon of ice cream from a small bowl cupped in her hand. A large tub of premium ice cream sat on the counter between them. Michael was filled with pleasant surprise as he witnessed the scene.

"Carolyn?"

She turned at her name and saw Michael standing in the doorway. Suddenly self-conscious about her playful mood with Adam and her comfortable perch on the chair, she sat the bowl of ice cream on the table and uncrossed her legs.

"I was looking for you," Michael said as he joined them at the counter.

"Are you ready to leave? Adam invited me to join him for dessert and I couldn't resist the invitation," she responded.

"Yeah." Adam smiled as he raised his spoon to his mouth. "She's an ice cream nut, too. You want some?" Adam asked Michael. "It's cookies and cream."

"No, I'll pass," he said to Adam, though his eyes remained on Carolyn. "I hope you're still hungry," he said to her.

He came to a stop and rested his arm along the back of her chair, the edge of his hand a faint caress at her shoulder. At the bare touch, Carolyn suppressed the pleasant sigh that tried to escape her lips.

"Oh, I'm good for dinner. Ice cream I can handle any time," she managed to answer.

Michael bent so that he was close to her head. "I promise dinner is not forgotten. Because it's so late, I had the chef prepare our meals and arrange to send them over."

Carolyn turned to face Michael and, again, enjoyed his heady, masculine scent. "Dinner is coming here?"

He nodded as he studied her face. "In fact, it should be arriving shortly. I was hoping you wouldn't mind."

"No, I—" She found herself lost in Michael's dark eyes. Pulled into them was a better description. She tried breaking off the contact, and batted her eyes in defense. "—I don't mind."

He grinned. "Good."

"What happened to Rollie?" Adam asked.

Michael reached over and playfully bumped Adam's head. "Mr. Anderson to you."

Adam tried to dodge the bump. "He said to call him Rollie because 'mister' makes him old."

"He's joining us for dinner, too."

Carolyn's disappointment showed through, and a frown began to form on Michael's face.

"I hope you don't mind," he said. "Rollie's okay when you get to know him."

"So, what's a person to do in the meantime?" she asked good-naturedly. She watched as Michael grinned at her humor, his mouth spread wide with an appeal that had begun to affect her.

"We can only hope the food keeps us occupied." He drew in a deep breath before he turned to Adam. "And what about you? Shouldn't you be heading off to bed?"

"It's the weekend," Adam said, slurping the last of the ice cream from his spoon. "But I promised Mrs. Pitts I'd go upstairs and finish my sketches in my room."

Carolyn glanced at the loose-leaf tablet Adam had placed on the counter. "Are you an artist?" she asked curiously.

Michael bowed his head near Carolyn and explained, "Adam wants to be a cartoonist."

"Do you mind if I look at your sketches?" Carolyn asked.

After a second's hesitation, Adam said, "All right." He passed her the loose-leaf drawing tablet. "I still have a lot to learn about different styles and stuff. My collection of comic books helps me out."

"Carolyn's family owns a gallery, Adam. The Hardy Gallery downtown."

Adam's eyes searched Carolyn's with interest. "Is that true? You have an art gallery of your own?"

She nodded proudly at Adam as she leafed through the tablet of comic characters colorfully drawn with distinctive style. "My family operates one, yes. We showcase all kinds of art and artists, too. You'll have to come and visit it some day."

"Will you take me?" Adams eyes were bright with expectation.

Carolyn was too surprised by her own blunder to do more than nod for a moment. "Of course, if . . . if Michael thinks it's all right."

Adam looked at Michael. "Can I go?"

Michael readily agreed as he met Carolyn's eyes. "Sure. Maybe your sister and I can join you." With a satisfied grin on his face, he winked at Carolyn.

"The more the merrier," she said in her best audacious voice. She had been bested, true, but this loss didn't seem as painful as the ones of two weeks before. She frowned at the confused changes in her emotions before she slanted a look at the man who seemed to bring them on.

The dining room in the house had pleasantly muted light that shone intimately down on the three diners from the chandelier. Carolyn and Rollie sat on either side of

Michael at one end of the table, and they all leisurely dallied over dessert while Rollie spoke of old times.

"Back at Michael's first house," Rollie said, "he had a room with all these giant, full-color posters of him in action, catching the ball on the fifty yard line, that sort of stuff. Most were easily nine feet tall, and all of his game balls were lined up in a trophy case. I mean, when you saw it, you knew who lived there. But now, I don't see any of it up in this place. How's anybody gonna know you're a football player, man?"

"I wondered the same thing myself, Rollie, when I first got here," Carolyn said, smiling easily with them.

"Okay, give me time. I just moved in, but I'll put it all back out again, no matter how tacky it looks." At Carolyn's look of horror, Michael said, "Well, maybe not all of it." They all laughed.

Dinner thus far had turned out to be nothing like any of them had imagined. While Carolyn had expected an obnoxious appearance from Rollie, he had prepared himself to be the unwanted third wheel, and Michael waited for Carolyn's disappointment and biting tongue to explode.

With low expectations running high, it had made for an amazingly quiet dinner. But by the time dessert was savored, and each of them had been surprised by the other's restraint of their most objectionable trait, the table conversation finally became less stilted.

"This stuff is good, man. What is it?" Rollie lifted the half-eaten plate of layered, caramel-and-brown colored dessert for a closer look.

"Tiramisu," Carolyn offered. "Careful, though. It's a high-calorie treat."

"I know you don't worry about stuff like that," he said. "If I had known what you looked like two years ago, I would have made my man go find you and then apologize. I wouldn't have let him give up on you so easy."

"What do you know about that?" Carolyn asked, and looked from one man to the other.

"I didn't tell you." Michael straightened in his chair, choosing his words carefully. "Rollie was with me that night when you called my hotel."

"Oh . . ." She turned to Rollie. "So you know all about what happened firsthand?"

He nodded as he dug into the remaining dessert. "If you ask me, you should have hung up on him a lot earlier."

Michael leaned back in his chair and laughed. "I don't remember it quite that way, bro."

"In fact," Rollie continued without skipping a beat, "a good slap up side his head at the bank might have knocked some sense in him. See, I figured you were different, and not used to his street ways, but he didn't take my advice." He looked over at Michael, a gleam in his serious eyes. "Look where it got him. Two years of lost time."

Michael smiled as he tented his hands. "Yeah. Remind me to take your advice next time."

"Is he kidding?" Carolyn asked Michael. "I can't tell."

"I'm as serious as a drive-by," Rollie said with a straight face. "I try to keep him out of trouble, but it's hard when the women—not you, of course—throw themselves at him."

"Okay, Rollie," Michael interrupted. "Enough of memory lane."

Carolyn smiled and settled back against her chair, realizing that Rollie, with his off-center sense of humor, was harmless. Michael had been right—he took a little getting used to.

"Michael said you were only in town for a short while," she said. "What do you do for a living back in . . . Baltimore, is it?"

Michael quickly spoke up. "He does car detailing—"

"When I'm not dealing with a city matter," Rollie added matter-of-factly. "I plan on being around, visiting with my old friend Michael."

Carolyn frowned at the odd answer. "I see." Actually, she didn't, but it didn't seem important.

"I've got to play a little b-ball with Adam," Rollie said, turning to Michael. "That kid is growing like a weed. Last time I saw him was just after his mama's funeral."

Carolyn darted a glance at Michael, the obvious questions in her eyes.

"Your wife is deceased?" she asked Michael.

"Michael told you he was married?" Rollie's snicker turned into a laugh. "You got to be kidding."

"No, Carolyn," Michael clarified, "I've never been married."

So, it was a girlfriend, after all. Carolyn's heart contracted with disappointment. "Oh, I understand."

"Probably not." Michael drew her stare as he explained. "It was my sister who died two years ago this spring, Carolyn. Adam and Halina were her children. I'm their closest living relative and guardian, and now, soon-to-be adoptive parent."

It was as though a light had been switched on and Carolyn could view Michael from a whole new perspective.

"I'm sorry about your sister," she said. "But it's a wonderful thing you're doing for the children, Michael."

"Yeah, I've grown pretty close to those two rug rats."

"So, what is it that you do?" Rollie asked Carolyn. "Of course, a fine young thing like yourself probably doesn't need to go out and look for work."

"And, why not?" Carolyn asked, looking shrewdly at Rollie.

"Watch yourself, Rollie," Michael warned.

"Hey, you can't be hurtin' for money too much," Rollie pointed out.

Michael straightened in his chair and looked at Carolyn. "I mentioned your family's business and influence around Atlanta, that's all."

"The way I see it," Rollie said, "if you got the clout, use it."

Carolyn folded her arms on the table. "Well, I don't see it that way. I'm a working engineer. Industrial management."

"Whoa, what the hell is that?" Rollie asked, seemingly impressed. "Which means I still don't know what it is that you do."

Carolyn could only laugh at his comic manner. "To put it simply, I help companies operate more efficiently in their businesses, from human resources to programmed software."

"I told you, Rollie, not only is she a beauty, but she's smart, too." Michael turned to Carolyn. "I was surprised you'd have your own place after I saw your parents' home. I figured you'd stay there."

"I wanted to declare my independence. Why should I stay there?"

"Well, for one thing," he said, leaning back in his chair, "it's a huge house, and a showplace, too. You know, you never did offer to show me around when I was there."

"Things were a little bit strained that night, if I remember." She leaned forward on the table, a secret smile on her face. "Your house has its interesting points, as well."

He nodded as he leaned forward, too, his hands brushing against hers. "Mrs. Pitts told me you wanted to look around. We could make another deal, you know," he said, and covered her hand with his. "If you show me yours, I'll show you mine."

Carolyn eyes narrowed. "Maybe I don't want to see yours as badly as you'd like to see mine."

Michael arched his brows as he whispered, "Give me some time, and I can change your mind."

She laughed. "Are you flirting with me, Michael Hennessey?"

"All right, that's it," Rollie said, slapping his hand on the tabletop. "I don't need to be sitting here listening to you two get your freak on." He pushed his chair back and shook his head at them. "I'm outta here, and I'll see you in the morning." He strutted from the table.

When he disappeared from the room, Carolyn and Michael both let out soft chuckles.

"That was one way of getting rid of him," Michael said.

"He's got the right idea, though." Carolyn looked down at her hand and realized it was still trapped beneath Michael's. "It is late, and I should be going." After a gentle squeeze, he let her hand go.

They looked up at each other and smiled in earnest.

"It's been a pretty unconventional evening," Michael admitted.

"But it was nice; something I didn't expect."

Michael nodded as he stood from his chair and moved to help Carolyn from hers. "Come on, let's get your coat."

"Are you sure you aren't cold?"

"I'm fine," Carolyn said as Michael walked with her the short distance to her car. Her coat was draped over her arm.

When they arrived at the vehicle, Michael reached out to pull open the door, but Carolyn's question stopped him.

"Can I ask you something before I leave?"

He turned to her. "Sure."

"Adam and Halina. Why didn't you mention them before tonight?"

"You didn't seem too interested in spending time with me, so it was never an issue as far as I was concerned."

"Oh, I see."

"So, you want to make it an issue?"

Carolyn smiled. "Every time I see you, you change from what I think you're supposed to be."

"Is that good or bad?"

"Mmm . . . after three consecutive weekends, it's all mostly good."

He nodded, his smile growing.

Carolyn basked in the warmth that emanated from his eyes. "I don't think you understand. I don't see the same man on three consecutive weekends. I don't even have time to see men at all." She hugged her arms against the cold.

Michael stepped close and briskly rubbed her arms and shoulders to keep her warm. "I've pretty much run out of leverage to force you into a fourth one." He dropped one hand and opened the car door. "You should get on in; you're shivering."

Carolyn saw the open door. Extremely conscious of Michael's virile appeal, his touch had made her feel daring, and she wanted to relish it some more, but was disappointed that he hadn't attempted another date. She turned to look up at him.

"Aren't you—"

His hands slipped up her arms and tightened to draw her closer. He kissed her first with a gaze from his eyes; and then his lips, warm and full, covered her mouth. Carolyn experienced a free fall of ecstasy during the heady, though too short, contact, and blinked her eyes open again.

"What were you going to say?" Michael's voice was thick.

Carolyn swallowed. "Only that I was way off base to think you were simply a dumb jock."

"Really?" He raised his brows at her.

"Quite the contrary—you were smart enough to stretch one simple dinner into three interesting evenings."

"I hoped that, given a chance, I could change your opinion of me."

"So, what am I to think if you don't ask me out again?"

Michael cocked his head to the side with a grin. "You mean, if I ask you out, you won't refuse?"

"You'll never know if you don't try," she replied cockily.

He backed away and laughed. "Then, maybe I'll just never know." He turned away to go back to the house. "Goodnight."

Carolyn's eyes stretched at his retreating figure, each step gnawing at her confidence. "Michael?" she shouted.

Still laughing, he turned around. "What?"

She stood there, slowly gaining enlightenment about Michael, and emotionally vulnerable. "Well?"

Michael strode back to her, and pulled her into his arms. "Damn, you're beautiful."

This time she felt his lips touch her brow before he tilted her chin and moved his mouth over hers with an urgency that devoured her womanly softness. Surprised by her own hunger for his touch, Carolyn returned his crushing kiss and was racked by a shock wave of pleasure. It was pure bliss.

And then, the exquisite contact was broken.

Michael smiled down at Carolyn. "I've been fighting a powerful urge to do that. It feels good to let go." He brushed her hair back from her face. "Can I see you next week?"

Carolyn nodded. "After the things I've thought about you, I can't believe I'm admitting I'd like that."

"Then we start over, and this time with no preconceptions," he said. "It's cold out here and I'm asking you out, just like I did before, but this time you're actually accepting."

"A replay of when we first met," she said quietly.

"You know what else? You're beginning to shiver again." He massaged her arms before he stepped back and pulled open the car door. "Get in and get warm. I'll call you tomorrow."

Shortly after, Carolyn maneuvered down the driveway and thought it was curiously reminiscent of that time in their past when she had spied Michael in her rearview mirror and had wondered "what if." And even as a warning voice whispered in her head to be her usual cautious self, she smiled at her unlikely decision to take a chance. . . . Just this once.

Ten

"I don't know what came over me," Carolyn said, "but suddenly, seeing him again didn't seem so bad after all."

It was the middle of the week and Carolyn had met her sisters for lunch in a restaurant near the art gallery, a luncheon date they had demanded of her when she revealed she'd be seeing Michael again.

"It was stubbornness on your part from the start," Stephanie said as she pushed her salad away and leaned forward. "Admit it, you were determined not to give the man a second chance if you could help it."

"That's right," Alli agreed. "And he's so handsome with those sleepy, bedroom eyes and that big old sexy mouth." She sighed at Carolyn. "You almost gave up on a prize catch, and only because you're a perfectionist who hates, more than anything else, being wrong."

"You're the one who leaps before she looks, not me," Carolyn quickly retorted, not ashamed of the traits that had served her well in the past.

"Anyway," she began again, "everything started out normally—we were getting ready to leave the house, and I knew this would be our last time seeing each other, and I could deal with that."

"But you got all weak-kneed when you saw that cute

little child, right?" Stephanie asked. "Kids do it every time."

"That biological clock mama's always talking about must be ticking for you," Alli added.

"Actually, at the time I was livid that he might be married or separated or something and still trying to go out with me," Carolyn continued. "So when I finally learned he was their uncle, I was touched, to say the least, and embarrassed that I had thought the worst. It changed everything."

"Yep," Alli agreed. "Men have been using kids and dogs to scoop women since the beginning of time."

"I know, but he was pretty sincere about the whole thing." Carolyn looked from Stephanie to Alli. "Anyway, I couldn't help but start thinking about what he'd said before, that he was a different person. To me, what he did for his kids wasn't the action of the self-centered jerk I met before." She fiddled with her dinner napkin. "Plus, this time he won't be paying for a date, either." She looked up again. "That makes a lot of difference; at least, to me."

"So you're going for it, huh?" When Alli tented her manicured hands, it set off a musical jangle from her arm bracelets as she gave her sister a sage look. "You realize what you're in for with a man like him?" She narrowed her eyes at Carolyn's blank look. "If you're interested in him, and you want to keep his interest in you, you're going to have to loosen up a bit, Caro."

"What's wrong with me now?" she asked.

Alli darted a glance to Stephanie for help before her attention returned to Carolyn. "You know how conventional you can be and, well, he's not, to say the least. You're pretty much a teetotaler, for heaven's sake. Anything stronger than light wine and you're done for." When silence met her words, she blurted out, "Say something, Stephanie."

Stephanie smiled as she looked at Carolyn. "What Alli's trying to say is, are you sure you're up to dating a celebrity like him? There's a lot of extraneous stuff to deal with, you know."

"I thought you two wanted me to go out with him—with anybody, for that matter."

"Oh, we do," Alli said.

"Then what's the big deal?"

Alli leaned across the table. "I don't think she realizes how famous and utterly popular he is, Steph."

"What I do realize is that I may not be in the know like you, Alli, but I think I can hold my own."

"Well, then, you understand the need to be wary," Alli said.

"Girl, what are you talking about?" Carolyn asked.

Stephanie laughed as she picked at her Caesar salad. "She's talking about all those women he attracts, being in sports."

"Nope," Alli clarified, "I'm talking hoochies, honey. Real, live hoochies who can smell a prospect before they can see him, and who'll do anything to get their hands around a rich athlete's—"

"Alli, stop it." Carolyn laughed, too, as she fluttered her hand to dismiss the idea. "It's not like that. I'm interested in learning who he is first . . . and slowly, I might add." At the sight of Alli's devilish grin, she added, "and so is he, so don't you even try to go there."

"Leave her alone, Alli. You'll scare her off before she gets a taste of 'there,' " Stephanie teased.

"You're right. Let her get a little smooching in first," Allie agreed. "She'll be screaming for our advice by then."

Carolyn snorted at them. "It's obvious you don't know everything," she said, and casually raised her glass of tea to her lips. "We already did."

Alli yelped in delight before Stephanie slapped her arm

as a reminder to behave in public. But it was a natural reaction to an unexpected revelation from their usually reserved sister who had seemed to flourish without a normal connection to the opposite sex. It was also atypical for the sisters to discuss with Carolyn such matters and emotions of the heart and flesh. They now looked at her in a new light.

"Oh, my goodness," Alli crooned to the others, "and he's got that gorgeous mouth, too. So, share some details . . . how was it?"

"None of your business, Miss tell-everything-you know."

"What?" Alli looked from Stephanie to Carolyn in mock surprise. "Like, both of you expected all this two weeks ago? This is news. Wait until Mom and Justin hear about it."

"See what I mean?" Carolyn complained.

"Well, he's going to know," Alli explained. "He's back in town and said he'd drop by to see you."

Carolyn's eyes brightened at the chance to talk with Justin. "Where is he?" she asked.

"With Davina, of course," Alli said.

"What's the deal with the friend you said showed up and spoiled your going out to eat?" Stephanie wanted to know.

"I'm not really sure," Carolyn answered. "They apparently grew up together, but Michael was also surprised when he appeared. He'll be staying at Michael's house for a few days."

"If you ask me, better watch out for that," Alli said. "You don't want your man ditching you for his friends on a regular basis."

"I got the distinct impression that something pretty important came up. But Michael managed to save the evening."

At that moment, Carolyn's cell phone buzzed from

where it sat beside her salad plate. With an apologetic look to her sisters, she picked up the phone and frowned at the screen. It was one of her team members. The call took less than a minute, but it managed to break the fun-loving mood of their lunch.

"Listen, guys," Carolyn explained as she packed the phone into the side of her purse. "I enjoyed my salad and the company, but I have to go. I've been delegated as the back-up speaker for a project planning meeting this afternoon. I've got to go by the loft and pick up some notes, and then head back to the office."

"Aw, Caro," Alli complained. "We've only just gotten through our salad."

"Carolyn," Stephanie said, and looked her sister in the eyes. "Pace yourself. You've got to learn to squeeze some personal time into your schedule. And the only way you'll get it is to demand it," she said. "I've been there."

"I know, I know, but it won't be today," Carolyn sighed. "The way this meeting is shaping up, I may end up sharing a working dinner with my team."

"Good grief, how boring," Alli pointed out. "And just when I have so many more questions about your sports boy."

"I know you do," Carolyn said with a smile as she looked from one sister to the other. "I promise we'll do this again and I'll . . . I'll turn the phone off next time."

"And get caught unprepared? I doubt it," Stephanie said. "Go on, dear; we understand, and I'll take care of your tab."

"I wonder how understanding Michael will be when he learns how you and G & G are attached at the hip?" Alli asked. "I hope you cut off that phone on your date. Where are you going, anyway? You should make it someplace where you can show him how open-minded and original you are."

Carolyn slid the strap of her purse onto her shoulder

as she prepared to leave. "Don't be so nosy." She reached over and tweaked Alli's nose. At Alli's yelp, Carolyn said, "I may take you up on that idea, though. I can loosen up if the occasion calls for it."

"In that case, my advice is, don't wear any of that black stuff in your closet. Look at you, wearing a black suit now."

"What's wrong with it?" Carolyn looked down at her dark suit, relieved only by a silk lavender blouse.

"Alli," Stephanie cautioned.

"No, no, I've got the perfect sweater she should wear on her date, that's all," Alli continued, unperturbed by the warning. "And it's blood red."

"What's happening to me," Carolyn groaned, and stood up to leave.

"What do you mean?" Stephanie asked as she looked up.

"I'm actually considering borrowing clothes from Alli's closet, that's what."

Michael, Adam, and the Pittses made up the audience as they listened to Halina's recording of her most recent rendition of "I Believe I Can Fly." Her young, a cappella voice rang out clear and pure from the juvenile player/recorder, filling the room. Michael watched as she moved her mouth in synchronization with the recording.

Singing—it was something Halina never seemed to tire of; she eschewed the stereo system in the family's entertainment room in favor of the player/recorder Michael had given her at Christmas. Wherever she went, it was usually at her side. She could be heard throughout the house, singing and then recording her songs, all of which were meticulously labeled on cassette tapes and kept in her music box carryall.

The child therapist Halina had been seeing since they

arrived in Atlanta felt that her singing was an excellent outlet for the unresolved resentment that had manifested during the traumatic aftermath of losing her mother. And it seemed to be working as a means through which the little girl could put her fears in perspective and shape her self-csteem. Her bed-wetting had been curtailed, and she was less introverted around others.

As her solo concluded, Michael had to admit she was very good for her young age, but he was reluctant to let her take voice lessons or allow the singing to become anything more serious than a pastime she could enjoy with the family. Music had been her solace since the early days of her mother's death, and he would leave it at that.

"Okay, that's the end," Halina announced, and pressed the chunky button that ejected the tape. While they all clapped and told her how good she had sounded, Halina pulled the tape from its holder and held it out to Michael. "If you want, you can listen in the car.

"I want," he replied and pushed the tape into his pocket. "Thank you."

"Mr. Pitts listens to them all the time in the car, don't you, Mr. Pitts?"

The older man nodded as he ruffled her ponytails. "Every chance I get," he said before he turned to Michael. "Mr. Anderson asked to have a car available for him this evening." He looked for Michael's tacit approval of the visitor issuing commands. "I'm on my way out to the garage now to make sure everything is in order."

Michael frowned at the knowledge. "Sure, it's all right." Deep in thought, he watched the older man leave the room.

"It's almost bedtime, sweetie," Mrs. Pitts said to Halina. "I'll expect you to go with me upstairs in a bit, okay?"

"Okay," Halina said before she turned to Michael. "I know, I can play the tape for Carolyn, too," Halina suggested cagily, "when she comes back over here."

"How do you know she wants to come here again, anyway? After the last visit, with everybody dropping in, maybe she doesn't want to come back."

"Well, I hope she does," Halina insisted. "Adam says she's taking him to her art gallery."

"So, you two have been discussing her, huh? I think she wants to take you to the gallery, too."

"She'll be back," Adam predicted as he dropped to the sofa.

"Oh," Michael said as he turned to watch his son. "What makes you think so?"

"Because you aren't crazy and probably asked her back," Adam replied.

Michael grinned at Adam's insight, and shot him a manly thumb's up signal.

"I like her better than that 'Shamu' lady," Halina said.

As the kids laughed, Michael remembered Sharma, a woman he had dated briefly before moving to Atlanta. "Hey, that wasn't her name."

"I like 'Shamu' better. That's a good one" Adam said.

"Can Carolyn go to the PTA meeting with us, too?" Halina asked.

Michael carefully monitored Halina's interaction with those who were outside the family.

"I thought we'd have a family trip. Me, you, and Adam."

"You aren't going to sit with us," Halina said. "I want Carolyn to go with us or I'm not going," she added and pressed her point home by running from the room.

"Halina," Michael said and followed her to the door, but she was gone.

"I'll take care of her," Mrs. Pitts said, and was up and headed for the door before Michael could reply.

Michael pushed his hands into his pockets as he turned to Adam. "What was that about? Why is it so important that Carolyn go to a PTA meeting? I thought she liked her new school and wanted to show off her classroom—"

"Maybe she thinks the same thing's gonna happen as last time."

"Oh, that." While Michael was used to the stares and autograph seekers in public places, the kids were not, and made no bones about their dislike of this interference during their time with him.

The uproar that had accompanied his first PTA visit to his kids' school last month had been one such occasion. It had taken a while for the administration to settle both the parents and children down for the business meeting, which had been temporarily disrupted by autograph seekers and gawkers who had followed Michael into the building.

"She didn't like it when you left us to go to that other room where the principal set up a place for you to sign autographs and see your fans." When Adam looked up at Michael, his brows were raised. "Truth is, I didn't either." Adam slumped back onto the sofa.

Michael sighed. "Why didn't you say something before now?"

He hunched his shoulders. "It happens all the time. You're supposed to already know that sort of stuff," Adam said.

Michael sat next to him. "That's the problem, sport, I'm going through all this with both of you, and I need your help."

Adam grinned in disbelief. "Really?" He sat up. "What can I do? I'm just a kid," Adam said.

"Hey, we got trouble in paradise?"

The voice came from the door, and both Michael and Adam looked up to see Rollie at the door.

"Hey," Michael said, and stood up from the sofa as he signaled Rollie through the door. "Come on in."

"Hey, Rollie," Adam said. "Are you up for a rematch, yet?"

"Aw, man, you put a hurtin' on me yesterday, and got me good," Rollie said, feigning pain. "You watchin' the game tonight?"

Adam cut a look to Michael. "I can't stay up past nine on a school night unless it's for homework."

"What?" Rollie exclaimed, looking over at Michael. "I know you not making my man here go to bed?"

"Come on, don't start trouble. I see you're getting ready to go out?"

"You're not going to Jemahl's sports bar to watch the game tonight with the rest of your boys?"

Michael looked at his watch. He had completely forgotten that some of his friends with the Wildcats were meeting at Jemahl's restaurant downtown to throw back some brews and watch the basketball game; Rollie had even been invited to come along.

"I forgot all about it," Michael said. "Why don't you go on without me? Mr. Pitts has the keys to the cars—he can set you up." He rubbed his chin in thought for a moment. "Listen, there is something else. It's about Mr. Pitts. Don't go around throwing orders at him, okay? We like to think of him and his wife as more than just people who work here."

"I hear you, man; but you know, I don't think the old dude likes me," Rollie whispered away from Adam. "Whenever I tell him to do stuff, he sort of rolls his eyes at me, man."

Michael looked at him quizzically and grinned. "Maybe that's why. Try asking next time."

"Mr. Pitts is cool," Adam said in defense of the handyman. "He doesn't talk a lot like Mrs. Pitts, so you just have to get to know him."

"Adam," Michael turned to his son. "Why don't you

go on up? You have school tomorrow. Besides, I need to talk with Rollie a minute."

"Sure," Adam said as he launched himself upwards from the sofa. "See ya later, Rollie."

"Right on, li'l bro'," Rollie replied.

When Adam left, Michael turned to his friend. "Don't be encouraging Adam to get a tattoo like the one on your shoulder. He's just eleven, you know."

"Aw, he was just admiring it the other day when we were playing basketball. Nothing wrong with that, is there?" He turned in a circle around the room. "There ain't no bar in here? The other house had one in every room. Man, you ain't no fun anymore. I know you're a daddy and all, now. Hell, I been one ever since I turned sixteen, but that don't stop me from living."

"It depends on how you define living."

"I sure as hell don't define it as sitting at home tonight when your boys are waiting for you. Unless, of course, your girl is coming over and you want to get rid of us."

Michael laughed. "Nope. That's definitely not happening tonight."

"What's with you and her anyway, man? I tell you, she's worth a second look. But she also looks like the kind of chick you don't get down with unless you meaning to make some promises you don't want to be keeping later on."

"Only you would describe a relationship in those terms."

"Come on, man. I'll be leaving town soon, and you sure as hell ain't invited me out to dinner this weekend, so let's kick back a while tonight."

Michael stood up. "Yeah, I think I will." He looked down at his jeans. "Give me time to change and tell Mrs. Pitts where I'll be."

"Cool. I'll either be in the game room or checking out

the bar, so no rush." He winked and walked toward the library. "See you in a few."

"Always Rollie," Michael muttered at his friend's back. "You'll never change."

Eleven

Jemahl, along with two men from his security staff, greeted Michael as he arrived on the sidewalk just outside the sports bar's front door.

"Hey, you made it in time for the second half," he declared, and clasped Michael's hand in a hearty shake. "Come on in. The other guys are already here. I've got everything set out upstairs; it's all sweet. That way, you have a bit of privacy and won't be out in the open area."

"Thanks, man. Glad I didn't miss it," Michael said, and stepped through the door as the small entourage trailed a few steps behind.

"Stay and hang out afterwards," Jemahl said. "The place gets loud and loose later on." He grinned at Michael. "You're gonna like it."

"Yeah, I can see that." Michael glanced around the low-lit restaurant and bar, and into the informal crowd. Some of the customers stood, while others sat near one of a few large television screens; still others occupied intimate booths or tables against the dark wood paneling, choosing their own mood.

As he and Jemahl strode through the crowded aisle side by side, the place teemed with conversation and activity generated by customers who seemed to be both sports buffs and starch-shirted business types from the buildings that surrounded the downtown establishment. Jemahl had mentioned how great an investment the business had become. From the looks of things, Michael judged him to be right.

"This place is live, man, and I like it," Rollie said as he brought up the rear. "Michael, I don't see your picture in the place." Rollie motioned toward the signed sports photos and memorabilia along the walls.

"Hey, we're gonna fix that tonight," Jemahl said, "if Michael agrees."

"Sure, my pleasure," Michael nodded. "Is it always like this—packed in the middle of the week?"

"I have my regulars," Jemahl laughed, "but everybody shows up when a big game is on TV, like tonight." Straight ahead, a group enjoyed themselves on the second-floor balcony that looked down into the restaurant. A burly guard at the bottom stair protected an open staircase, which led to the balcony.

"Usually, they're pretty good at leaving celebs alone and giving them their space, but every so often—"

A fan reached out and shook Michael's hand, immediately stopping their progress.

Jemahl hunched his shoulders in humor as he hustled Michael toward the stairs. "See what I mean?"

"No problem, no problem," Michael said and turned as he heard a hail from a fellow athlete, a friend whom Michael hadn't seen in a while. He stopped a moment to greet him before he and the others moved on.

By now, Rollie had taken the lead as they neared the staircase and their group.

"Oh, by the way," Jemahl said to Michael. "I already seated the two ladies that were meeting you here."

Michael looked puzzled before his gaze moved ahead to Rollie, who now glanced back. "What gives, bro?"

"He's talking about Carleshia and Randy, that's all,"

Rollie explained over his shoulder. "I met 'em the other night." Glancing back, he grinned at Michael. "Nice."

Michael frowned as Rollie's plan became clear. "You didn't mention meeting up with any women, nice or not."

Jemahl stopped and turned to Michael. "Hey—if you want me to get rid of them, I can do that. I didn't know—"

"No, no. It's okay." Michael looked ahead and saw that Rollie had already climbed to the balcony, where he was being greeted with high fives and elaborate handshakes. "This is some of Rollie's doing, but I'll handle it."

Jemahl also followed Michael's gaze to the balcony. "He's your friend, but all you have to do is say the word."

"Hey, it's done. It'll be okay," Michael decided.

"Come on," Rollie looked over the balcony and gestured to Michael as he lifted a wine bottle in salute.

"Go on up and enjoy yourself," Jemahl said, and slapped Michael's back. "I'll check on some more appetizers for us and be back in a minute."

Michael climbed the stairs and greeted the easygoing group one by one as someone pressed a cold beer bottle into his hand. It was good to see a few of the faces he called friends and played against on Sundays during the season. He grabbed a few more hands. Yeah, he was glad that he'd come, after all.

As the game prepared to start up again, Michael moved through the small group until he reached Rollie and the two women he'd invited. When Rollie introduced them, it was clear that Randy, tall and statuesque, was intended for Michael's entertainment. She was young and pretty in the overblown way that Rollie preferred women, and curvaceous, to boot—from the looks of the abundant creamy flesh that seemed to hover above her sweater. Michael swallowed, unexpectedly challenged by what was laid out before him.

"Come on, bro," Rollie engaged him with a grin. "I got you here to enjoy yourself tonight."

Michael raised his eyes from Randy and lifted his beer to his friend in a silent toast of disapproval.

"Did you see that?" Roger Burrell, a self-described "techie" asked the group of five at the table. "I swear it was Michael Hennessey. He walked right past me with his posse." He stood at the table with a pitcher of beer in one hand and a plate of quesadillas in the other as he continued to look down the aisle.

The surprise announcement alerted Carolyn, and she jerked her head around to follow his stare.

"Where'd he go?" Kurt, the systems analyst, craned his neck to get a glimpse, too.

"Aw, man, they don't call it a posse anymore, and sports celebrities are always in here," George, another member of the project team, chuckled. "Set the pitcher of beer down, please, and stop gawking."

"Carolyn, what's wrong?" Anthony Wright scooped up another quesadilla from the plate Roger had set in the middle of the table. "You look like you're upset about something."

"Yeah," George added as his attention darted back and forth from the big screen television to Carolyn in quick succession. "We thought you'd figure out why we wanted to come here."

Carolyn abandoned her attempt to get a glimpse of Michael. Indeed, the sighting had disturbed her, but not in a way she could reveal to her work group.

"No, I'm not upset," she explained good-naturedly. "It's not like it's the first time you've played a trick on me. I can take a joke." When dead silence accompanied their looks of comic seriousness, her own face dropped. "Well, I can, can't I?" she protested.

They broke the silence and laughed at her expense, and she joined in.

"I'll remember, though," she said, "to think twice when a work session is adjourned to the local watering hole."

While George waved down a waitress to get Carolyn another Coke, she looked around the room, her surreptitious glances intended to seek out Michael.

"You're only safe in this place when it's off-season," Roger said. "Right now, basketball is king."

"Yeah, Carolyn, March is here, and that means college basketball, and the final four," Kurt, their systems analyst, explained in the middle of gobbling up chips. "Why do you think they call it 'March Madness'?"

"March Madness?" she repeated.

"Well, you better add baseball; and football is right around the corner," Anthony, the design engineer said.

"Sounds like there's always a sport in season." Carolyn's head whirled with their sports advice. "Or maybe I'll just avoid dinner meetings when a TV is present," she suggested. But the men had already diverted their attention away from her and were caught up in the action on the big screens.

The restaurant radiated a vibrant air and was filled with business types who appeared, like Carolyn and her team, not to have made it home yet.

Carolyn bit into her sandwich as she listened to the lively sports banter between her team members. Their talk had quickly moved from system processes, which she easily absorbed, to basketball, a totally foreign language to her. The two large screens that broadcasted the game to either side of the restaurant also captured their attention. Caught up in the multiple stimuli of the room, she bobbled her sandwich and it fell apart into her lap.

She sighed in disgust. "Excuse me, guys," she said as she scooped the remnants of the sandwich up with her napkin. "I'm going to the ladies' room." Leaving her jacket on the back of her chair, she rose from the table.

"I'll be right back." She shook her head, seriously doubting they would even notice her absence.

Carolyn waded through the active crowd on her way to the bathroom, all the while conscious that Michael was somewhere in here, too. After the staff meeting, she and her team had continued their strategy session past the dinner hour—not unusual when new projects were being assessed—but all in all, it had made for a very long day, even by Carolyn's tough standards.

As both senior engineer and team leader, Carolyn acknowledged that her team's wish for the project's success was as strong as hers but, unlike her, they needed a break. So she had agreed with their suggestion to adjourn to the restaurant down the street from the office for dinner, a custom practiced in the past. It was a popular sports bar, after all. Why *wouldn't* Michael be here?

A loud "whoop" went up around her, and Carolyn was pulled back into the present by the energy the game evoked. She looked back to her table and could see the men cheering as they stood to give each other hand slaps like young boys.

Carolyn smiled, thinking she should have suspected their plan all along had been to watch the game. Alli was right; sometimes Carolyn did feel like a stick-in-the-mud. It wasn't that she wanted to be like that, it was just that nothing around her interested her as much as her work.

Why hadn't she known it was the height of basketball season? How hard would that have been to figure out? Once this project was up and running, she would do better, she promised. And then she remembered that Michael was here tonight. Just as she chastised herself for the direction of her thoughts, a vision of him flitted into her head, of his mouth lowering onto hers. . . .

Carolyn touched her mouth, embarrassed by the personal thought, so real that it produced a shock to her center. She shivered over this new reaction to a man she had wanted no part of a few weeks ago. Of course, that was because she had only a first impression of him. And though she didn't know much more now, she recognized in him something other men interested in her had lacked: determination. It was almost admirable that he hadn't been scared away like the others.

She set aside her musings and suspected that, being the man he was, Michael was somewhere watching the game, not thinking about her. It made her recall something else Alli had said. While Carolyn knew Michael liked her outward appearance, what did he think of *her?* Would he, like her sisters, think she was too conventional for his tastes?

She entered the bathroom full of thoughts and unfastened her soiled skirt. Alone in the small space, she stepped out of it and then went about the task of cleaning the stain.

After a few minutes, finally satisfied that she had done her best with the spot, Carolyn dropped the wet paper towels into the wastebasket just as two women came through the door, laughing as they talked.

"I can tell when a man is on the make, girl, and he wants me," the tall one with the cascade of curls boasted to her friend in the leather suit. "You saw how his eyes haven't left my chest from the get-go." She walked past Carolyn to enter one of the stalls, and then closed the door.

Carolyn held tight to her smile when she caught a glimpse of the woman's brazenly exposed breasts. Wasn't that her purpose in walking around with them bared like that? She shook out her skirt.

"Aw, they all do that, girl." The leather-clad woman produced a lipstick and poised herself in front of the mirror to apply the bright color. "Just make sure he's the one who takes you home when we leave, and that'll tell you all you need to know. I hear he's loaded, too."

Carolyn darted a friendly smile at the woman who was blocking her access to the automatic hand dryer.

"Excuse me. I need to get to the dryer." By way of explanation, she lifted the skirt draped across her hand.

"Sure," the woman replied, and moved aside. "Messed up your skirt, huh? Been there, done that."

Carolyn's pumps clicked over the linoleum floor as she took the few steps to the wall and pushed the start button on the wall dryer. She held her skirt aloft under the blast of warm air.

"Luckily, I'm wearing good old black," Carolyn said above the whirr of the blower.

"Not underneath, though."

Carolyn looked over her shoulder and saw that the woman was referring to the short, lacy lavender chemise that barely covered Carolyn's pantyhosed bottom.

"I bet your man likes your style, huh?" The woman returned her attention to her image in the mirror.

Carolyn's eyes narrowed as she lowered her skirt from the stream of air and quickly stepped into it. Fastening the waistband, she gave the curious woman a stealthy glance before she reached for the doorknob to leave.

"With those legs, girl, you could make them work for you at the Sheik's Harem."

At the woman's words, Carolyn paused at the door and looked back.

With a haughty laugh, the leather-clad woman winked before she returned to the mirror. "I can tell you don't even know what I'm talking about."

Carolyn shook her head and quickly left the bathroom.

When the women had disappeared for a minute, and there was a break in the game, Rollie used the moment to persuade Michael to meet a friend of his who was a big football fan.

Michael followed Rollie to a table downstairs where two men sat at a table watching the game.

"Charlie, my man, what it is?" Rollie shoved out his hand to greet the friend, who was already standing in anticipation of the meeting.

"Rollie Anderson." Charlie spoke as a toothpick dangled precariously from his mouth and a drink rested casually in his grasp. His attention, though focused through a pair of shrewd dark eyes, remained on Michael the entire time. "And I know who this is," he laughed. "Michael Hennessey, wide receiver extraordinaire. I've been following your career since you were first drafted."

Michael extended his hand, first to Charlie and then to the grim-faced man just behind him, who remained anonymous.

"I appreciate the interest in me and the sport," Michael said. "Rollie's a good friend—"

"Yeah," Charlie nodded. "That's what he says."

"And when he told me a fan of the game wanted to meet me, of course, I was glad to oblige."

Rollie grinned and gave Charlie a thumbs-up sign. "See, I told you he'd come over and say something." Rollie turned to Michael. "Charlie didn't want to come to our table and interrupt things over there."

Nodding, Michael smiled. "That was, uh, considerate of you." He looked past Charlie to his stone-faced friend still standing like a sentry. "If you'll both excuse me, I'll get back to my table so I can enjoy the rest of the game."

"Of course," Charlie agreed.

Michael turned on his heels and left, but he heard Charlie's parting greeting.

"Hey, until next time."

Michael sucked in a deep breath when he saw that Rollie had caught up with him. "So, who the hell is he really?"

"He's just Charlie, Charlie Madden," Rollie answered.

"And what does he do?" Michael asked. Before Rollie could answer, Michael stopped and vented his misgivings in his friend's face.

"On second thought, Rollie, I don't want to know what Charlie does. I don't want to know, and don't want to be involved in any scheme. Are we clear?"

"Yeah, I hear ya, man; but you don't have anything to worry about—"

"Good," Michael said, and started up the stairs. "Let's keep it that way."

"Tell me what you think about the women. You think we ought to invite them back to the house?" Rollie asked.

"I think I can choose my own company, that's what," Michael said, and moved through the group to the balcony rail. He glanced over at the TV screen and saw that the game had resumed. "Where'd you find them, anyway?"

"They're just a couple of dancers over at the Sheik's Harem."

"Figures." Michael twisted the cap from a fresh bottle of beer and tilted it up to his mouth.

"Hey, man, I was looking out for you. What do you mean by that?"

"What do you think?" Michael set the bottle down before he turned and spoke for Rollie's ears only. "You want them, you go home with *them*. Just keep me out of it."

When Rollie attempted to speak, Michael's cold glare stopped him. Launching his own frown, Rollie walked off.

Michael ran his hand across his head as he tamped back the rising impatience he had begun to feel with Rollie's continued attempts to revive a past lifestyle that was best left buried. He shook his head. Rollie could be a hard case, but sooner or later he would get it through his head that Michael was serious this time.

Leaning into a shadowed corner near the balcony rail, Michael looked out over the restaurant. He could see that Charlie still sat quietly with his unnamed friend. Michael's gaze strayed past the TV and picked up on a woman who slowly picked her way across the room. Carolyn? Michael stood away from the wall, sure of it, now, and took long, purposeful strides to the stairs, hoping to catch her.

"Hey," Jemahl called out. "Where're you going so fast?"

"I'll be right back," he replied absently as he took to the stairs, training his eyes on the straight-backed figure that was quickly disappearing into the crowd.

As Carolyn made her way back to her table, she looked down at the barely visible damp spot in the lap of her black skirt. At least she had managed to miss her blouse. And the two women who had come in the bathroom— what was that about? Suddenly, a strong hand closed around her arm and jerked her to a stop.

"Carolyn?"

She whipped her body around and looked up into Michael's face, surprise eclipsing her unexpected pleasure at seeing him.

"Michael? What—" Someone jostled them in the tight aisle and she bounced into his chest. "What are you doing here?"

He put his hand on her shoulder in a possessive gesture, and drew her from the aisle. "Come on," he said as he led her a few steps away to the edge of the bar. "Don't you think it's more appropriate for me to ask you what you're doing in a sports bar?"

When he let go of her shoulder, Carolyn crossed her arms in front of her. "I'm working."

Michael laughed as he glanced around the room. "Here?"

She nodded, enjoying his humor. "Sure. I have a table here with my team." At Michael's blank stare, she explained. "My project team. We closed out a late meeting with dinner. Here."

He motioned toward a TV. "And a game, too?"

She smiled as she prepared to exaggerate the knowledge she'd picked up tonight. "Basketball's a great way to wind down. Why do you think they call it March Madness? It's only football that I can't seem to get a grasp on."

Michael shook his head as a grand smile covered his face. "I'll have to work on that. Still, I would never have thought—"

"That I'd frequent a sports bar, and on a big game night like this?" At his nod, she said, "Well, that just goes to show you shouldn't presume anything about me."

He took hold of Carolyn's hand. "Since we're both here, why don't you join me at my table? The guy who owns the place is a friend, and he's set up a spread for a few of us upstairs on the balcony."

Carolyn took a deep breath as her heart beat rapidly, but she made no attempt to retrieve her hand.

"Thank you, but I should probably rejoin my own group."

"You said your meeting was over."

"Oh, well, I—"

"And you're a big basketball fan."

"Yes, but . . ." She bit her lip as her eyes darted to Michael's.

"And it'll be my pleasure to spend another evening with you, Carolyn. It'll give us another chance to get to know each other, like we promised the other night out by the car."

"Okay, okay." Carolyn smiled as amusement flickered in his eyes. "You didn't have to bring up the car."

"Why?" Michael teased. "I liked it when you lost control for a while."

She arched her brows, liking this gentle camaraderie. "My jacket . . . I left it at the table."

"I take that as a 'yes you'll join me.' " As Carolyn turned, Michael pulled her hand to draw her back, and then stepped behind her. "I'll go along with you . . . just in case you get scooped up by some player from a sport you like."

Shortly thereafter, Carolyn's introduction of Michael to her co-workers produced the expected surprise, but she hadn't been prepared for their excited responses that bordered on embarrassing. He even signed autographs for all four of them. When she and Michael left the table, Carolyn apologized, but Michael assured her he hadn't minded at all.

Now, as they returned to Michael's friends, Carolyn took notice of her surroundings and was amazed by the reactions Michael continued to draw from the patrons they passed.

"How do you put up with grown men acting like this around you?" She glanced over at him. "If men act this ridiculously, I gather the women are probably worse."

Michael chuckled at her reaction. I suppose it's okay now that I'm used to it, and as long as they don't get physical."

"Physical?"

"Yeah, I've come across men who want to prove they're bigger and badder, and the women—" he bent near her ear, "—they usually just want to jump my bones."

Carolyn laughed. "You sound like my sister, Alli."

Michael slowed as they reached the staircase. "After you," he said to her.

Carolyn climbed the heavy wooden staircase, conscious that Michael was very close, right behind her. As she stepped onto the landing, she saw a noisy group that numbered twenty or so who were either watching the game, standing in conversation, or eating from the trays of appetizers nearby.

"Michael, I was looking for you, man."

Carolyn recognized Michael's friend, Rollie, as he separated himself from others near the railing. Another man she recognized from the auction was right behind him.

"Hey, Michael, you found somebody to join us who looks a lot better than Rollie," Jemahl joked as he squinted his eyes at Carolyn. "You're the date he won at the auction, aren't you?"

"Her name's Carolyn Hardy," Michael announced. "She's a friend."

Jemahl grinned at Michael. "You sly devil, you two made a connection that night, huh? Admit it, you connected."

Amid the back slaps to Michael and the not-so-innocent comments addressed to them both, Carolyn could feel the heat rise up her neck and envelop her face as the football players, and the few with dates, introduced themselves to her.

Michael moved on to his friend. "Rollie, you remember Carolyn, don't you?"

Carolyn's attention had already whisked past Rollie only to fall on the two women next to him who, likewise, had taken a serious interest in her. She stiffened as she recognized, first, the leather-suited woman and then, the woman with the mounded cleavage. They were the same two women she'd encountered in the bathroom.

"And these are two of Rollie's friends, Randy and Carleshia."

Carolyn barely heard Michael say their names. But the memory of the women's conversation came back like a brick through a window. Surprise lit her face as she glanced at Michael, her body vibrating with what could only be described as an unusual case of jealousy.

Twelve

Carolyn sipped at her wine and masked another of her glances that wandered in the direction of Randy, who seemed to be having a good time despite the fact that Michael watched the last of the game at Carolyn's side.

While Rollie's friends laughed and enjoyed the game with him and other guests from an adjacent table, Carolyn stole a sidelong glance at Michael, who was involved in the game action with the other men, laughing as they pressed their teams to victory.

Carolyn felt totally out of place, and edgy at her predicament, fidgeted in her booth seat, absently gulping swallows of wine, more from habit than enjoyment.

Earlier, when Jemahl had posed the question "What's your poison?" Carolyn had searched for an answer more suitable than her normal Coke. Though amber beer bottles had dotted the tables, Carolyn didn't have a hope of getting that bitter brew down, let alone keeping it down. And she didn't want her secret—that she wasn't much of a partygoer—to be revealed to this group of partygoers. A slender bottle of red wine, along with a more sturdy scotch whiskey bottle, also graced the table, either of which she knew could be nursed, if necessary, through an entire evening. She had decided to nurse the wine.

"Come on, you got five more seconds, pass the ball,

pass the ball," exhorted one of the huge ball players at the TV screen, amid the shouts of encouragement from the others.

Suddenly a "whoop" went up as the group jumped to their collective feet while the announcer shouted victory. The game was over.

Carolyn rose from the booth to join the others as they all redirected their emotions after the game with randomly offered hugs, hand slaps, and laughter. Someone to the right of Carolyn bumped against her. It was Randy; even taller in heels, she looked straight at Carolyn and spoke in a low voice.

"You're not his type, you know."

"What are you talking about?" Carolyn asked, slightly intimidated that the woman would actually speak what Carolyn had only suspected.

"Look at you, all prim and buttoned up." She let out a laugh meant as pity. "How long you think you're gonna keep his attention playin' hard to get?" she asked before she laughed again. "He's a man, honey, and a real man wants a good time, which is what he was gonna get before you showed up."

Taken aback by the words, Carolyn wouldn't deign to answer the woman. She shared a hard glare with Randy before turning to reclaim her booth seat. She fingered the front of her blouse before she pressed her skirt down to sit, and realized that Randy was right. She was prim, and buttoned up in black, too.

She stared in the direction Randy had gone, and watched as the woman made a seductive beeline toward a group of the men that included Michael. Within a few moments, Randy had insinuated herself into their space to become the center of attention.

Mesmerized by the woman's obvious abilities, Carolyn squinted with disbelief as she gulped another swallow of her diminishing glass of wine.

* * *

Most of the TV screens in the sports bar had been turned off and the music had been pumped up for the crowd that remained to simply hang out and deflate from the game. Carolyn felt more than saw Michael rest his dark eyes on her in the booth they shared. As she managed another sip of her wine, she returned his gaze, alerted by the piercing stare.

She narrowed her eyes. "What?" she asked, and took in a deep breath, innocently drawing in his deep fragrance.

"Why do you keep looking over there?" Michael's arm rested across the back of the booth as he turned to Carolyn and gestured with his head toward Rollie, who sat with Randy and Carleshia at another table.

Carolyn scooted straight up. "I wasn't doing that," she said and darted him another glance before she cringed. "Was I?"

Michael's grin was bright and sexy, and Carolyn decided he knew it as he leaned in close to her face.

"I've been watching you and, yeah, you were doing that."

She drew her head back, and blinked him back into focus. When he reached out to tuck a strand of hair back behind Carolyn's ear, the seductive touch was fleeting and delicate and, for a moment, her eyes fluttered closed of their own accord.

"Why did you ask me to join you if you were with Randy before I arrived."

Frowning, Michael turned in the booth to confront her more comfortably. "What makes you think that?" he asked.

She didn't answer, but continued with her take on things. "Maybe you were having a better time with her," she said, and took another sip from the wineglass before she set it back on the table, licking the residue from her lips under Michael's studied stare. "From the looks of her, she sure knows how to have one."

"For the record, I wasn't with her this evening, and I'm having a pretty good time with you," Michael said. He reached out and lifted her hand into his. "What about you? Are you enjoying yourself with me?"

"Maybe I just don't know how to have a good time. You know, my sisters tell me that all the time." She raised the wineglass to her mouth again.

Michael chuckled at her before he slipped the glass from her fingers and set it down on the table. "That's bull. A woman like you, beautiful and smart—I know you've had chances to get it on on the dance floor and let your hair down."

This time Carolyn chuckled and dropped her head back against the padded booth, her chest rising and falling with each laugh.

"Yeah, right, but not the same way your friends do."

Carolyn's reference was easy for Michael to follow, and he took a quick glance back at Randy. Carolyn was right—the woman knew how to party, and he'd read her offer to him right from the start. If he wanted, he could easily have had a warm bedmate when he left tonight, but Randy wasn't who he wanted to ease his unreachable itch.

He turned back to Carolyn. Her head was thrown back on the booth, looking up, and exposing her face with its wide mouth and white teeth. Her creamy smooth throat lay open to his gaze. Unbidden, his eyes traveled along that line of skin, down to her blouse, his progress coming to an abrupt stop at the first button high on her chest. Michael returned his attention to her eyes, large and bright with laughter . . . and something else he had already suspected. She was high from the constantly replenished wine in her glass.

At first, Michael thought she was aware that her glass was continuously being topped off. Now he realized she was simply naïve and didn't realize she was working on a high, and well on her way to becoming drunk.

She rolled her head in Michael's direction. "Alli says guys like you don't have the same kind of good times as regular people. In fact, she warned me about Randy, and I don't even think she knows Randy."

Michael touched a finger to the side of her chin. "Alli's an expert, I'm sure. And I'm beginning to understand, now. You think Rollie's friends—"

"Know how to have the kind of fun you're used to," she finished for him, still staring into his face.

Michael didn't stop himself. He dipped his head down to hers and lightly kissed her mouth, her body's perfume combined with the bouquet of the wine on her lips making for a heady combination. With a deep sigh, he raised his head again.

"Did anyone ever tell you how good you smell?" Carolyn asked as her giggle turned into a yawn. "I could smell you all day."

Smiling at her wine-induced comments, Michael said, "I can do you one up. I could kiss you all day."

"You're just saying that," Carolyn said. "In fact, I know you're interested in Randy because she told me."

This time Michael let out a hearty laugh as he ran his hand across his hair. "When did she say that?"

"I ran into both of them in the bathroom. Randy said you couldn't take your eyes off her chest." When Michael let out a humorous grunt, Carolyn's bright eyes narrowed. "Of course, I should have known she was talking about you. Isn't that where your eyes were when we first met?"

"That's where they are now, too."

Carolyn's hand went to her chest. "The difference is, I'm all buttoned up and prim, right?" She pushed herself upright on the chair again, and Michael moved over to give her room. "All I want to know is, did you bring her here tonight?"

"No, I didn't," Michael said, and briefly explained how the women came to be there. When Carolyn remained silent, Michael felt compelled to explain more fully. "Rollie likes to party and have a good time. He hooks up with people all the time."

"I have to give it to him. The man knows your type."

"Not for some time, Carolyn." He brushed back more strands of her dark hair that had become tangled when she laid against the booth, and looked into her face. "Let me try to explain it this way. When Rollie finds women, they are more like . . ." He searched for the right description. "We call them party girls who are just out to have a good time, too, and that's all. It's all about attitude, nothing more."

"Girls who just want to have fun," Carolyn suggested flatly.

"Yeah, that's one way of putting it. You have a good time with them and then . . ." He looked at her again, but this time he didn't smile. "And then, you go your separate ways."

"I thought you said you'd changed. Rollie doesn't think so—he's still setting you up, like with Randy tonight."

"It didn't happen that way." Michael drew in a deep breath before he admitted, "Okay, maybe it did happen that way; but, Randy and Carleshia are grown women, and they like having fun with, well, athletes."

"Really?" Carolyn asked incredulously. "And that makes you proud to be an athlete—that some woman wants to have way too much fun just because of that?"

He sighed. "I know, it's shallow, but it's what some girls like to do; so before you decide that anyone's being used, you should find out how they feel about it."

"Maybe I will, then." Carolyn stifled another burgeoning yawn and made to get up from the booth.

"Whoa . . . Hold on," Michael said, and pulled her back down into the booth by the waist. "I don't think you're in any shape for a confrontation tonight," he whispered in her ear.

Carolyn slipped from his hands before she picked up her wine glass and expertly tilted the stem to drink the last of the wine from it. "So, any type can be a party girl, right? Even me?"

"Mmm . . . I don't think so," Michael said, and wondered what she was up to.

"Well, you're the one who said it's all about attitude. So, I'll get some attitude." She sat up and began to unfasten the top button of her blouse.

"Now what are you doing?" a laughing Michael asked, his eyes trained on her fingers.

"Getting a party girl attitude." She started on the next button. "You know, Randy's not the only woman in here who has br—breasts." She giggled as she stumbled over the word.

"I can see that." Michael's brow rose a fraction as he continued to watch her fingers. He looked around to see if she had drawn any undue attention. "Carolyn, I think you've had a little too much to drink."

"Why? Because I want to claim my right to be a party girl for the evening?" She eased a third button loose. "You don't think I can pull it off, do you? You think the way Alli does—that I'm too straight and boring."

"Not on your life. I think you're smart and self-assured. You're the kind of woman who knows exactly what she wants and how to get it, but without being a party girl."

Michael found Carolyn's revealed insecurity both amusing and enlightening, and watched as she shook her shoulders so that the loose blouse settled against her curvy frame; a sliver of lavender at the now deep neckline kept an enticing view of cleavage contained within its borders.

"So, what do you think now?" she asked, and brushed her hair back from her face.

Michael's eyes drank her up.

"Do I pass enough to be at the Sheik's Harem?"

With a speechless frown, Michael swallowed hard as he felt a familiar tightening in his loins.

A young waiter came up with a towel-wrapped bottle of wine and without asking, prepared to fill Carolyn's glass again.

"No more for her," Michael said, dragging his eyes from Carolyn and waving the waiter away.

"What's this one?" Carolyn asked as she reached for the whiskey bottle in the center of the table. "I've seen this around before. A classic bottle, don't you think?"

"Here, let me get that for you."

Michael scooped up the bottle of Chivas Regal from Carolyn's grasp and then looked at her. She had had enough, and was definitely on the way to tying one on; but he remembered how her family had described her as an unapologetic workaholic, which meant tonight was more than just a rare event. Maybe it was something she needed to do to prove something to him, or even to her sister, Alli.

In a quick decision, he decided that, under his guidance so she wouldn't totally embarrass herself, he'd let her play out her evening. Michael unscrewed the cap and splashed a small amount of the liquor into her glass.

"Take small sips, not a gulp, okay? It'll feel real smooth going down, and then comes the kick."

Carolyn looked up at him. "So, how do you know I'm not a regular whiskey drinker?"

"I don't know. Just a guess," he said, and replaced the cap on the bottle. "I do think you've decided to take a walk on the wild side tonight."

"Are you walking with me?"

"All the way," he said.

At that moment, a ring came from somewhere under the table. "My phone," Carolyn said, and looked to either side of her for it; but Michael stayed her hand.

"Don't answer it. You'll spoil your magic, your walk on the wild side, party girl."

She giggled and put her hand over her mouth. "You're right, you know. What would I say, anyway?"

"Exactly," Michael agreed, as the phone stopped its ring. "See, the world didn't come to an end because you didn't answer."

"Yeah, I think I like that." She sipped the whiskey, and grimaced as she swallowed it down. "Ugh . . . it's hot. Give me some of your ice cubes."

Michael watched as she fished ice cubes from the glass he'd offered her, and then used her finger to swirl the liquor around them. He crooked his arm on the table.

"You have now become a full-blown mystery, Carolyn Hardy. There's a lot more below your surface than I first figured." He leaned in closer and rested his hand under her hair and against her soft, warm nape. "You know something else?"

Carolyn grinned at Michael as she sucked the scotch from her finger. "What?"

"You never told me where you live."

"I didn't, did I," she teased, and leaned in close. "My place is right here downtown, in the Phoenix Loft high-rises," she said, and giggled again. "Get it? Atlanta? Phoenix, rising from the ashes?" She giggled again as she sucked the scotch from another digit. "Never mind. Why?"

Michael smiled at her peculiar humor as he caught a signal from Jemahl a short distance away. He dropped his hand from Carolyn's neck as Jemahl came over and leaned his head near Michael.

"I think I'll get something to eat while you two talk football," Carolyn said, and slid out from the booth.

"Wow, she sure perked up," Jemahl observed. "What's up with that? Is she road-ready?"

"Don't worry about her." Michael spoke low as he followed Carolyn's movements across the room. "She's pretty busy and doesn't get out often for fun, so I'm letting her make up for it tonight. I have her keys and I'll make sure she gets home."

Jemahl patted his shoulder. "Good. You know, that's the downside of owning a bar—making sure everybody who's had too much knows it."

"So, I gather from your signal you found out something about our boy downstairs?"

"You were right. He is well-known on the back streets. One of my guys in the back says he's known as Charlie "The Brick" Madden. Seems he beat some poor dude to death with a brick a few years back—he was a bad loan risk."

"Damn," Michael exclaimed.

"Yeah, he only did a couple of years by claiming it was self-defense. But his trade of choice is the usual racketeering stuff: drugs, prostitution, loan sharking." As Michael shook his head, Jemahl advised, "Listen, he sounds like trouble and I'd stay clear of him if I were you."

"Yeah, I intend to, even if he is a football fan."

"He's not one of my regulars or I would have remembered. I suspect the unknown friend attached to him at the hip is his ever-handy heat."

"That was my guess, too."

"You know I have to keep my nose clean on account of my own position in football. No betting, no drugs and stuff go on around here," Jemahl declared. "I can't kick him out unless he gives me cause."

"Hey, man, thanks for the info. Tell your source I owe him one."

"No problem. I already took care of him." Jemahl looked to his left and right before he added, "One more thing. You're not the only one interested in The Brick. Somebody else was asking about him, too." He slapped

Michael on the back again. "Let me know if I can help you with anything else."

As Jemahl left, Carolyn trotted back toward Michael. "What was that all about?"

"You," Michael said with a grin, and reached for her hand to pull her back beside him in the booth. "Come over here with me because I want to ask you something." When she settled on the seat, he turned her to him. "Tell me, do you trust me?"

The skewered bacon-wrapped shrimp she held stopped halfway to her mouth, and she looked around the room for a moment before a smile began to form. She answered with a nod. "Yes, I do."

"Good, because I'm going to make sure you get home safe tonight. You probably have a buzz on now that won't wait."

"I do not." She chewed on the shrimp.

Michael leaned back and pinned her with his mischievous grin. "Oh, yes you do, and I've decided to sit back and let you have a good old time tonight, because I'm going to have the supreme privilege of telling you all about it in full detail tomorrow."

Thirteen

"You're Michael Hennessey?" the young doorman at the Phoenix Lofts exclaimed. He pushed open the double glass doors and backed into the lobby; his oversized burgundy and gold tasseled uniform looked ridiculous on his slight form.

Michael was more concerned with keeping a barely awake Carolyn upright at his side; her arm encircled his waist as added support. She had fallen asleep during the short drive from the sports bar; and after being coaxed from the car, she had giggled an unintelligible protest over having to put one foot in front of the other so soon. Michael had almost decided it was simpler to just carry her. He relished the humor in this situation, and was glad that at least she was a happy drunk.

As they followed the doorman to the elevator, Michael could see the guard from the desk up ahead coming their way.

"You're really Michael Hennessey," the doorman continued to mutter.

"Do me a favor, okay?" Michael asked the young man. "Sure."

"Would you see to it that Miss Hardy's car gets parked in the garage?" Michael nodded his head toward the lobby door, where her silver Acura could be seen sitting at the curb in front of the building.

"Hey, I'm on it."

Michael tossed the kcy to the doorman with one hand as he balanced a fidgeting Carolyn with the other, and then continued on to the elevator. "You can bring the key up when you're done," Michael called out.

With a big grin on his face, the doorman backed away a few steps before he turned and rushed through the doors to the car. Meanwhile, the desk guard, an older man in a burgundy suit, met up with Michael at the elevator.

When Michael greeted the man, Carolyn interrupted.

"Are we there yet, Michael?" As she tried holding her eyes open by tilting her head up, she saw the guard. "Gerald, is that you?" she asked slowly, and peered at him. "How are you doing?"

"I'm fine, Miss Hardy." He rocked on his heels as he observed her carefully. "I should ask the same of you, ma'am."

Carolyn had closed her eyes again, though she kept the smile on her face as she slumped against Michael. "I could do with some hot tea, I think." She dropped her voice to a whisper. "Michael promised he'd make some if I let him bring me home. Are we home yet?"

"Does that mean you'll be wanting me to add Mr. Hennessey to your guest list, ma'am?" the guard asked Carolyn.

Michael smoothed Carolyn's hair back from her sleepy face. "I think the answer is yes, but you can ask her again tomorrow."

The elevator arrived, and as Gerald held it open, Michael entered with Carolyn. "Oh, another thing," he cautioned, and reached for his wallet while he balanced Carolyn against him. "You wouldn't want Miss Hardy to be embarrassed by all this later on, I'm sure."

"Of course, not," the guard said as he darted a glance

at the sleeping Carolyn on Michael's arm. "Miss Hardy's a nice lady."

"Good, then let's keep this between us." He reached into his wallet and withdrew two large bills. "She's had a long evening, that's all, and I'm sure she'd appreciate it if you'd honor her privacy." He stretched the bills out to Gerald. "Both of our privacy, in fact. Extend my appreciation to your doorman, too."

Gerald looked at the notes Michael passed to him and smiled. "Thank you, Mr. Hennessey." He looked at Carolyn again. "She's gonna be all right, you think?"

"Oh, she'll be fine by morning. Nothing a little tea and sleep won't cure."

Carolyn grunted sleepily as she continued to hold onto Michael.

"I'll buzz you onto her floor when the elevator arrives," Gerald said.

Michael nodded. "That'll work." He pressed the button to Carolyn's floor, and the doors closed smoothly.

The contemporary design of the elevators allowed the occupant to look out onto the city from one side, but it insured privacy from outside viewing. Carolyn began to stir at his side and turned so that her face pressed against his chest. It was as she circled his waist with her arms, and her body pressed against the length of his, that Michael's loins began to stir.

"Mmm . . ." She murmured through closed eyes. "You smell so good."

Michael couldn't manage words for a moment as he guiltily enjoyed the unexpected pleasure of her posture, and with a heavy sigh, tightened his grip on her shoulders. He did recognize, however, that this seemingly uninhibited Carolyn could mean trouble—more for him than her.

"So do you," he said as he rested his head against the top of hers. "So do you."

"Why can't we just stay here and smell each other all night?"

She mumbled what Michael suspected were her private thoughts. He looked down at her, comfortably nestled against his chest. With all the fun she'd had tonight, he wondered how much of the evening would stay in her memory. A good sleep was in order for her.

The elevator doors slid open and revealed a private, unobtrusive foyer that led to a rich, mahogany-finished door. Carolyn's, he presumed. With some gentle urging, Carolyn finally unclenched his waist and took the steps necessary to reach her door. Michael unlocked it and led her through.

"We're there already," Carolyn announced gaily. She let her purse slip from her shoulder to the floor, and managed to step away from him and into the room.

Michael watched her walk off into the dim light cast by the illuminated windows. He looked to his left and right. From what he could see, her loft appeared to be one huge room that she had sectioned off into large living spaces. Two walls of windows that overlooked the city flanked the space. It was a very urban feel for a woman he had come to think of as quite traditional in her tastes.

In the span of a few seconds, Carolyn had disappeared into the darkness ahead without making a sound. Michael touched around the wall behind him and, discovering a switch, pressed it.

The front living area was instantly bathed in light from two tall floor lamps and an overhead source emanating out of the deep black ceiling. Her floor was dark hardwood, and certain areas were covered by Persian area rugs. Artsy dividers and other art pieces, all touched by Carolyn's good taste, defined the separate living areas. What he saw now was much closer to what he considered her traditional roots.

Michael moved in the direction that she'd gone when

she first entered. He passed one of the large windows, and could see the distant, twinkling city lights.

Apparently, Carolyn had only gotten as far as a spindly-legged chaise lounge somewhere in the middle of the apartment, a chair that looked way too delicate for Michael's large frame. She had dropped onto it without taking her jacket or shoes off, her legs and arms splayed the way she had slumped there.

"I wondered where you had gone," he said, and stooped near the chair so he could see her face. "In fact, I'm trying to decide what I should do with you since I don't think it's a good idea to leave you this way, at least until you're settled in."

She rolled onto her back and looked up at Michael. "I thought you said that's what you do. You leave party girls."

Michael scratched his head as he looked at her trusting face and too bright eyes. "You're not a party girl."

"But you like me anyway?" She laughed with her eyes squeezed tight. "I can tell."

"Yeah, well, I don't think it's a secret that I like you . . ." He gave her a pointed look. "Very much."

She cringed as she tried to rise to a sitting position. "Whoa . . . Michael, I don't think I can stand up," she slurred. "My head just swims"—she lolled her head as she spoke—"when I hold it up," she continued. "What's wrong with me?"

"It's called being drunk." Michael smiled at her sagging form. ". . . Party girl," he finished. He stood and gathered her up in his arms, making an instant decision not to leave her like this—sprawled over a chair to sleep off the buzz.

"I told you I could be one," she said and draped her arms around Michael's neck. "But I'm not sure it's all it's cracked up to be."

"I think I need to get you sobered up a bit before I

leave." He looked around for the direction of her bedroom and saw that it was set up behind a glass-blocked wall near the chair. When he entered the space, he was surprised to see a king-size bed.

He set her down on the edge and she immediately dropped backward onto the coverlet. Michael steeled himself for what he knew would be a challenge: helping to undress a woman he was desperately attracted to. He bent down on one knee and slipped her shoes off first, and then, pulling her back up, eased her jacket from her shoulders. For now, he left the partially buttoned blouse and skirt in place.

He looked over her shoulders to a set of double doors in the wall behind the bed, which probably led to the bathroom.

"Carolyn," he said, looking back at her, "why don't you finish getting undressed while I start the shower? I promise you, you'll feel a lot better after you get a good soaking of water."

"Are you going to stay and help me?"

Michael thought any further help he gave would be a bad idea, and it would be like taking advantage of her, since he would doubt any decision she made tonight. In fact, he thought he should stay as far away from her as possible.

Carolyn raised her hand to stroke the side of Michael's face. "Thank you," she said, before she followed with her head and kissed his mouth.

Michael didn't ask what she meant, nor did he push her away. And at first, he let her direct the gentle kiss, enjoying the delicious sensation her mouth sent through his body as she gave herself freely to her passion. He thoroughly sampled her soft lips, his emotions still tightly controlled, but things changed abruptly when she opened her mouth to his.

As the kiss deepened and he tasted her tongue, his control began to unravel. His tongue traced the soft fullness of her lips before he explored her mouth with amorous abandon. As Carolyn worked her hands under his shirt so that she now stroked his bare skin, he took over the tempo, as well. He dropped his hands to her sides and began a caress that circled around to her stomach, and ended with his hands cupped beneath her breasts. Soft, full breasts with firm nipples.

Carolyn's low groan of delight entered his head, and he pressed her backwards onto the bed as he followed to bury his lips against her neck. She had worked his shirt up and now stroked his back, her wanton abandon a strong elixir for his own lust. Michael pushed her blouse up and exposed her stomach. And though the lavender chemise covered her, he placed a lingering kiss there before he moved to her breasts and kissed the softly plumped fruit that flowed out of its confines.

Carolyn drew Michael's hand to her blouse, and he began to unbutton it with lightning speed. He lifted his head and looked into her eyes, half-lidded with pleasure, anticipation . . . and wine. He stopped his hand's exploration and tried to steady his pulse.

"Michael?" Her breathing was heavy as she touched his hand. "Why did you stop?"

As he waited for his control to return, he could see her lips were still moist from his mouth. "Because I'm the sober one, and if I let this go any further, you'd never forgive me. Anyway, when I make love to you, I want all of your senses there for all of me."

When she gave him a puzzled look, he shook his head and blew out a breath. "Trust me, this is not the right time." He got up from the bed. "Come on, Carolyn, get in that shower, while I go out to the kitchen to find some coffee."

She started to giggle. "I don't drink coffee."

"You don't drink wine, either, but that didn't stop you tonight."

"You promised me tea."

"All right, tea it is. Come on," he urged, and pulled her back up before he tugged the open blouse down her arm. It slipped over her fingers as he pulled it away, exposing the slip-like chemise beneath and the delicate skin above—delicate skin now marked with a russet spot where he had nibbled earlier. The peach soft mounds rose and fell with each breath she took.

Michael drew in a deep breath of his own as his eyes refused to quit the luscious picture he was presented. He had to get out of there.

"All right, you can do the skirt," he said, and left her at the bed.

He took the quick steps to the bathroom and, after opening the shower stall, cut the water jets on before he returned to the bed to check on Carolyn. In his absence, she had managed to stand, and now the skirt slipped to the floor and puddled at her feet.

"The shower's running," Michael said, her bare legs only a fleeting vision as he continued past on his way to the kitchen.

Once there, he went about searching for utensils, his mind on autopilot as he wondered on what had just happened between him and Carolyn on that bed. Sure, he had it bad for her, but playing it out tonight wasn't smart at all, he concluded. In fact, he wondered how smart it had been to let Carolyn imbibe as much as she did when it became obvious that she wasn't a drinker. He didn't think this was what her family had in mind when they gave their consent for a date. Nope, getting Carolyn drunk and then taking advantage of her was not what they had in mind at all.

The doorbell's ring streaked through Michael's thoughts. He looked up from what he was doing and immediately remembered the young doorman he had instructed to deliver Carolyn's keys upstairs after the car was parked. A knock had now followed the ring.

"Hang on," Michael yelled, and turned out of the small kitchen on his way to the door. The shower was still going; hopefully, Carolyn had stepped into it.

He opened the door to greet the doorman.

"Hey, man, thanks—" Michael's words and smile froze as he met a scowl from a man whose height and weight was similar to his own.

"What are you doing here?" the man asked angrily. "And, what did you do to Carolyn?"

"What the hell—" Michael was shunted aside as his stare followed the stranger who had barged past him through the door and into the room like a bull.

"Look at you, already breaking your promise," a melodic female voice declared in the vicinity of the door. "You were supposed to find out what was going on, first."

Michael looked back toward the door and now saw that the man was accompanied by someone else—a curly-haired beauty whose focus seemed geared on keeping the man under control. Michael turned back to the man who was entering the kitchen.

"Who the hell are you, and where do you get off barging in here like this?" Michael followed him.

"I'll ask the questions." He left the kitchen, traversing the place as if he knew it well. "Where is my sister?"

Michael blinked hard as it all began to make sense.

The woman came up from behind Michael and held out her palm. "These are Carolyn's keys. I'll put them on the counter."

"Carolyn invited me here," Michael said as he followed the man again.

"After you got her drunk?"

"Well, if you know all the answers, why ask?"

"Both of you, stop yelling," the woman demanded, as

she caught up with and then stood between the two of them.

"Now, in case you haven't figured out our names," the woman said, "I'm Davina." She turned and looped her arm through the man's. "And this is Justin the Terrible, Carolyn's brother."

"Oh," Michael said, his eyes turning shrewd as the names and their particular history registered. "I'm Michael Hennessey."

"You still haven't told me where Carolyn is," Justin said, still none-too-friendly. He cocked his head toward the bedroom. "Isn't that the shower? Carolyn," he called, and left the kitchen, only to stop in his tracks.

"Justin? Davina?" Carolyn giggled as she stood at the edge of the living room area, wearing only a dripping chemise and pantyhose. Her hair was also wet and plastered to her head, hanging to her shoulders in clumps. She looked as though she'd taken the shower without taking anything else off. "Alli said you were back in town."

Michael and the others had frozen at Carolyn's greeting, but now Davina went to her side.

"Carolyn, honey, are you all right? Let me get you a robe, okay?" At her nod, Davina left for the bedroom.

Both Justin and Michael took a step toward Carolyn.

"Is anything wrong?" Justin asked. "Did he do anything to you?"

Michael darted a frown at Justin. "Of course, I didn't."

"No, but he did let me be his party girl for the night," she giggled again. "And now, he thinks I'm drunk."

Michael drew in a deep sigh as Justin shot him a decidedly unhappy frown that demanded an explanation, and fast.

Fourteen

Carolyn slowly awakened and stretched her toes against the soft bed linens. She even leisurely flipped onto her back before the events—or at least part of the events—from the previous evening permeated her brain. It was then, cloaked in a miasma of indistinct, hopscotch memory, that she sat straight up in the bed; it had all started with running into Michael at the restaurant. She rubbed her forehead to hasten the clarity.

It was morning—she could tell by the clean white light that poured through the east windows; but something wasn't right. It appeared to be late morning, much later than she normally awakened. She jerked her head around to view her alarm clock, and in the process, set off tiny explosions in her head that reminded her of the brain freeze you get from drinking a Slurpee too fast.

Carolyn focused on the clock and was disbelieving of what she read. It was after nine o'clock, so why was she still in bed? She tried moving swiftly from bed, but stopped as her head blazed with bright stars each time she made a quick, sudden move.

This time, she was more careful as she tossed the covers back, and was startled when she looked down at what she wore—a short silk gown that had bunched up around her waist. This only added to her confusion as she slid from the bed, her mind already muddled about the morning's events. It was, after all, still late winter, and she could have sworn she always preferred pajamas this time of year. She gingerly made her way to the bathroom.

When Carolyn reached the doors, she pushed them open as she stifled a yawn. She looked up at the back of a strange toweled man, who stood at the sink. Carolyn's knees buckled in shock and she stumbled back against the doors. The stranger turned to her and—why, he was no stranger after all. It was Michael in all his broad-chested glory. He gripped a toothbrush between his teeth and wore one of her pink towels swathed low around his hips.

"Carolyn!" he exclaimed.

"Michael, what are you doing here?" She sputtered the question as she took in his dishabille. A nervous possibility raced through her thoughts as the next natural question formed in her head. What had happened last night?

She watched as he quickly tossed the toothbrush on the sink, rinsed his mouth, and dried his hands, all in a matter of seconds, before his powerful, well-muscled body moved with easy grace toward her.

"I thought you'd be sleeping it off for at least another hour."

"What?" The unspoken question came back to haunt her. "Oh, my goodness, don't tell me," she said to him, and then looked away. Shock slammed through her as one hand flew to her head, the other to her chest.

"I let you—" She couldn't finish the sentence and tried again as she gave him a seriously strained look. "Did we have . . . I mean, well, did we do something . . . last night that we're going to regret?"

"Well, if we had," he spoke cockily as he stopped in front of her, "I sure as hell wouldn't be regretting it, and I would have made sure that wasn't your take on it, either."

"Be serious, Michael!" she exclaimed.

Michael laughed at her shock. "I am serious. Nothing happened, I assure you. Your honor is intact."

"Then, why are you naked in my bathroom?" She glared at him for making fun at her concerns and ran back into her bedroom.

Carolyn reached for her robe in the closet as she realized how ridiculous she must sound discussing her horror at having sex with him, when all the while they talked, he wore only a towel and she, a short gown. What the heck had happened last night that made them so familiar, that she would even allow this familiarity?

"If you'd stop and breathe a moment, I'll tell you what happened last night," he said. "It was all pretty innocent."

She looked over her shoulder and saw him standing in the doorway. He had pulled on his pants from last night and stood with his hands crossed over his chest. He was a massive, self-confident presence, and it did nothing for her own insecurities.

Carolyn sighed, and did stop. "I was trying to find my robe." She peeked in the closet again. "Nothing seems right this morning."

"Your robe is in the laundry."

"The laundry?"

"You don't remember?" He smiled. "You took a shower in it."

Carolyn frowned as Michael came over to her and pulled her to the bed's edge, where he sat facing her. As he began to explain the previous evening, he helped her to slowly recall the events at Jemahl's restaurant. She even remembered the two women that Rollie had brought to the group, but she didn't seem to have much of a handle on detail after that.

"Things were going fine here until that bullheaded brother of yours showed up."

"Justin?"

"Seems he intercepted your poor doorman, and both

the doorman and guard were only too happy to fill him in on what they witnessed."

"That's right," Carolyn said, and rubbed her head. "I do remember talking with Justin. It seems like a dream now, but I guess it was real. Davina was here too, wasn't she?"

Michael nodded, and crossed his arms, a smile on his face. "Davina was something else; very nice. Pretty, too."

"Don't let Justin hear you say that. He's sort of a Neanderthal when it comes to her."

"You should have seen Justin's face when you came walking out of the shower soaking wet. I needed a camera," Michael laughed. When he saw Carolyn's look of shock, he quickly explained. "You still had on the little lavender number, but Davina got your robe and wrapped you in it."

She sighed. "Well, thank goodness for Davina."

"She was probably the only reason we didn't duke it out. The man doesn't know how to listen, and talk about stubborn. All he wanted to do was throw out these ridiculous questions and never give me a chance to answer any." Michael looked at Carolyn. "Actually, that reminds me of you."

"I know my brother. So what calmed him down enough to leave you with me?"

"Davina convinced him that I'd be crazy to try something now. I told them your mother and sisters knew me well enough to know I wouldn't do any harm to you, so he called Alli."

"He left me with you on Alli's advice?" Carolyn was crushed. "That's comforting."

Michael grinned at what she perceived as a slight. "Whatever she said to him, I owe her one."

"You still didn't say why you stayed. You didn't have a way home?"

"I could have called a taxi, or Mr. Pitts; but when

Justin and Davina left, I wanted to make sure you were safe the rest of the night."

"Oh, I bet your little Halina missed you this morning." Carolyn remembered how the little girl had clung to Michael before.

"I've already called her, and she's fine. Oh, and thanks for the toothbrush. I found an extra one in the bathroom."

He nodded toward the living room. "You realize you have no decent furniture to offer a man on a sleepover?"

"Sure I do. There's the chaise lounge right outside my bedroom and the living room couch."

"That couch was made for a tea party. Don't you think a six-foot-three man would look pretty silly trying to sack out on either of those chairs?"

Carolyn laughed with him. "So, what did you do for a bed?"

"I slept in here with you, of course."

Her eyes grew wide. "You slept in here? With me? That's impossible. How could I not have noticed you in my bed? Is there anything else I need to know about last night?"

Michael smiled at her. "Not that I can think of right now."

She looked down at the gown, and hugged her arms around her. "How did I manage to get this gown on?"

"You didn't," he said mysteriously.

Carolyn's eyes grew shrewd. "You didn't . . . I mean—"

"It's not as if you're a virgin," he quickly interrupted, a gleam in his eye. "You're comfortable being undressed by men."

"What?" Her eyes grew wide, and she tried to fathom if he were teasing. She couldn't tell. "I am not . . . I mean, I am—"

"Oh hell." Michael straightened up on the bed and gave her a stricken look. "Tell me, you're not a virgin, are you?"

Carolyn's look mirrored his and she swung her arm back to slap him. Instead, she only managed to unseat him from her bed as he caught her hand in his. "You don't ask me a personal question like that unless you're ready to be slapped."

"So, what was that? A yes or a no?" He chuckled at her anger as he held onto her hand.

"It's none of your business," she retorted, steadfast.

He stroked her hand. "You're not into getting undressed by me, huh? Maybe one day I can remedy that."

"One day?" Carolyn asked, her brow arched.

He nodded and smiled. "Davina did the honors last night."

She snatched her hand from his. "That's not funny. You let me think you . . ." She flashed her eyes at him.

"I hope you learned your lesson last night," he said, leaning back on his arms. "You shouldn't be out drinking when you don't know how to do it. Lucky for you, I was there."

"I . . ." She sighed. "I can't believe I did that. I don't know what got into me."

"You seemed obsessed with being a party girl for an evening, something about them having all the fun."

"I said that?" She hugged her arms across her chest.

"Maybe the green-eyed monster reared its head last night," he said, raising his brows at her.

"Oh, my goodness, look at the time." Carolyn scooted off the bed and trotted to the bathroom, determined to avoid any talk of jealousy on her part. "I almost forgot. I have to shower and get to the office for a team meeting."

"They called earlier."

She looked back at Michael from the bathroom door.

"I told them you'd be in this afternoon."

She put her hands over her mouth. "Michael, you didn't."

"After that, I turned your phone off, in case they called back." His words were laced with humor.

"I'll get you for this later," she called from the bathroom. "Now, turn it back on. I've got a board meeting later on at the gallery, too."

"Can you drop me by my house on your way in? I can always call a taxi if it's a problem."

"No, no," she called out. "I can do that. She stuck her head from the bathroom. "And thank you."

Michael looked up from sliding his belt through the loops at his waist, his expression changing ever so slightly at her words.

Carolyn lightly tilted her head. "For staying to watch over me last night."

"Of course," he said.

Carolyn smiled as, finally, a certain detail from last night began to crystallize.

Carolyn exited the elevator and headed for the end of the hall and Justin's office. As she rounded the corner, she came to Nora Watt's desk, a small fortress to be stormed before one could gain access to Justin. Nora was Justin's executive assistant, and the small woman, who now sat behind her desk, was no pushover.

She looked up as Carolyn arrived. "Well, look who's here. How are you doing, dear? It's been a while since you came by for a visit."

"I'm fine, but my own schedule's been a bear lately."

Nora looked at her watch. "Aren't you a little early for this afternoon's board meeting?"

"Probably," Carolyn laughed. "Actually, I came by to spend a few minutes with my big brother. Is he free?"

"For a while. Go on in."

"Thanks," Carolyn said, and walked through Nora's fortress and into Justin's open office. He sat behind his desk with his head buried in paperwork that was stacked neatly on his desk. The big office that had belonged to their father suited her dynamic brother.

She glanced toward the long wall where her father's portrait hung, a portrait that had been painted long ago by Davina's father. This office, that portrait—both continued to make her anxious. In this room, she couldn't help but wonder if her father still judged her accomplishments.

"Carolyn? Come on in."

She looked away from the wall and greeted Justin as he came from around his desk. She gave him a broad smile as she announced from the door, "So, how long will you be in town this time?"

When he reached her, he gave her a hug and then held her from him so he could look her up and down. "You're okay behind those sunglasses?"

She laughed as she slid the glasses from her face. "I forgot about these. You know how it is when you've tied one on and you can't stand too much light."

"That's not funny," he chastised, as she settled in one of the chairs across from his desk. He sat across from her. "I leave town for a couple of weeks and you're the same Carolyn. I return, and I think you've turned into Alli. So, what was up with the big dude last night?"

"What did Alli tell you?"

"That you and Michael were serious, and that I should back off and let nature take its course."

Carolyn ground her teeth. "I'm going to kill her."

Justin sat up. "So, it's not true? I can't believe she'd let me leave you there with some guy you're not interested in."

"No, no," she explained to Justin. "It's not that, it's just that we're hardly serious, and nature was not going anywhere last night. That was all in Alli's little plot-heavy mind."

His eyes twinkled. "But you are interested? Mom thinks the same about him as Alli."

It was Carolyn's turn to sit up. "You told Mom about last night? How could you, Justin?"

"No, Alli told Mom, who called me this morning."

Carolyn's eyes rolled heavenward. "So the whole family knows I spent a drunken evening with a man I hardly know." She sighed. "Are there any private moments to be lived in this family?"

Justin laughed. "Cheer up. Davina and I can't remember having any. So why should you be any different?"

"Speaking of Davina, where is your rising artist?"

He smiled. "She's probably still in bed where I left her this morning." He turned in his chair so he could look more fully at Carolyn. "But I'm more concerned about you and this Michael Hennessey. I know he's a well-known football player, and during the season, his name is all over the place."

When Justin became silent, Carolyn said, "Well, go on."

"Rumors are rife right now that he's going to be playing with the Atlanta Wildcats this coming season. Do you want Connie to check him out? He can do it quickly and quietly."

She waved her hand. "That's not necessary, Justin, and didn't that get you into trouble with Davina once already? Connie has bigger fish to fry in his P.I. business. Michael and I are just . . . dating. I guess that's what you call it."

"That's what I mean. When was the last time you dated, or even went out to dinner with someone when it wasn't business or family related? And Edward doesn't count."

She frowned. "Okay, I see your point. This could be cause for alarm."

"I figure two years." He tented his hands as he talked earnestly to her. "You've given all of your time to your work, so don't get upset if news of your interest in someone gets everybody in the family whipped into a frenzy." He looked at Carolyn for a long moment and seemed to absorb the situation. "So, you're really interested in him after all?"

She smiled. "I don't really know how it came about," she said as she looked at her brother. "I hated him when we first met; he was rude, egocentric, and football was so . . ."

"Foreign to you?" When she nodded, he asked, "So, what happened?"

"It may sound silly, but he didn't give up on me the way I did on him. He made me want to continue seeing him."

Justin leaned back in the chair. "You didn't scare him off; instead, he took you on, full steam."

"No one's ever pursued me that way. You know me, I need to be the driver, in control. He's not afraid of me."

A knock came at the door, and they both looked up. It was Davina. Justin stood up.

"Davina, come on in," he said. "Carolyn's here."

"Nora told me," she said.

When Davina, willowy and graceful, moved across the floor to join them, Carolyn thought her brother actually glowed with pride. Justin pulled her onto his lap where they shared a chaste kiss, and then he trapped her in the circle of his arms. Carolyn thought they made a magnificent couple, although no one ever dreamed of this ending when the two first met. In fact, they had fought like cats and dogs. She pondered her own future.

"Alli's on her way down from the gallery," Davina said to Carolyn. "Thought I'd warn you."

"You're right. I don't need her comments this morning," she said. "Michael asked me to send you his thanks." As Davina raised her brow, Carolyn said, "For refereeing him and Justin."

"Oh, I'm a pro at keeping Alpha males apart. I do it all the time with Justin and my brother."

"At least I now know David," Justin said of Davina's brother. "To be honest, I don't know Michael except what I've read in the papers about his sports heroics. Other than that, he has a strong reputation for being in the middle of all the parties with a host of boys from his hometown in the East."

"I don't know, honey," Davina said and squeezed Justin playfully. "He reminded me a lot of you. Brash, self-assured—cocky, even."

Carolyn laughed. "That's him, Davina."

"Well, if he's anything like me, I might as well have gone ahead and kicked his—"

"Justin . . ." Both women interrupted his expletive, and Carolyn threw her head back in laughter.

Davina smiled as she looked at Carolyn. "I take it you like this Michael?"

Carolyn took in a deep breath and nodded. "I think so," she said, and out of nervous habit, tucked a strand of hair behind her ear.

"Good," Davina said. "It wouldn't do any good to sport a bright passion mark from someone you disliked. Better yet, I wouldn't advise you letting Alli see it."

Carolyn sank back into her chair as she pulled her hair back around her neck and looked up to Justin and Davina's grinning faces.

Bruce Witherspoon leaned back in his chair in his twenty-fifth-floor office in the Federal Building and studied, in detail, the series of photographs laid out on the table in front of him.

His mind carefully considered what they meant, and the direction they could lead him and the investigation. He shook his head. This could all be good news or it could blow up in his face. He'd have to tread through this with care.

He selected one of the pictures and, grabbing his jacket from the back of the chair, headed for the door and the elevator lobby.

The Federal Building was busiest in the afternoons and the elevator was usually the first place to feel the crunch. It took forever to arrive, and was packed when it did.

When his elevator stopped on the thirty-second floor, the other floor that housed Justice Department employees, he stepped off, greeting a myriad of people as he made his way through one secure door after another to the inner sanctum of the U.S. Attorney's office.

He whizzed past Jean, the receptionist, and a line of glassed-in offices before he found the one that belonged to the U.S. Attorney, Mitchell "Mickey" Abrams, his boss.

"Bruce, what you got?" Mickey asked as he looked up.

"The daily surveillance shots came in on my case. Look who got snapped."

Mickey reached for the photo and looked at it. As it dawned on him who the men were, he leaned back in his chair and whistled. "You got more?"

"Lots, but only during this same incident."

"Did we have any inkling, or did this come at us out of left field?"

"None, sir."

"Any history?"

"Nah, but he's gotta start somewhere. I'll start working up a file, though. Known priors, friends, that sort of thing."

"Let's keep our eye on it, then."

"I'm expanding the surveillance to include him. I'm checking out the other man in the picture as well."

"Good. Let's keep an eye out and see what happens." Mickey tapped his pencil against his desk as he looked at the picture again. "Greedy lawyers always have their crooked clients like Charlie Madden around. It's all part of the food chain."

"Yeah," Bruce agreed. "If we play our cards right, and draw him into our sting, maybe Madden will cooperate and give us the scoop on why he's meeting a celebrity as well-known and with such deep pockets as Michael Hennessey."

Fifteen

With a deep grunt, Michael released the dumbbell weight and let it bounce to the floor. Exhausted, he dropped heavily onto the weight bench in the room he had turned into a gym. Grabbing a towel with one hand, he scooped up a nearby bottle of water with the other and gulped a considerable amount in a series of swallows.

"Ah . . . now, that's good," he said to Rollie, who he had watched limp sadly to a chair on the other side of the room.

Rollie, on the other hand, reached for an opened bottle of beer that waited for him on the table.

"Man, I don't know what the hell got into my head, agreeing to spot for you," he said, and brushed a speck from his shirt as he sipped from the bottle.

Michael grinned before he tilted the bottle to his mouth again. Rollie had no practical use for exercise or involvement in sports other than a casual pick-up game of basketball. His involvement in exercise was limited to acting as spotter for Michael, who diligently worked out in an off-season conditioning program.

"How long you been at this, old man?" Rollie chuckled as he took in Michael's sweaty face. "What is it? You afraid of losing your edge now that you turned thirty?"

"Hey," he joked, and flexed his biceps. "I'm a prime piece of work ready for the new season."

"Nah, you know those young players are gunnin' for you, man. When you want to make a name for yourself fast, what do you do? You knock off the top dog, that's what. They know you the top dog to knock off."

"Nothing like a little confidence-building from a friend," Michael said as he loosened the bands around his wrists. "I'd be crazy to get on the field and not be in shape when some three-hundred pound tackle, who's done his homework, is ready to clock my lights. So, hell yes, I'm working out; and as often as I can."

"So, you ready to sign with the Wildcats?" Rollie took another sip of the beer, though he kept his eye on Michael for an answer.

"I don't know, man." Michael leaned against the bar on the weight bench and let out a sigh. "Their offer isn't bad." He looked at Rollie and smiled. "In fact, it's damn nice. But I'm leaving that up to Jeffrey; my job is to stay in shape so I can pass the physicals, no matter whose camp I'm in."

"Oh, but, man, the cash is fierce, and not even for a full year's work. You don't know how lucky you are, man." Rollie shook his head and swigged another gulp of the beer.

Michael had heard that sentiment from others, and often from Rollie. "Yeah, but hear this. It takes its toll, and it's hard work, too. The average player only gets about four good years in the league."

Rollie grunted. "The other brother on the team—Jemahl—he's a pretty okay dude. He's got a nice bar, too. I'd like to own something like that someday."

"Aw, man, get off it." Michael swung his legs to the side of the bench. "Who are you fooling? Jemahl says that place is hard work, and you know you don't want any part of something where you have to work that hard."

They both laughed at the truth in the statement. "Don't you already have a business waiting for you up the way?"

"Yeah, you're right," Rollie admitted grudgingly.

"Talked to Glenda lately?"

"Nah. She's still pissed."

"I don't blame her for kicking your butt to the curb. I mean, how do you think she feels. You get out of jail and don't even tell the woman where you're heading."

Rollie turned to Michael. "How'd you know——"

"She called to see if you were here."

Rollie frowned. "Damn," he said, "that woman'll worry you to death."

"How about showing her and your daughter a little respect, man? The least you can do is stop your cattin' around."

"You talking 'bout Carleshia last night, huh?"

"Since you brought her up," Michael said, sitting up to remove the weight belt, "yeah; both of them."

"Well, damn, listen to you. You mess around with that high society chick, Carolyn, who showed you the road before, and now that she knows what she passed up, she's baa-ck . . ."

Michael darted a frown at his friend. "Shut up about her, Rollie. It's not like that."

"Now you want to tell everybody else what's best for them like you suddenly got the knowledge. What's that chick done for you, man, besides get you hot last night? Not a damn thing."

Michael tamped his rising annoyance. "You better chill, buddy, before you say the wrong damn thing." He stood from the bench and released the weight belt. "I see trouble, and I was only trying to warn you, that's all."

"Aw, man, c'mon; you losin' your edge." Rollie slapped Michael on his back as he passed to the other side of the gym room, where he turned and smiled. "Remember, I knew you when you'd take both of the chicks home with you; so don't try and make yourself believe you wouldn't have hooked up with your girl, Randy, if Carolyn hadn't been there." He lifted the beer bottle in salute.

Michael didn't answer; instead, he raised the bottled water to his mouth for another swallow before he set it down. He had learned there was no point in getting ticked off at Rollie ten times during one sitting. It was best to just let him dish out all of his jive-time crap at once and get it over with.

"I got to hand it to her, though," Rollie said. "She's one sweet looker, that Carolyn. All refined and healthy right where you like it." He curved his hands in the shape of a Coke bottle, his grin a knowing one.

When Michael didn't respond, Rollie said, "Okay, I get it, now. I'm hitting close to home, huh? You didn't make it back here last night, so that means you two must have gotten it on when you left." He whistled as he walked back to Michael. "Lord, have mercy."

Michael patiently shook his head as he flexed his tight shoulders. "You're not funny, man, and now you're pissing me off."

Rollie stopped in front of Michael. "Nobody's gonna blame you for working her, man. That way, you can get her out'cha system and move on to the next lucky lady."

In a flash, Michael had gripped Rollie's lapels in his fists, and now roughly shoved him backwards. "Hey, I told you not to talk about her."

Rollie stumbled backwards to a stop, chuckling the whole time. "Oh, hell, I think I hit a nerve."

Michael turned away from Rollie, needing only a moment to regain control of his anger. Rollie liked to talk smack, and he did it all the time. And it was a given that he'd do it again. *So, why did I lose my cool?*

"Maybe I don't want to move on just now," Michael said, and dropping back to the bench, he picked up the bottle and drained the last of the water. Liking the conviction in his voice, he glanced up at Rollie. "I'm taking my time with her, that's all. I don't want to scare her off again."

"Damn, man, I think you got it bad." He joined Michael at the bench. "I swear, if you ever get inside her pants, she's gonna have a hold on you like you never knew before."

Michael laughed richly as he rose from the bench. With a perfect arc to his arm, he tossed the empty bottle into the wastebasket before he turned to Rollie and spoke in a way his friend would understand.

"If she's half as good as she looks, I'm gonna hold onto her like nothing *she's* ever known."

As Michael headed for the door, he glanced sideways at Rollie's puzzled stare and laughed again. "Get your slow, sorry butt outside with me while I throw some footballs with Adam."

"Caro, he gave you a hickey, girl."

"Alli." Carolyn pushed her sister's hands away as she reared precariously backwards in her chair in the Hardy Enterprises board room. "Would you please get off my neck."

"I bet you didn't say that to Michael last night," she giggled. "And, look at this, another one."

Carolyn sighed as she scooted her chair away from her sister. The monthly board meeting of Hardy Enterprises had concluded about fifteen minutes earlier and now, in the empty conference room, Carolyn suffered Alli's inspection of the soft discolorations along her neck, remnants of her evening with Michael.

"Those little suckers can be the source of a good time," Alli admitted, and dropped back into her own chair. "But make sure you don't go dishing out too much dessert before he can show you he's willing to sit through a main course.

"Alli—"

"I'm telling you from experience." Her voice was serious. "I know men. They'll drop a girl like a hot potato if you let them gorge too fast. Of course, I'm sure Michael isn't that kind of guy, but he's a guy and you never know."

"You're barely into your twenties, *Baby Girl*," Carolyn emphasized the hated title. "And have you ever dated anyone over twenty-five?" She grinned at the petulant frown her sister now wore.

"Well," Alli responded, "Before Michael, I don't think you've had a date since you were twenty-five."

Now Carolyn wore the frown, as she said, "Anyway, I thought you were admiring the flowers Michael sent, not my neck."

"Well, what do you expect when I find passion marks on my saintly sister? I'm in shock." She turned to the brightly colored carnations that sat on the table in front of them. "But your flowers are beautiful. How did he know you'd be here today?" When the flowers had arrived downstairs, Alli was present, and had been the one to bring the arrangement upstairs to the board room.

"I think I mentioned to him this morning that I had a meeting here this afternoon."

"This morning . . . ooh, that sounds so sexy. What did you do with the card that came with the flowers?"

"Don't fake it," Carolyn said as she sniffed the bouquet. "I know you read the thing before you brought it up here."

"So, what did he mean about looking forward to more thank-you's?"

Carolyn remembered vaguely that it had been the intro to the kisses that followed and, shifting uncomfortably in her chair, smiled. "Leave it alone, will you? I don't want to jinx things by picking over every detail with you and Stephanie."

"I can tell . . . you like him."

Carolyn stretched her eyes wide and smiled as she nodded. "Yeah, and I don't think I've had the pleasure of expressing that sentiment in a while."

Without warning, Alli stood and leaned over her sister, grabbing her shoulders in a hug. "I'm so happy for you, Caro," she whispered. "And to think you didn't want to give him the time of day until Steph and I bullied you into it."

"We're not engaged or anything, just seeing each other again," she said.

"I know," Alli agreed, and dropped back into her chair. "But, this is, what, the fifth time you're seeing each other? The fifth date?"

"What's that supposed to mean?"

"Well, you're obviously hot for him, and he is for you, and if you-know-what isn't on your mind, I'm sure it's on his. Are you going to have sex with him? He is so gorgeous, Caro."

"Alli, that's none of your business."

"You know it's going to come up—"

A ring interrupted their conversation. It was the cell phone in Carolyn's purse. When Carolyn dug it out, she saw that it was Michael. She sucked in a deep breath, surprised at how her heart jumped in anticipation. She answered with a bright hello.

"Hi, it's me." Michael's deep voice flowed through the phone. "Did you get the flowers?"

Carolyn looked at them again. "They're beautiful, and my favorites, Michael. My board meeting is just now over, and I wanted to call you first to say thank you. How did you know to send them here in time for me to get them?"

His chuckle was deep. "I didn't, so I had them sent to your office, the loft and the gallery."

Carolyn's face lit up. "Michael, you didn't?"

Alli stood up. "Uh-oh, I'd better go," she teased.

"Michael, can you hold a moment?" she said into the phone while she motioned for Alli to wait. When Alli turned to her, she pressed the phone against her chest.

"Remember lunch yesterday?"

"Uh-huh," Alli grunted.

"You think I can still borrow the red sweater?"

"Gotcha!" Alli grinned and flashed a thumb's up. "Come by the house later on, and I'll have it ready."

Carolyn returned the phone to her ear. "I'm sorry. Alli was just leaving."

"So," Michael said, "Are we still on for Saturday?"

"Yes, but, why are you being so secretive about what we're doing?"

"Because I want you to be surprised, that's all. I want it to be a special night. I'll pick you up," he said. "Is eight okay?"

She thought about Alli's comments, which continually suggested that Michael was an experienced sophisticate, and that sex, being a part of that worldliness, was never far from his thoughts. Though she was no untried virgin, self-doubt about her abilities in this area began to build, and she wondered if she was up to his standards. Last night's fiasco as a party girl said a lot. With the little experience she'd bring to the table, she wondered how they'd end up.

"Hello, Carolyn?"

"Oh, I'm sorry, Michael. Eight will be fine."

"Good, I'll see you then."

When she rang off, she stuffed the phone in her purse, and was set to leave for her own office when Nora, Justin's assistant, came in.

"Nora, would you see to it that these flowers get taken up to the gallery floor?"

"Sure, Carolyn. They're beautiful. Are you sure you don't want them sent home?"

She smiled. "I have them waiting for me there, too."

"Now, that's a smart admirer," Nora said.

Carolyn walked into the hallway and toward the elevator. When she stepped in, it was occupied by two men. Both wore dark sunshades, and one had the hard look about him of a street thug outfitted in an expensive suit. They wore visitor's badges and had apparently been up to the art gallery level.

Carolyn smiled to herself. There she was, being judgmental again. Hadn't she been very wrong about Michael? These two men were probably upstanding citizens getting a little culture in the afternoon.

When the elevator door opened on Justin's office level, she stepped off, and threw a smile backwards to the two quiet men.

"Have a good day."

Their reply was a simultaneous grunt.

Sixteen

"Aw, man, all he did is loan me the damn SUV. What's wrong with that? I use your cars all the time. I thought you'd be fine with it."

Michael turned from the mirror to look at Rollie, and held his hand up to stop the arguing. "Listen, if you want to borrow a car from somebody you say you barely know, then that's your business. But think about it, Rollie. You got the ride from Charlie Madden. Are you gambling again?"

"No, and you beginning to sound like my mama."

"That dude is bad news, and you know it, too." He turned away and proceeded to slap aftershave along his jaw.

"Charlie's okay. He is, man. He's okay."

"Yeah, keep telling yourself that even though you know he's a thug—and a big time one, at that," Michael emphasized.

"Where'd you hear that?"

Michael switched off the light in the bathroom as he walked past Rollie, heading for his closet on the other side of the room.

"Don't worry about that," he said. "I just don't want him around me, and I'd feel better if his property wasn't parked on mine." He reached into the closet for a jacket.

"So, where you going tonight?"

"Out," Michael said as he shrugged into the jacket and adjusted the collar. "With Carolyn. I've got something special planned for her tonight."

"Yeah, yeah." Rollie walked over near the door and propped himself in the opening. "Why don't we throw a party next week? You can invite Jemahl and some of the other players and friends from around these parts. I can invite a few. You know, do like we used to do it up in Jersey."

"I don't know, man. Those parties always got out of hand, and the kids will be home next week." He picked up his keys from the dresser. "It's a bad idea right now."

"Damn, man. You are domesticated. I was only out of circulation a year and you changed on me." He snapped his fingers. "Like that."

Michael walked to the door and grinned. "For the better, I like to think." He closed the door behind him. "I'll see you later. I've gotta say goodnight to the kids."

He left Rollie in the hallway and took a path that led him to the children's wing. When he turned the corner to their rooms, he saw them sitting on the carpeted floor in the open foyer that stretched between their rooms. Adam looked up first.

"Michael, you look spiffed. I bet you're going out," Adam deduced, dropping his pencil to the sketchpad, the ubiquitous headphones encircling his neck.

Little Halina fiddled with her cassette player. "Daddy, are you taking Carolyn with you?"

Michael kneeled down near her, and answered. "Yes, why?"

"You like her?" She darted her eyes at Michael.

It was the one thing Michael had been apprehensive about—how the children would take to Carolyn. He decided he'd tackle any problems in that area as they surfaced.

"Yes, Halina, I like her a lot."

"So do I," Halina announced.

"Guess what?" Michael reached out and tweaked her cheek. "She likes you, too."

"If she likes me, can I call her sometime?"

"I think that'll be okay," Michael said, curious as to why she'd want to call Carolyn.

"Look, I made another tape," she said and presented the cassette tape to him. "You and Carolyn can listen to it in the car."

"Give it a break, Halina. They've got better things to do than listen to you sing in the car," Adam teased. "You're such a baby."

"Daddy listens to my tapes in the car all the time—"

"Hold on, you two," Michael said, and turned to Halina. "Thanks for the tape, and we'll remember to listen." He now turned to Adam's grinning face. "What about you? What do you think of Carolyn?"

"She's cool. Anybody who eats ice cream like her can't be all bad."

Michael tousled his head affectionately and stood up. "Take care of your sister. Mr. and Mrs. Pitts are downstairs, but I still want both of you to be on your best behavior, or I'll hear about it."

After eliciting the kids' promise, Michael made his way downstairs. He bid a goodnight to the Pittses and soon after, left the house in the car. As he stopped at the end of his private drive to turn onto the main road, he saw a nondescript gray panel truck parked on the shoulder. Two men worked on a length of the fencing that surrounded the property across the street. One of the men, dressed in appropriate work gear, tipped his cap to Michael. Nodding in response, Michael pulled out onto the road in the direction of Carolyn's high-rise.

* * *

Carolyn did a little twirl in front of the mirror and smoothed her hands down her skirt. She actually felt pretty, sexy even, and it was all for Michael. The red, cowl-necked sweater she'd borrowed from Alli went well with the cream colored suit—it was much more of an eye grabber, as Alli put it, than the standard black blouse she usually matched with it. And the red shoes Alli had insisted she wear—

The phone interrupted her appraisal, and spying it on the bed, she answered with a rushed, "Hello?"

"Hello. This is Halina."

Surprised, yet concerned that something had happened, she dropped to sit on the bed. "Halina, how are you doing? Is something wrong?"

"No." She paused a moment. "Daddy said I could call you. Adam got your number from his room."

Carolyn smiled at the simple answer. "All right, then. It's very nice of you to call." She patiently waited for the child to continue.

"When you take Adam to your art gallery, can I come, too?"

"Well, of course, Sweetie, you'll come. I hadn't planned on leaving you out."

"Okay."

"Is there anything else?"

"Oh, daddy has my singing tape. Make sure he lets you listen to it."

"All right." Carolyn smiled at the phone. "I'll make sure he doesn't forget."

Carolyn exchanged goodbyes with the little girl before she hung up the phone, all the time marveling at how it must feel to have a child totally reliant on you. As she shook her head and stood up, she realized Michael would be there any moment now. The next minute, she heard her intercom sound, and knew it would be Gerald, from downstairs.

"Hi, Gerald," she said into the intercom.

"Good evening, Ma'am. Mr. Hennessey wants to come up."

"That's fine, buzz him through." She released the button and figured she had a minute before he got to her door. She checked her hair and outfit one more time before the doorbell sounded. If dating someone made you this nervous, then maybe it was a good idea not to do it too often, she ruminated.

When she reached the door, she counted to five to regain her composure before she opened it.

Michael wasn't there. Puzzled, she stuck her head outside the door and saw that he had stepped to the window in the foyer that looked out over the city.

"Michael?" When he turned from the window before he strode back to the door, his appreciative eye traveled from her sleek heels to the red sweater. Carolyn saw the frank admiration and quietly thanked Alli even as she admired the clean, sharply urban look he presented in a dark suit and burgundy silk shirt.

"The other night, when I brought you home, I didn't see the window. It offers a nice view from here—the window and you." His smile widened in approval. "Are you ready?"

"Yes." Carolyn enjoyed the warmth emanating from his eyes, and was loathe to leave just yet. "I'll just get my purse."

Once the purse was retrieved, they left in his car for dinner. And though Carolyn detected a cool reserve in his manner, it didn't stop her from keeping up a steady barrage of questions in order to pinpoint their destination; but Michael wouldn't relent, saying it would spoil his surprise.

When finally they arrived at the valet parking for a restaurant in midtown, known for its intimate atmosphere and superb desserts, Carolyn suspected this was the surprise. The parking attendant opened her door just as Michael came around for her.

"I know this restaurant," she said. It's where we were supposed to have dinner last week. Of course, Rollie showed up."

He placed his hand lightly at her back as they started for the front door. "Don't forget, the kids showed up, too."

"That's right," Carolyn remembered.

"In fact, between all that, a fund-raiser audience, and your family, I don't think we've had a private dinner yet." He chuckled as he held the door open for her. "So I made sure we wouldn't get disturbed tonight."

Her curiosity peaked, Carolyn entered the restaurant, and upon looking around, found it empty, with the exception of four waiters who stood in single file and at attention. When she looked at Michael, he only smiled.

One of the waiters led them up the stairs to a private, glass-walled rooftop where carnations were in the majority in the dozens of flower arrangements set around the room. The centerpiece of the room was a table set for two.

"Michael!" Carolyn exclaimed as he pulled the chair out for her. "This . . . this is a surprise, and it's beautiful up here."

He dismissed the waiter and they took their seats. "I wanted to make up for all the missteps."

"Don't think of them as missteps." She smiled. "If you remember, something came out of each one, right?"

"Michael, you're here. Welcome." A tall man with a shiny bald pate, who looked to be in his early forties, had come up the stairs and was walking their way.

"Gregory," Michael stood to greet the man. "I want you to meet Carolyn Hardy." He turned to Carolyn. "This is Gregory Robelot, a superb chef."

"You sent those wonderful dinners to the house last week."

Gregory laughed. "Ah, you were right, Michael, she is a beauty and well worth closing down my restaurant for a few hours." After presenting them with the menu for the evening, he left them on their own as waiters began to set up appetizers and pour drinks.

Carolyn leaned forward on the table. "Be careful what you wish for," she advised.

Michael cocked his head to the side as he relaxed comfortably in the roomy chair. "What do you mean?"

"You wanted privacy, but you look as though your mind is somewhere else."

He reached across the table for her hand. "You have no idea how much I wanted this. Unfortunately, what I want doesn't stop the rest of the world from interfering."

"Is something wrong with the children?" She thought of Halina's phone call.

"No, it's Rollie."

"Oh, him."

He sighed as he gently stroked her hand, and then tried to smile. "What can I say? He's been my friend all of my life. I want him to go back to his family. That way, he wouldn't be my immediate worry."

Quiet strains from string instruments reached their ears, and Carolyn turned to see three musicians playing on the stair landing, quietly out of view. Carolyn turned back to Michael. "I believe you've thought of everything."

"Maybe we should wait until the end of the evening before we decide on that." He pushed his chair back. "Come on, I want to dance with you. That way, I can hold you in my arms."

Carolyn liked the way he took charge with bold assurance, and felt a warm glow flow through her.

"On one condition," she said as he pulled her chair out. "Let's not talk of problems—which rules out family and friends."

"There you go again. You have to be in control with

some kind of condition," Michael whispered in her ear. "All right, it's a deal," he said, and turned her into his arms. "I'll teach you some football basics and, maybe, how to enjoy wine without getting drunk; and you can try and explain to me again what it is that you do."

They both laughed as he pulled her close and they moved as one across the floor.

It was a good beginning to what would become a relaxed evening, and by the time they had made their way halfway through the delicious entrée, Carolyn was quite comfortable with the man she had once considered an obnoxious jock.

"It's not that I'm controlling," Carolyn said as she set the water glass down. "But I have to go to job sites where ninety percent of the people taking orders from me are men. I learned very quickly to be assertive in order to get the job done, and it's not something I can turn on and off."

"I think that's good in a woman," Michael said. He looked up from his plate as he paused with his fork and smiled. "Not the controlling part, the assertive part."

She laughed. "You're making fun of me," she accused.

"Never." He set the fork on the plate. "You know, my mother would have liked you."

"Oh? Why do you say that?"

A grin spread over Michael's features as though the memory were a warm cushion. "She never made any bones about how she disliked the girls I had dated since tenth grade. I guess she didn't like the fact that I seemed to have an easy time of it; and I admit, it wasn't tough as an athlete.

"After I was drafted, she knew the spoils would become easier, and she said to me, 'Michael, remember that the lightweight material will always float to the top for an easy pick. The material of substance will stay hidden below, and you're going to have to learn to dig for it.' Turns out, it was good advice for when I met you."

They looked at each other and smiled in earnest.

"She sounds like she was pretty wonderful. How long ago did she die?"

"About a year after I was drafted. A car accident."

"Michael, I'm sorry. I gather you were very close. It must have been hard on you and your sister."

"After mom died, it was just me and Vivian, my sister, and Rollie, who was like a brother. And you know, for the three of us, after growing up ghetto poor and with no other family for guidance, losing my mother was like losing the rudder of your boat."

Carolyn saw him drink from the wine glass, as though for fortitude. She looked away, ashamed that she had continued to broach what seemed for him a difficult subject. "I . . . I can't believe I'm asking all these questions," she said. "We agreed not to bring up family."

"Oh, that's okay," he said, and wiped his mouth with the napkin. "I'd like you to know. Then maybe you'll understand why I owe a better life to Adam and Halina."

"Speaking of Halina, she called me tonight, before you came over." She then told him of their conversation.

"I hope you didn't mind. She's still . . . delicate. I thought she wanted to remind you to listen to her tape."

At Carolyn's frown, he smiled. "I'll tell you about it later. For now, though"—he stood up from his chair and held his hand out for hers—"how about we squeeze in another dance before dessert?"

Carolyn stepped from the elevator and into the foyer ahead of Michael. The evening had gone well: the food, music and Michael's company had all meshed beautifully; yet, she still sensed that Michael hadn't completely divorced himself from the thoughts that had intruded upon them earlier in the evening and during dinner.

She slid the key into the lock, and as she turned it in the slot, she looked back at Michael. His hands were in his pockets as he regarded her with dark, unreadable eyes. Carolyn felt a momentary burst of panic. Should she invite him in, wish him a pleasant goodnight at the door, or just thrust her face up at his for a kiss? He had given her no hints as to where he wanted the evening to go, and she . . . well, she didn't think she'd given any hints, either. Had she?

"Are you having problems with the door?" Michael quickly stepped forward to grasp her hand in his as he took over the key.

In an instant, the door was pushed open, Michael was halfway through it, and drew her after him.

Carolyn let out a sigh of relief as she followed him in. At least that decision had been made.

She closed the door behind her, dropping her purse and keys on the counter.

"Can I get you anything?" she asked and turned to reach for the light switch on the wall.

"No."

Carolyn felt his hands at her shoulders as he gently turned her to face him in the dimly lit room.

"This will do just fine," he said.

With one forward motion, it happened so fast. Carolyn was in his arms—arms that had become hands; hands that had found their way beneath her sweater to caress her bare waist. As she leaned into Michael, her body tingled from the sensations that swirled around: his smell, touch, and strength.

Her arms wrapped of their own accord around his neck before she looked up. His breath, warm and moist against her face, made her heart race in anticipation of his kiss.

It began with small nibbles to her lips. Then his mouth

took hers hungrily. She returned the enthusiasm with abandon, her fingers playing over his wide shoulders.

What Carolyn felt, Michael experienced in spades. He held in tight control a storm of energy that begged for release; the exquisite weight of her breasts pressed into his chest and her slender waist tapered down and then outward . . . His fingers stroked, then splayed around the firm flesh of her bottom, and he pulled her against him, her soft curves molding erotically to the jutting contours of his hard, lean body.

Carolyn's body jolted from the contact of his thigh on her hip; she was trapped against his rock hard form. And then, she was being consumed. Blood pounded her brain and heart, and her knees trembled with healthy lust. She couldn't think of anything except . . .

"I think . . . maybe we've had enough for the evening," she whispered, their lips still making contact as she spoke. She pulled her hands from his neck, breaking the lusty, electric contact with Michael, and tried to push away.

"I don't think I can ever get enough of you."

Reclaiming her lips, he crushed her to him again, his thrusting tongue forcing her lips apart before he made a searing path along her jaw line.

"Mmm . . . Michael," she murmured through a haze of pleasure.

"Mmm . . . you like that," he responded. "I do, too."

"We should stop," she managed to say during the onslaught and raised her hands to his chest, "before things get out of hand."

Michael stilled his mouth against her ear before he drew his hands back up to her waist. Straightening her sweater, he set her from him. "You're right. I think if I stay any longer, I may have to try changing your mind."

"I can always let you try," she said suggestively.

He grinned, as he drew a hand across his head in a

frustrated motion. "Maybe my bad news will change your mind."

She frowned as she climbed onto a barstool at the counter. "What are you talking about?"

"I have to go to L.A. for two weeks—to shoot a commercial." He lifted his brows in disdain. "My agent called about it."

"When do you have to leave?"

"In the next few days. The only problem is the kids are in school and Rollie's still around. But the Pitts are becoming like family to them, so they'll be okay."

"Well, I can't do anything about Rollie, but why don't I drop in on them? We could schedule our gallery visit. That way, they'd at least get an outing while you're gone."

He shook his head. "No, Carolyn, you're busy with your—"

"I insist. It'll work out fine."

"In that case, I think they'll like that. Whenever you're ready, just arrange it with Mrs. Pitts."

"Done. Oh, and tell Halina her music was beautiful." She regarded him through the dim light and saw that his earlier, tight expression had relaxed. She preferred him this way. She slid off the barstool. "I had a great time tonight, Michael."

"So did I." He leaned over, and gave her a kiss that was surprisingly gentle. "I don't trust myself to get too close again. I'll call you before I leave town next week, okay?"

"Okay." She followed him to the door where he managed to squeeze in one more peck to her mouth before the elevator took him back downstairs.

Carolyn stood and watched the closed elevator doors for a while before she went back inside. Smiling, she saw they had spent the entire time in the room with the lights out. Of course, they didn't need lights for what they had been doing. She hit the wall switch and the lamps illuminated the space.

She slipped from her high heels and left them at the door, then walked ahead to her office area. As she passed the TV, on a whim, she turned it on. She had not had time to read the paper today, and the late news would be on now. She settled onto the window bench and looked down on the streets from her window —perchance to spot Michael as he left—only partially attentive to the TV.

She was amazed at the depth of her feelings for Michael at this juncture. His absence for two weeks would give her a chance to step back and consider what she was truly feeling. She closed her eyes.

"New indictments are expected to be handed down soon by the federal grand jury convened by U.S. attorney Mickey Abrams in his ever-widening net designed to bring to justice former local high-profile attorney Eugene Preston and a bevy of his former clients. Sources now tell us that Abrams has requested that the grand jury remain in session longer than expected. This can only mean more evidence will be brought forward, and soon. In a related story—"

Carolyn groaned at the newscaster's intrusion into her pleasant thoughts. That was why she preferred the newspaper. A fifteen-second blurb never offered detail, only headlines. She looked at her watch. There was still enough time left in the night to work on the project notes she'd brought home yesterday. She dragged herself from the bench and, first things first, she cut off the TV.

Seventeen

The weekend was fast becoming a distant memory as Carolyn's workweek began with its usual hurried activities.

Carolyn glanced at her watch as she raced down the hall, her black pantsuit perfect for the occasion, with papers clutched in one hand and a pen gripped between her teeth to jot in last-minute notes as she tried to catch Roger Burrell, her team's technical consultant, before he left for the client's office. Strangely enough, only a few minutes earlier, no one seemed to be available in his office. When she'd been told Roger was last seen heading for the elevators, she decided to make a last ditch effort to head him off there.

As she neared a small gathering up ahead in the office lobby, she angled off and chose an alternate path to the other side. That's when she noticed a group crowded there, as well.

Not sure what was going on, she slowed down and took her pen from her mouth. That's when she saw a familiar face and build at the center of the tempest. Michael was standing in the lobby area, talking with both Roger and Kurt, two of her team members he had met at the sports bar the other night, and a bevy of other people from the office.

She took tentative steps toward the area and with her ears pricked, tried to figure out what was going on.

That's when she saw him passing something back to one of the workers; and just as quickly, another paper was pressed into his hand. He was signing autographs, and his admirers were using anything available: magazines, napkins—one of the secretaries had extended her arm for his seemingly magical signature. She stopped short of the area with a sigh, crossed her arms, and viewed the scene with awe. It was a revelation.

"There she is. Carolyn."

Kurt had caught sight of her and now called to her over the heads of the group.

She acknowledged him, but met and returned Michael's raised-brow smile, though she continued to stand apart from him, all the while watching as he wrote and slowly waded through the group toward her.

"I was on my way back to your office to tell you Michael had stopped by," Roger called out, offering an explanation for Michael's sudden appearance.

"Carolyn, this is a surprise. We didn't know that Michael Hennessey is a close friend of yours."

The gravelly voice came from behind her. She turned and found Alex Geary, one of the firm's partners, being ever so chummy as he came up to stand next to her. He also held several sheets of the company's letterhead in his hand.

"Oh, he's just Michael to me, nothing special," she said, smiling at the facile lie to her boss.

"It shows you know how to keep a secret. You wouldn't mind getting an autograph for me later on, would you?" He shifted closer to her as he spoke low. "It's for my grandson, you see. Just have him make it out to Alex."

Carolyn smiled and took the sheets from her gray-haired boss. "Of course, Mr. Geary. I'll be happy to do it."

"Good, good. You know, this makes me wonder if he'd

want to do something, along the lines of charitable work, under the firm's name." He raised his heavy white brows as he turned toward his office. "Just a thought to consider, you know."

Carolyn watched until he was a half dozen steps away before she turned to see that Michael had finally managed to sign his way through the group, which had begun to disperse. She nabbed Roger, who stood nearby, and thrust the notes into his hand.

"I was worried that I had missed you, and here you are, out in the hall talking with Michael." She playfully slapped her co-worker in the chest with the papers. "Men and sports. These are the client's proposed changes to the program. Check it out before you bring their system up. If they're not compatible with our suggestions, don't accept them."

Roger stuffed the papers in his bag. "Done." He turned to Michael and they shook hands. "Hey, nice seeing you again."

"Same here," Michael said.

Roger left Carolyn and Michael in the hall outside the lobby.

"So, do you always manage to cause havoc when you show up places?" Carolyn asked, and folded her arms across her chest.

"I'm getting ready to leave for L.A."

"Ooh, so soon? I thought it was later in the week."

"So did I. What's this?" He lifted her hands into his and noticed the letterhead sheets.

"My boss is infatuated with you. So much so, he wants your autograph. His name is Alex."

Michael smiled and, using the pen she held, autographed both sheets. He handed the papers and pen back to her.

"I wanted to see you before I left, so I took a chance you'd be here."

"I'm glad." She folded the papers into her hand.

"That I'm leaving?" He closed his hands around hers.

"No." Carolyn grinned, and squeezed his fingers. "That you came by." She tried to draw him away from the lobby. "Come back to my office."

"Actually, I'm on a tight schedule, and I can't stay." He stared at Carolyn, as though he'd discovered some new attribute of hers. "You're beautiful," he said simply. "I don't know how I'm going to stand being away for two whole weeks. But I will call you, okay?"

Carolyn blushed crimson, and she knew he would notice it; but she didn't care. He didn't think her odd at all, with her dark-hued wardrobe and conservative sensibilities. In the short span of a few weeks, he had acquired the magical ability to make her feel beautiful and sexy, both at the same time. And now she beamed with pleasure.

"I'll wait for your call, then."

Michael looked around, and saw that no one was in their vicinity. He leaned down and brushed Carolyn's mouth with his, stalling for a delicious moment that was not nearly as long as either of them wanted it to be.

"Later," he said, and backing to the door, he turned and was gone.

Carolyn sighed as she returned to her office, a satisfied smile on her face as she met the faces of coworkers. Taking a much more leisurely pace this time around, she decided it was going to be a beautiful day today because . . . well, because Michael thought she was beautiful.

"Adam, is Daddy going to call tonight?" Halina's tired voice rose up from the backseat of Carolyn's car.

"I dunno." Adam fiddled with his Gameboy in the front seat.

"We can check with Mrs. Pitts when we get back to the house," Carolyn replied.

"Next time, I get to sit in the front with Carolyn," Halina said. "If Daddy was home, he'd let me."

"Stop being a crybaby," Adam complained. "And Michael never lets you sit in the front, and you wanta know why?" He shifted around in his front seat, and holding his fingers apart about an inch wagged them up and down, chanting in a sing-song tone, "Because you're short people."

"Okay, you two, settle down." Carolyn squinted through the deepening darkness for their turnoff onto Michael's drive. Of course, she knew her warning wouldn't stop their good-natured teasing, and shaking her head, she turned and smiled at Adam before she looked in the rearview mirror at Halina, whom she suspected might be more than a little tired from their earlier food and fun.

"Before you know it, Halina, you'll be tall enough to sit in the front seat. Adam's just jealous because you outskated him tonight." Carolyn's comment touched off another round of teasing between the children.

It had been Stephanie's idea to invite Michael's kids, along with her own two, to the skating rink, and it had turned out to be a great idea. As a mother, Stephanie's heartstrings had been pulled when she learned that Halina and Adam were orphaned and in the process of being adopted by their guardian uncle. She had even insisted Carolyn bring them for the family dinner on Sunday.

Halina and Adam had thoroughly enjoyed the skating and pizza, and Halina, at least, didn't seem at all constrained by the fact that Carolyn was still, more or less, a stranger. Adam had, in some instances, exhibited more reserve when it came to opening up to her.

Recognizing her turn-off up ahead, she maneuvered the Acura off the main road and onto the long, private drive.

She was traversing Michael's universe as well as attending to his children; so, being as immersed in his life as she'd become, why should she be missing him the way she did? She smiled as she recalled how his visit had kept the office abuzz for two whole days before the talk died down and things returned to a normal pace.

But of late, her favorite pastime late at night, and when no one was around, had been to recall the feel of his hard body, his touch on her, and his parting words before he left town. The warm thoughts brought on an electric jolt.

"Carolyn, watch out."

She looked up at Adam's shout and swerved just in time to avoid crashing into the back end of a car parked along the bend in the drive.

"Where did that car come from?" she asked no one in particular, shaken by the close call.

As Carolyn eased up on the brakes and gained control again, she continued around the bend only to see a line of vehicles illuminated in her lights, all leading up to the main house.

"Hey, what the heck's going on?" Adam asked as he let his window down and peered from it.

"I don't know," Carolyn replied, and slowly drove past the vehicles. All of them were partly set onto the shoulder and parked with no occupants. The house was fully in view now and it was bright with shimmering white light. Something was definitely happening at the house.

Halina had released her seat belt and her face was now pressed to the window. "Mrs. Pitts may be having a party," she said.

Adam looked at Carolyn. "I don't think it's Mrs. Pitts. I think it's Rollie."

Carolyn remembered the doubts Michael had expressed about his friend. "Oh, dear. We'll find out what's going on inside when we see Mrs. Pitts." Carolyn drove beyond the cars and the front door to the garage on the other side of the house. It was closed; but when she stopped her car in front of it, a shadow separated from the ground and came towards the car. It was Mr. Pitts. He came around to the driver's window.

"Hello, Miss Hardy."

"Mr. Pitts, is something going on at the house?"

"I guess you could say that." He looked down the long line of cars. "That Mr. Rollie Anderson is having a get-to-gether with some of his friends, so Mrs. Pitts has me standing out here to make sure none of those rascals inside leave with anything they're not supposed to."

Carolyn smiled at their plan to protect Michael. "I'm going to take the children inside. Is there another way to get in without going through the front?"

"Sure. I'll show you."

He opened the back door and helped Halina from the car with her stuffed bear, bucket of tapes, and cassette player. Then they all trouped into the kitchen by way of the garage. Strains of music and voices were coming from another room.

"Well, hello there." Mrs. Pitts held her arms wide as Halina ran into them. "Did you two enjoy yourself with Carolyn?"

"I outlasted Adam in the skating contest," she said.

"Yeah, but you still didn't win," Adam countered.

"I think they enjoyed themselves," Carolyn said, and set Halina's things down on the table. "I see you've got a full house tonight, huh?"

She looked at Adam and Halina and said, "Adam, why don't you take Halina upstairs and I'll be up shortly to help her prepare for bed?"

"Sure." He stuck his Gameboy in his back pocket and scooped up his sister's belongings from the table. "Come on, short stuff."

"Stop calling me that," she complained. She looked back at Carolyn. "Are you coming back tomorrow so we can go to your mother's house for dinner?"

"I sure am. Mrs. Pitts said she doesn't mind if I steal you two for another afternoon."

"And are you going to come upstairs and say goodnight before you leave, too, like Daddy does?"

Carolyn smiled and smoothed back Halina's ponytails. "I sure will, right after I talk with Mrs. Pitts."

The little girl ran off after her brother who had already left for the wing that housed their rooms.

Mrs. Pitts turned to Carolyn once the children were out of sight and growled her anger. "Oh, I'm so mad," she grunted.

Carolyn crossed her arms and leaned against the counter. "Mr. Pitts told us that Rollie decided to have a party tonight."

"I know Michael isn't aware of this. He would never have strange people in the house with the children when he's not here; I just know he wouldn't. But Rollie is his friend, and I don't feel comfortable 'telling on him.' "

"Where is the party, anyway?" The music and voices seemed to be coming from a part of the house she had not yet had a chance to visit.

"It's going on around the back terrace and the entertainment room. They're using the Jacuzzi, the billiards room, everything."

Carolyn raised her brows in curiosity and ventured in the direction that Mrs. Pitts had indicated. With the housekeeper in step behind her, muttering about the unsavory guests walking off with anything not nailed down, she moved beyond the solarium.

Another hallway served as a bridge to the opposite wing, one she had not yet visited. Here, the music was clear and loud, and she saw people as they walked and sat about, leaned against walls with drinks in hand, and enjoyed a party. And food. She could see a small buffet spread set up in a sunken area that held a billiard table near the doors to the terrace.

Carolyn stayed at the wall in the hallway and looked back at Mrs. Pitts, who read her thoughts.

"He had it catered himself. All he told me was he was having a party tonight and he knew how to clean up after himself."

Carolyn turned back to watch surreptitiously from her position at the wall. She didn't see Rollie, but heard his voice in the distance, a gregarious and joyfully loud one that continually exhorted his friends to party. Carolyn's eye caught a man of a slender but powerful build, dressed in an expensive, three piece suit, who crossed into her view from the billiards area. A thin cigar played at his lips. His face was terribly familiar, but Carolyn couldn't place it; she couldn't remember where she'd seen him before, and she knew it would plague her until she could.

"Mrs. Pitts, that guy in the charcoal gray suit up ahead—do you know him?"

"Honey, I don't know any of these thuggish-looking people, and I suspect you don't, either."

Carolyn smiled at the woman's candor. "Maybe you're right. At least, I don't know why I'd know him, either."

She turned with Mrs. Pitts and they quietly left the hallway together, with Carolyn throwing one more silent glance over her shoulder at the man who stood in the middle of the room.

Bruce Witherspoon rolled over in bed on the phone's second ring. It wasn't going to stop so he picked it up.

"Yeah," he growled sleepily.

It was his counterpart, Derrick Easley, in the East. "Our informant's talking for you, and he's got some stuff on Roland Anderson."

"Damn, he couldn't talk Monday through Friday, nine

to five?" he asked, rubbing his face. "All right, what you got, and that is the ID for the other guy we caught in the pictures, right?" Bruce was slowly coming awake.

"Yeah. Our guy says Rollie joked all the time in the slammer about how Michael owed him big time and he could get anything out of him he wanted."

"He's talking blackmail?" Bruce asked.

"Nah, more like tit for tat."

"So, Rollie likes to milk his best friends?"

"Looks like he's been doing it most of Michael's career."

"Rollie is our linchpin, looks like. He's the common thread linking Michael with our target, Charlie Madden," Bruce surmised.

"Your case can start pulling together the more those three get interconnected."

Bruce yawned. "It's all sounding good. I got a call from surveillance earlier. Seems they're gonna be spending a lot of time checking out car tags."

"You hit a party?"

"Yeah. These guys have the run of Michael's place, even when he's away, and Madden's cars have been making it in and out of there on a regular basis." He finally sat up on the bed. "When can you get me a fax of your guy's full statement?"

"I can do it Monday."

"You know," Bruce frowned, "this is pretty sad stuff."

"What do you mean?"

"I don't know." He scratched his head as he dropped his feet to the floor and sat on the side of the bed. "I like the guy—so much so that I almost hate to turn the spotlight on him. It's gonna be a crushing blow to a lot of people who believe in him, and all because he was in the wrong damn place at the wrong time, and shaking the wrong small-time hood's hand."

"Don't sweat it. It happens to the best of America's celebrities. Shake it off and get some sleep."

"Yeah, you're right," Bruce said. "Thanks for nothing." He rang off, and taking Derrick's advice, went back to sleep.

Eighteen

"Ah, Caro, she's such a cute little thing," Alli said of Halina as the curious little girl stuck her head in the gallery's business office.

"Yes, she is, isn't she?" Carolyn had grown fond of the time she'd spent with the child over the last week and watched as Halina now showed off her cassette case to Rosa, the hostess of the Hardy Art Gallery.

The children's promised art tour was over, and Adam had hurried off to the magazine floor with Stephanie for a chance to see and talk with a real cartoonist in action.

"I mean, doesn't she just make you want to squeeze one out?"

"You do have a way with words, Alli, but don't include me in your nightmare." She looked around. "And where's Steph? I thought she and Adam were on their way back down here?"

"There they are," Alli said. Stephanie was leading Adam through the gallery doors.

"Carolyn." Adam talked in a rush of words as he joined them. "It was so neat up there. They even let me ink in one of my characters on a drawing board." His eyes were bright as he showed her a pad-sized board.

"That looks really great." Carolyn smiled at his enthusiasm.

Stephanie squeezed his shoulders. "You're a good kid, Adam; just keep on working hard at your sketches."

He left them to show his work to his sister.

Stephanie slammed her hands on the hips of her suit. "I don't know what to make of this, Alli. I can't remember the last time we've seen this woman this many times in one week." She smiled as her eyes twinkled devilishly at Carolyn. "Let me guess, you've been fired."

"No," Carolyn smiled smugly. "I promised the children an art gallery visit after school today, and I'm delivering, that's all."

Alli and Stephanie exchanged glances.

"You missed my birthday party because of a G & G meeting," Alli snorted at Carolyn. "Nope, there's more going on here."

"I only missed part of it, and you were late, too."

As if on cue, Caroline's cell phone rang.

With an apologetic shrug, she walked away and looked at the ID. Her heart literally skipped a beat. It was Michael.

"Hello? Michael?"

"Hi." His deep voice seemed rushed. "Did I catch you at a bad time?"

"No," she replied. "I'm at the gallery. Adam and Halina are with me, too. Where are you?"

His deep chuckle rumbled through the phone. "I'm walking through the airport. The Atlanta airport."

Carolyn's heart leaped. "You're home early? That's great."

"I'm trying to make good on a promise to Halina that I'd see her school project at the PTA meeting tonight. So I managed to speed up my part of the production in order to get back in time."

Carolyn was impressed by his commitment to the children. "The kids are going to be excited that you're home."

"I know you have a busy schedule. Mr. Pitts and I can swing by the gallery and pick them up."

"No, no—"

"Things will be a little crazy between now and after the meeting tonight. Do you mind if I stop by your place to see you later?"

"I have a better idea. We were getting ready to leave, anyway. So, I'll just return the kids home, and then see you before your meeting."

"Can't wait." His voice broke with huskiness.

They exchanged goodbyes, and Carolyn clicked off the phone.

"Guess what?" She turned back to her sisters, who had now been joined by the children. "Michael's home."

While Halina cheered and broke out in a wide smile, Adam asked, "He is? I thought he wasn't getting back until the weekend?"

Amusement flickered in Carolyn's eyes as she shared her suspicion. "Don't tell him I said it, but I think he missed you two, and was just anxious to get home.

Stephanie smiled. "Something tells me he's anxious to see all three of you."

"Why don't you two get your things," Carolyn said to the children as she darted a warning eye to her sister. "And we'll meet him at the house." When the kids left to get their jackets and school bags, she lowered her tone for her sisters.

"I'm not sure how Halina and Adam might react, so I try not to act like there's anything going on between Michael and myself."

Stephanie dropped her voice, too. "Take my advice, Carolyn, and be honest about your feelings. Kids see a lot more than you think they do, and it won't pay to lie."

Returning with their backpacks, the children bid a goodbye to Alli and Stephanie, and then left through the gallery doors with Carolyn. As they walked through the hallway to the elevators, Halina reached over and grabbed Carolyn's hand.

"Don't forget," Halina reminded her. "You promised we could go to McDonald's if we were good."

"You're right," she agreed. "Then McDonald's, it is."

Michael passed his travel grip and bag over to Eldridge Pitts's waiting hands as they cleared the front door. It was good coming home; yet he knew there were things he had to deal with—come to terms with. He didn't hear any movement in the house from either of the children, so he assumed they must still be with Carolyn. An unexpected smile of pleasure crossed his face because he knew he'd see them all soon.

He walked toward the library, expecting to run into Mrs. Pitts. Instead, it was Rollie he met coming out of the kitchen.

"Whoa . . . Hey man," Rollie said as he strolled forward. "When did you roll back in from La-La land?"

An edgy intensity invaded their space. Michael wondered if the bad feeling that washed over him was being felt by his friend of twenty years.

"I just got here," Michael said. "Listen, I need to talk with you. You got a few minutes?"

"Sure. I want to run something by you, too."

"Then let's talk now." He motioned up ahead. "Come on in the library."

Michael led the way into the room and then closed the door after them. He watched as Rollie made a beeline for the bar. When he splashed a shot of liquor into a glass, he threw a glance at Michael from over his shoulder.

"You want me to pour you one, man?"

"No, nothing for me." Michael said and walked over to the desk. "I've got a PTA meeting tonight."

"I tell you . . . a damn PTA meeting," Rollie mumbled

as he set the bottle down and picking up his glass, turned to sit in one of the arm chairs.

Michael leaned against the desk and watched Rollie get comfortable. "You first. What's up?"

"I have a proposition to lay on you." Rollie looked at Michael above the rim of his glass. "And before you knock it down, just listen. Because this time, it's the real thing."

The bad feeling Michael experienced earlier had returned.

Mrs. Pitts opened the door for Carolyn and the children, but waylaid the kids' search for Michael, explaining that he'd be tied up for a few minutes. After they ran off with instructions to clean up for the PTA meeting later on, Mrs. Pitts turned to Carolyn.

"He's in the library with Rollie."

Carolyn raised her brows in understanding. "Did you tell him about the party?"

"No, I haven't had a chance to talk with him since he got back; but Mr. Pitts said he asked him in the car about how things went while he was away, and, well . . ."

"He told him?"

She nodded. "But Carolyn—" She touched her hand to Carolyn's as though she needed to talk. "That all-night party on Saturday wasn't the worst that happened. The next day, when I cleaned up, I found"—she whispered her next words—"some of that wild bunch's drugs, and a little pipe, even. Eldridge was livid."

Carolyn's surprise at Rollie's betrayal of Michael's trust registered on her face. Knowing Michael for only the short time that she had, she sensed that he might have a problem with the party; but he wouldn't easily forgive drug use around his children.

"What did you do?" Carolyn asked.

"Well, Eldridge wanted to find Rollie and throw him out right then and there; but I told him Michael was our employer, and that was a decision he had to make."

Carolyn wondered how this disloyalty would affect Michael, because it was a given the friendship would suffer; Rollie would pay heavily for this. But she felt no sympathy for him.

"Anyway," she patted Carolyn's hand, "let me get upstairs and make sure those two clean their necks before they change clothes."

Carolyn smiled as Mrs. Pitts left for the staircase. On her own until Michael was free, she moved through the hallway in the general direction of the solarium.

"We go too far back, man, and I've always been there for you. Remember, I was there when it counted, and when no one else cared."

Rollie's distinct, raised voice caused Carolyn to jerk her head around to the closed library door.

"And I've paid that debt, ten times over, and you know it." Michael's voice was angry.

"You gonna just break our pact, man, you gonna dog me out for something—"

"Don't look at me like I did it, Rollie. You screwed up, and under no circumstances are you going to drag me into drugs. So you'd better figure a way out of this."

Carolyn looked up the hallway, and didn't know which direction to walk, ashamed that she had overheard their private argument. She decided to retreat to the living room. There was less of a chance of hearing them there. As she retraced her steps to the front of the house, the library door behind her opened. She stopped and turned to see Rollie. He had a great scowl on his face as he quickly gained on her. When he came alongside her in the hall, he slowed momentarily to greet her with a sneer.

"You're bad news."

He moved on at a quick pace and stormed from the

house through the front door. Carolyn looked back toward the library where the door remained ajar. She went to look for Michael inside.

When she reached the library, she saw him sitting at the enormous desk, his head thrown back against the huge chair he occupied. She quietly walked around the desk and faced him as she leaned against it. His eyes were closed, as though he slept.

"Are you all right?" she asked quietly.

Without opening his eyes, he pulled Carolyn's arm, and she tumbled into his lap in the huge chair.

"Now I am," he said to her. "Are you welcoming me back?"

She smiled as his arms closed around her in his lap. "First, I should tell you I could hear a bit of the tail end of your argument with Rollie. I heard you refuse to have anything to do with drugs."

He shifted in the chair so he could see her face. "You sound surprised that I would."

"No, it's not that." She looked at him. "I know he's like a brother to you, Michael. And I can see that it's affected you, too. But you know how it is with relatives; you take them with their baggage, good and bad."

"Yeah . . . well, right now, Rollie's got a lot of lousy baggage." He pulled Carolyn's head down. "I don't want to talk about that. I want to be welcomed back properly."

They kissed in that delicious way that couples do when, after an absence, they're hungry for the other, gorging themselves outright at first before a pleasurable, sated pace is found. And that was how the kids found them.

"Daddy, you're back."

Halina's hail to Michael broke up their kiss.

"Oh, goodness," Carolyn said and tried to scramble from the chair. But, to her surprise, Michael's hand was still tangled in her hair, and held her in place.

"Don't run off so fast," he cautioned her with a smile, and slowly released his hold on her.

Halina ran to Michael as he stood from the chair with Carolyn nearby. Adam followed and also gave Michael a hug.

"I bet you two didn't believe me when I said I'd make it back in time for the PTA meeting, huh?" Michael grinned, proud of his effort.

Adam flopped onto the sofa. "Let's just go, okay? I want to get there early."

"Me, too," Halina chimed in. She turned to Carolyn. "Are you going to the school with us?"

Carolyn looked from Michael to the kids, and back to Michael again as he watched her with a keenly observant eye, giving no clue as to how he wanted her to respond. And then, she recalled Stephanie's advice. "If you and Adam don't mind, I'd love to."

"Sounds like a plan to me," Michael said. "We might as well leave now."

When Halina caught up Carolyn's hand in hers and began to swing it, Carolyn realized the decision she'd made from her heart was a good one.

"You have to meet my teacher, first," the little girl said as they all left the room.

Adam sauntered over to them with his Walkman in his hand. "My science teacher will think it's neat that you're a real engineer."

Michael laughed, and caught Carolyn's eye. "You see why I need help? No one's impressed with my skills."

She smiled, thoroughly enjoying their company as Michael hauled the entire group out of the house and into the car.

When they arrived at the elementary school, it was obvious that Michael had been kidding about not being able to impress anyone. In fact, he couldn't get through the front door without signing autographs and shaking more hands—all this before he reached the auditorium.

While Carolyn stood with the children near Michael, the group of people who'd recognized him pressed in on them. She looked down when Halina tugged at her hand.

"Let's go," Halina urged. "He'll be doing this for a while."

"Yeah," Adam joined in with a whisper. "Maybe if we go on in and sit down, they'll leave him alone. Or he'll stop and come with us."

Carolyn saw the resolute look in their faces. They didn't like the fact that Michael was being forced to share the time meant for them. She leaned near Michael.

"It's almost time for the school program to start," she whispered. "Why don't I go on in with the children and get us seats?"

Michael finished the autograph and darted a look at Halina and Adam before he turned to Carolyn again.

"We should go on in," she said, her words emphatic in their meaning.

He nodded reached out one hand to Halina and rested the other on Adam's shoulder.

"This is family night and you're right. We'll go in together." He led them through the thickening crowd and into the auditorium.

For the next ninety minutes, they sat through the PTA's business meeting, and then toured the children's classrooms with their teachers, all without Michael stopping even once to sign an autograph. Respectfully declining, he would say he was with his family for the evening.

Back in the car on their ride home, Halina asked for, and received, permission to attend a sleepover at the house of a friend whose mother Michael had met at the PTA meeting.

"Michael, that's not fair," Adam said. "Since Halina

gets to go at the last minute, why can't I go hiking with my friends at Stone Mountain this weekend?"

"Okay, okay, you talked me into it," Michael said, and smiled at Carolyn who sat next to him in the front seat.

"What about you, Daddy? What are you gonna do if both of us leave you at home?"

"Oh, I'll think of something," Michael said, and reached for Carolyn's hand on the seat between them. "I'll think of something."

Michael walked Carolyn out to her car on the crisp spring night.

"Between me and the kids, we've taken up pretty much all of your time this evening; and you went on not one, but three outings with the kids while I was gone. I hope you know how much I appreciate it."

Carolyn hugged her arms against the light chill. "I didn't do it just for you, I did it because you have two great kids and they wanted to spend the time with me, too."

They strolled on toward the car in silence. "You heard how they'll both be gone all day and night on Saturday," he said.

Carolyn smiled. "Actually, I heard how you dumped them."

Michael laughed. "So, you want to go out with me again this weekend?"

She glanced at him as they walked. "It's going to be hard topping last weekend's restaurant."

"We can try. I know lots of them." He named a few popular, trendy spots.

She wrinkled her nose and gave him a squinted look. "We could just stay in."

The look of astonishment on his face surprised her. "What's wrong?"

"I don't know." He rubbed his chin. "Most women like a night on the town."

"I thought you had learned I wasn't like most women."

"Jeez, I can't believe I said that." He looked properly chastised. "So, let me prepare dinner for you here on Saturday."

"You can cook?"

"My mama taught me a few things. She didn't want me to be at some woman's mercy simply because she could cook and I couldn't."

"You have nothing to worry about then, when it comes to me."

He laughed. "Something else I'll have to teach you."

They came to a halt at Carolyn's car. "What about Rollie and your blow-up this afternoon? Is he going to be here?"

"No, he's—" He started to say more, and then seemed to change his mind. "He's moving in with someone he met."

"So you'll be in this big house by yourself?"

"The Pittses will be in their quarters, but they'd never disturb us"—he paused with a grin—"ah, disturb me when I have a guest."

"Okay, you've won me over. I'm going to let you cook for me."

"Great." He massaged her shoulders and drew her closer. "The dress is casual, and all you need to bring is a strong appetite."

The double meaning wasn't lost on Carolyn. Her arms wrapped around him as his lips slowly descended before capturing hers. His mouth was tantalizing, devouring her softness and leaving a divine ecstasy in the pit of her stomach.

She felt his lips brush her brow after they had pulled apart and she caught her breath.

"Goodnight."

"I'll see you Saturday, Carolyn." He helped her into the car before he closed the door.

She started the engine and drove away, inexplicably taken by the idea that she would return to him that weekend, and the result would be that they would make love.

Nineteen

"Come on, open wide," Michael encouraged Carolyn. He leaned over her on the floor of the entertainment room and dangled more grapes precariously close to her mouth.

"No," she said, laughing hard as she already chewed on grapes they had been enjoying after dinner. Carolyn struggled to get up from where she and Michael lay sprawled together atop giant floor pillows. "No more," she cried. "No more."

"All right." He moved the vine of grapes away from her mouth and moved in with his own. "I'll eat them," he said against her lips, and proceeded to nibble at her mouth.

Carolyn enjoyed the hardness of his lips and body as they covered hers and pressed her back into the soft pillows. She stroked the sharp angles of his face as he explored the soft recesses of her mouth. A tiny groan escaped her mouth before Michael pulled away and stared into her face, his eyes glazed with passion, which she knew was mirrored in hers.

He smiled as he plopped the remaining two grapes into his mouth and then he sat up. Carolyn rolled away from him and straightened her shirt, which had risen above her slacks in their playful tussle. She brushed her hair back from her face, flushed by the continued intimate contact resulting from this pas de deux they had begun.

She drew her legs up as Michael rose from the floor to reach for the remote control that sat on the brick, raised hearth fireplace. The room was comfortably decorated and included the de rigueur large-screen television, stereo system, and game system. She smiled as she stood up from the floor. Men would be boys whenever they got the chance, she surmised, and walked toward the decorated screen door in the corner. Behind it sat a hot tub, soaking up sunshine through the glass wall.

The stereo music had changed from basic R&B to low vocals from a decidedly jazz-flavored selection. As she turned, she felt Michael come up behind her and encircle her waist.

"You have some collection of music," she said as she covered his hands with hers. "When you did that rap video—I forget the name of the group—"

"I'm shocked that you even know about it," he laughed as he hugged her tighter.

"My source was Alli, of course. Anyway, I thought you were more interested in rap music."

"Actually, it was a hip-hop video, and you're right, I do have an eclectic collection because I'm turned on to variety, just as I can tell you are."

When he nuzzled her neck, Carolyn closed her eyes as the pleasure burned inside.

"Dinner's over," he whispered. "How about a dip in the hot tub to relax before dessert?"

Carolyn lifted her head slightly. "I thought we had dessert already?"

He turned her around to face him. "Who says dessert can only occur once in an evening?"

Carolyn looked into his eyes, which were filled with promise. As he rubbed his hands slowly up and down her arms, she remarked, "I don't have a suit with me, Michael. You should have told me to bring one."

He dropped his hands and went over to the screen door. When he opened it, the hook on the inside had colorful pieces of cloth hanging from it. "I picked up a few suits for you to use." He unhooked them from the door and walked back to Carolyn.

"You didn't," she said, laughing as he held up the pieces of material for her to choose, each with store tags still attached.

He grinned. "I think I got the size right."

"Yeah," she added humorously, "One-size-fits-all stretch. I can imagine you in the store choosing these things." She snatched them from his fingers.

The chimes from the front doorbell rang out.

They both looked up.

"Now, who the hell is that?"

"Maybe it's the Pittses?"

"No. When they have time off, or I want privacy, they stay at the manor house in the back. Anyway, they don't have to ring the bell."

The chimes rang again, and this time it was more insistent.

"Go ahead and change," Michael said as he headed for the door. He looked over his shoulder at Carolyn. "I'll send whoever it is away and get right back."

Michael strode through the halls and reached the door as the chimes sounded again. He threw open the door, ready to blast one at the caller.

Rollie was lounged casually against the door frame, and he didn't look happy.

Michael shifted gears, his frown furious. "What are you doing here?"

"Man, for a minute, there, I didn't think you were home. But I saw Carolyn's car. Then I thought you weren't gonna answer because it was me."

"I thought we made it pretty clear about how it stands between us the other day."

"Yeah, well . . ." He stood away from the door. "I'm in some deep stuff, man, and I need your help." He looked at Michael. "I'm serious. I got nobody else to turn to."

Michael sighed deeply. "Come on in, Rollie."

They walked into the library where Rollie proceeded to explain his problem. This time, it was gambling.

"I'm trying to lay low until I can raise some cash, maybe the interest . . . something." He rubbed his forehead as he spied the locked bar.

"How much this time?"

"A hundred thou, a hundred and fifty with all the interest."

"Damn, Rollie." Michael slammed his hand at his friend's chest, literally pinning him to the wall. "How stupid can you be?"

"I came down here to raise it. These dudes—"

Michael dropped his hand and Rollie slumped against the wall. "Raise it how, Rollie? When was the last time you held a job?"

Rollie let loose with an angry expletive. "That's easy for you to say. You've always had it easy. So if you want to bust my chops, go ahead. I know I got a little gambling problem; but man, don't leave me hangin'. Not now. Carleshia found out about Glenda and threw me out of her apartment tonight."

Michael scratched his head and looked at Rollie. He really looked at him this time. And what he saw set off alarms. Rollie had become a desperate man hanging onto anything he could to save his own skin. If that meant lying, cheating, or stealing, he'd do it.

"All of those come-ons to me, about setting you up with money to finance some straight-up deal that I knew was all about drugs—that money was supposed to pay off your debt, huh?"

Rollie turned away and looked out the window. "Yeah. I can't deliver, so they want their money."

Michael's sarcastic laugh echoed through the room, and Rollie turned to him from the window.

"You're right," Michael said. "You couldn't deliver me to your buddies, so they're not forgiving your debt. Now all bets are off, huh? You're a rotten bastard after all, Rollie," Michael sneered. "I've always seen it, but I just didn't want to believe it."

He turned away and reached in his pocket for a small set of keys. He selected one and walked to the desk. Unlocking a bottom drawer, he selected from several packs of banded bills and, after closing and relocking the drawer, tossed the packets to Rollie, who caught them against his chest.

"That's five thousand, Rollie. Get yourself a place to stay for the night, then I suggest you get the hell out of town."

"Michael, you don't know these dudes. They're bad news. I need your help, just this one more time."

Michael shook his head. "There was a time when I'd give you anything, help you with anything; but you *know* what happened to Vivian and how it affected my family. She was my sister, man, so you know how I feel about drugs, and you still try to involve me, even bringing them into the house with her children. You've lost it with me." He turned away. "Maybe you can sell the business and raise the money."

"You know I put the business in Glenda's name when I was in jail."

"Then you better hope she's more forgiving than most wives."

"Aw, man, this is messed up."

"Goodbye, Rollie." Michael went to the library door, and walked through to the front door. He heard Rollie behind him as he opened it.

"I'm up at the Marriott downtown."

"Take my advice, Rollie, and get out of town."

"Yeah, sure," he said, and ambled off to the car he'd driven up in.

Michael stood against the closed door and realized his mouth was clenched with unspent anger. He heard the strains of music coming from the entertainment room and knew that Carolyn was waiting for him in the hot tub. He would worry about Rollie tomorrow because tonight was their time.

He pushed off from the door and headed back to Carolyn. They had waited patiently for this night and he wanted a slow and easy evening. No rushed passion for them. They had all night long, and he'd make sure it lasted all night long. He had to change into a suit, too, and began to unbutton his shirt, wondering which suit she'd chosen. Maybe it would be that little gold one, he thought as his mouth now curved into an unconscious smile, his imagination working overtime.

It was thirty minutes later, and Michael still wore a smile, though Carolyn suspected the last grin had been at her expense, due to her slipping in the hot tub.

Carolyn now stood at the edge of the sink and stretched like a satisfied cat, her yawn real. The hot tub had been totally relaxing until she had slipped and surfaced with a soaking wet head. She had sputtered water all over a laughing Michael as he left to get her a towel to dry her head, strutting off proudly in his sleek black trunks.

Clad only in the tiny gold two-piece bathing suit, with a handy terry robe tied discreetly for modesty while out of the tub, Carolyn towel-dried her hair under the overhead heat lamps, brushed it out, and then swept it into a ponytail.

"Are you sure you're all right?" Michael called out to

her from the other room. "Do you want something to drink?"

"No, I'm relaxed enough. Club soda is fine," she said. She was about to walk back out into the entertainment room to join him when he came up behind her.

"We got out of the tub just in time," he said.

"Oh?" she asked. "And why is that?"

"Because I couldn't do this in there."

He began to nuzzle against her neck, his breath warm on nerves already taut from the evening's fever. "I like this."

"So do I," Carolyn said, visibly shaken by the seductive attention she was receiving.

He reached around and gently stroked her shoulders, his hands slowly reaching for her waist where he untied her robe.

Carolyn's head fell back onto Michael's chest. As she was pulled against his hard loins, she could feel that his ardor was both strong and obvious.

His hands dropped lower and caressed the soft exposed skin near her belly on their slow journey to the delicate skin hidden beneath her suit.

Carolyn sighed, and covered his hands with hers as a pleasurable wave rolled through her.

"Do you want me to stop?" The words were whispered in her ear before he continued to kiss her neck.

Her head lolled back against him and offered him easy access to her tender skin.

"No," she replied urgently.

As his hands, guided by hers, slipped beneath the material to caress her taut stomach on their path to the juncture of her legs, Carolyn let out a groan of pleasure that was a scream within her body. His fingers burned into her mounded skin.

"What are you doing to me?" she whispered in wonder. He said nothing as he worked magic with his hands.

Slowly, no longer able to hold her trembling body, her knees buckled, and she sank to the pillows on the floor, with Michael following her there.

The door opened and a man in dark gear with a black cap pulled down over his head jumped from the gray-paneled van parked on the road near the entrance to Michael's drive. As he stretched his legs, his headgear lit up with a call.

"Yo," the agent spoke into his headgear.

"Are you aware that somebody besides us is curious about your mark?"

It was his backup who was positioned farther up the road.

"Anybody we know?" he asked as he walked to the other end of the van.

"I don't think so, but I'm checking. They picked up his tail not too long after leaving your spot. Want me to do anything about it?"

"No, just keep to our instructions and put it in your report. For now, we're strictly on observation patrol. No interaction."

"Gotcha." The backup signed off.

The agent leaned against the van and lit up a cigarette. A few more hours, and he could call it a night.

Instinctively, Carolyn's body arched upwards from the pillows as Michael's mouth tantalized her swollen, sensitive nipples now free of the suit. Pure and explosive pleasure radiated throughout her body as she found herself at the mercy of his skillful touch.

His mouth made a path down her ribs to her stomach, where he kissed the delicate skin.

And after slipping the golden material away from his

prize, the shapely beauty of her naked body open to his eyes taunted his own. Michael gently cupped her bottom in his hands, his tongue skimming the swell of her hips before he made the ultimate praise and explored her inner thighs—at his leisure and for her pleasure.

Michael's ardor was surprisingly restrained as he brought Carolyn's passion to a fever pitch. Her moans of satisfaction were foremost in his mind, but he didn't think he could withhold his own passion much longer as he felt her tremble with his every movement.

For Carolyn, the real world spun and careened on its axis as waves of ecstasy overtook her and throbbed outward. Had she cried out? She couldn't be sure. All she knew was that she had pulled Michael's head up, and clutched him to her, wanting to undergo a possession that only he could satisfy.

As she moved underneath him, he was reaching above her head, across the pillows, for something.

It was the phone. It was ringing.

"Hello," Michael said into the receiver.

Carolyn quietly listened as her breathing slowly returned to normal.

"No, it's all right." His body stiffened and then remained still above her. "What happened, Mrs. Pitts?" he asked.

Something sounded wrong. Quickly, Carolyn slid from beneath Michael as he continued to talk on the phone with the housekeeper. She spied the terry robe on the floor a few feet away and grabbed it up. Slipping it over her nakedness, she returned to Michael's side and waited as he hung up the phone.

Before he said a word, Michael reached out and pulled her to him, kissing her lightly on the mouth before he released her.

"That was Mrs. Pitts."

"Did something happen?"

"Halina wants to come home from the sleepover. *Now,*" he emphasized awkwardly. "And she wants me to pick her up."

"Bless her heart," Carolyn said, smiling. "Is this her first night away from home?"

"No, but there are special problems we deal with, and we have to take them one sleepover at a time."

"I understand," Carolyn said.

"Do you? I'm beginning to wonder if this house isn't bad luck for romance." He looked at her hard. "This won't be our last night together, I promise you. We've got a lot more of them in our future."

Carolyn nodded, thrilled by his enthusiasm.

"You believe me, don't you?

"Yes, I do." She stood. "But you need to go ahead and change. She'll be waiting for you."

He stood. "Yeah, I know." He took her hands into his. "Carolyn, I—"

She looked at the earnest look his eyes had taken on. "Yes?"

"Never mind. Another night, when the mood returns."

As he walked toward the bathroom to change his clothes, Carolyn crossed her arms and sighed as she admired the view. He was still looking nice in those black trunks.

"Halina, I promise you, it's okay that you wanted to come home."

"You don't think I'm a big girl, anymore," she said.

Michael drove the big Mercedes down the expressway through the light rain, ready to be home again.

"Yes, I do." Michael watched her carefully in the backseat through the rearview mirror. She had started to cry when he put her into the car. Miraculously, she had stopped only when Carolyn had coaxed her into her lap.

And that's where Halina had continued to sit for the entire trip home.

"Carolyn, do you think I'm a baby?"

Carolyn smiled and pressed the child's pigtails back. "I think you're quite brave." At the child's blank look, Carolyn said, "It took courage to call when you told everyone you'd be okay. Now, I think bravery and courage are signs of a big girl."

Halina giggled, and in the front seat, Michael let out a relieved smile.

"Wait until I tell Adam," Halina said, her good humor returning as she settled more comfortably against Carolyn for the rest of the ride home.

Twenty

"I'm fine," Carolyn said, and looked at the other three women in the salon of the Hardy house. They all stared back at her from their comfortable spots on the sofas. It was where they would gather after Sunday dinner to talk.

"What?" Carolyn demanded.

"Well, you seem less manic, very relaxed," Stephanie offered.

"And a number of times you've been deep in thought," Davina said.

"And the most striking change," Alli added, "is that you don't have that cell phone hanging around your neck beeping every ten minutes."

"So, things are okay with Michael?" Davina ventured.

Carolyn nodded. "Michael is fine." She swung her legs to the floor. "In fact, he prepared dinner for me last night at his house."

Three other heads now lifted from the sofas and turned to her.

Carolyn remembered her evening with Michael and couldn't stop the blush that crawled up her face, so she quickly changed the subject.

"We had to cut the evening short, though," she said. "His little girl, Halina, had to be picked up from a sleepover.

"When you have kids, that's a fact of life," Stephanie said.

"Well, Justin and I are going to look forward to that fact of life," Davina said with a grin.

"She gets anxiety attacks, Steph, when she's away from home, since her mother died. Michael says she's doing much better than she has in the past."

"Oh, the poor thing," Stephanie said.

"How did her mother die?" Alli asked

"I don't know," Carolyn replied. "Michael has never offered any details about his sister." She leaned back onto the sofa. "I'm hoping he'll feel comfortable enough to tell me soon."

"You two have been dating steadily for, what, not even two months?" Stephanie asked. "Give it time."

"Just make sure you don't use his decision to make revelations as a measure of how much he cares," Davina said. "You know how long it took me to open up to Justin. Only Michael can work his way through his barriers to get to you. And if he's what you want, you'll be there when he makes the breakthrough."

Carolyn reached over and squeezed Davina's hand. "Thanks. You don't know how much I needed to hear that. There's so much that confuses me these days."

"It's okay to be confused and question what you're feeling," Stephanie said. "Eventually, we all do it."

"That's why you talk with your girlfriends," Davina said with a laugh. "We've withstood the fickle finger of love and lived to tell about it."

"Leave me out of that finger-pointing," Alli said. "I like to think I'm a love story not yet developed, thank you very much."

"Alli's name spoken in the same sentence with sentimental love and romance?" Stephanie laughed in her hearty, pleasant way. "It'll never happen to the family cynic."

The others laughed, including Alli, at the implausibility.

* * *

It had been hard, but during the rest of that week, Carolyn was able to draw on her single-mindedness to put Michael aside in her thoughts long enough to get her project successfully off the board and her team members assigned for its implementation with the client.

With the first level of the project given the go-ahead, much of the onus was removed from her shoulders and had shifted to the separate teams, which would simply report results to her for overall review.

Normally, Carolyn would be antsy to start in on a new assignment project. But it didn't seem nearly so important now as it had, say, two months ago. Suddenly she had time that was free for spending a leisurely Saturday afternoon with Michael and the children eating homemade tacos.

"Can I be excused from the table," Halina asked politely, as she looked from Michael to Carolyn."

"Sure," Michael answered. "But first, tell me where you're going."

"I want to sing my new song for Carolyn," she said, sliding from her chair. "But I have to get my cassettes and microphone from the solarium."

"I bought her music for 'I Believe I Can Fly,' " Michael said to Carolyn. "After she practices, we have what we call recitals here at the house where she sings and records her songs on cassettes."

"She's pretty good, too," Adam added.

"I know," Carolyn said. "I've heard her tapes." She looked at Halina. "But why don't we just go into the solarium with you and listen to it there?"

"Good idea," Michael said, and watched Adam and Halina clear from the room in record time.

"You know the only reason they both sped from the

room is neither wanted to be tagged to help clean up the table," he pointed out.

She smiled as she crossed her arms on the table. "I'll have to remember to think like a kid next time. But I don't mind spending a few minutes alone with you cleaning off the table."

Michael stood and drew her up with him. "I like the way you think." He smiled down at her. "I figure we have about a two-minute window before they come looking for us."

"Then we should make the most of it," she suggested.

"Right," he said, and settled her within his arms. "And I don't mean cleaning off the table, either."

She raised up on her toes to meet his lips, warm and sweet on hers.

"Your project's done, right?" He landed small kisses against her eyes, her cheeks.

"Uh-huh," she murmured.

"So, no more late-night project meetings at a moment's notice, right?"

"Right."

"Think of us, Carolyn—restless with want, tangled together, doing whatever we want to each other, and having all night to do it." His mouth grazed her earlobe. "Can I come over one night, tonight, maybe?"

The imagery created havoc in Carolyn's mind and her breathing became thick as she remembered the bliss he could create.

"Of course," she said heavily. "You can come over any night."

"I'll remember," he said.

"Daddy, what's taking so long?"

Halina's voice screamed her demand from some other part of the house.

Both of them laughed as Carolyn dropped her head

against Michael's chest. "What did I tell you?" he said as he squeezed her in his arms. "Two minutes tops."

Arm in arm, they went into the solarium where Halina's 'stage' had been set up near the coffee table. Her audience had already increased by two—the Pittses. And with all of her equipment set aside and out of view, she looked the consummate singer, with only her cordless microphone in her hand.

"I'm ready," she announced. And at Michael's ready signal, she sang her version of 'I Believe I Can Fly,' her small voice surprisingly well-equipped to handle the intricate melodies without accompaniment.

As Carolyn listened with the others, it became clear how important it was to Michael that his life, both on and off the field, merge comfortably with the lives of his children, and not the reverse. That must be how it felt to be a parent, even when it was unexpectedly thrust upon you, as in Michael's case.

What had changed him so intriguingly from the hedonist of two years ago had to do with both his family loss and this family addition.

Halina's song was done. As Carolyn and the others clapped loudly for her, excited, she tossed her mike to the floor and took a deep bow. Michael, of course, then stooped to swoop her up in his arms for a big hug.

The doorbell could be heard in the distance, and Mrs. Pitts got up to answer it, with Mr. Pitts leaving with her.

"If you visit every week, Carolyn, you'll get to listen in on Halina's recitals," Michael said as he looked down at the little girl.

"Yeah, and then you'll be forced to listen to them again and again in the car," Adam complained jokingly.

"She will not," Halina argued.

Michael looked up and saw that Mrs. Pitts was at the door.

"You have a visitor," she said to him.

Puzzled over who it might be, Michael told her to invite him in. When she left, he looked at Carolyn and shrugged his shoulders.

"Who could be showing up in the middle of a Saturday afternoon?"

"Rollie, maybe?" she offered.

He smiled. "No, I don't think so. In fact, I haven't heard from Rollie since he dropped in when you were here last week."

Mrs. Pitts appeared again at the door, and standing behind her was the beefy form of Charlie Madden, dressed in a dark business suit. Michael's lips thinned in anger as he released Halina.

"Michael," Carolyn said. "Do you know him?"

"Take the children out of here for a while." He walked briskly across the room toward the man who had now stepped into the room and casually looked around.

"The other gentleman preferred to wait outside," Mrs. Pitts said as she turned and left the room.

Charlie Madden's path was blocked from further entry as Michael stopped in front of him. "What are you doing here?" he asked brusquely.

Charlie's grin seemed a mockery of humor as he squinted back at Michael. "Is that any way to talk to a long-time fan of yours?"

"We can always call the police and have them ask you the question."

Charlie took a step back, and held his hands up. "Hey, I'm not here for trouble. He looked around Michael's shoulders. "I see you got your family around you. But I only need a few minutes of your time. Just a few minutes and I'll be gone." He smiled and showed even small teeth nestled in dark gums. "I promise."

Michael turned and walked back to Carolyn, who stood at the sofa with the children, just as he'd left them. "I told you, take the children out of here for a while." The words didn't come out the way he'd intended, and three sets of eyes gave him a surprised look.

"Do you know him?" Carolyn asked.

"I'll explain later. Just, please . . ."

She abruptly turned away from Michael's tight face. Carolyn motioned for Adam and Halina to come with her even as she shot worried glances toward Michael.

"Halina," she said, "the weather's nice out. You can show me the spring garden."

"But—" the little girl protested, as she was pulled away.

"You come along with us, too, Adam." As Carolyn hustled them out of the room and through the French doors to the side garden, she gave a worried, backward glance at Michael before she closed the door.

When Michael saw them safely out, he turned back to Charlie Madden, who had made his way to Michael's side of the room.

"Now, what do you want to say that's so important I put my family out to hear it?"

"Our mutual friend, Rollie Anderson, is in trouble, and you're the only one who can help him out."

"Rollie's not here anymore, and his trouble is not my business."

"It's my business now, and I'm making it yours."

"You're threatening me?"

"I don't have to threaten." He reared back on his heels and pushed his hands into his pockets. "I state the facts and circumstances, and it's up to you to weigh the consequences." He turned his finger into his own chest to make the point. "That's how I operate, Mr. Hennessey."

Michael could not deny Madden's air of authority or his commanding manner; but simply put, he was a common-variety type thug, and therein lay the danger to Michael's family. He knew he'd have to tread carefully.

"State your facts and circumstances, and then get the hell off my property."

Charlie smiled. "Rollie Anderson owes me a hundred and fifty thousand dollars. Of course, that was the figure two weeks ago."

"Then you're a stupid businessman to allow a debt that size to somebody like Rollie."

"Oh I had pretty good collateral at the time. You."

At Michael's frown, he explained. "Rollie had gambling debts already due before he spent time in jail up the way. While he was in lockup, word got out that he had a good source with deep pockets that would help finance some business buys. I was interested. To make a long story short, not only did he promise to deliver your money, he promised to deliver you."

"That's bull," Michael challenged. "I have all the money I'll ever need. Why the hell would you believe I wanted to get involved in stuff with you when I can rake money in legally?"

"Yeah, I thought about that, and figured your little weasel friend was lying; but I had you checked out and learned you'd give money, and lots of it, to Rollie. Hell, you been doing that since you hit pay dirt with your first football contract. I guess childhood ties run deep. Unfortunately for me, it looks like you're just beginning to wake up to your buddy's ways and his well is about to turn dry. So, here we are."

"Now you know Rollie lied," Michael said, his voice cold. "I have no deal with you."

"When I came out to collect the other week, he was having a little party here, so I had a chance to get the lay of the land, so to speak, and I left him in one piece because I could see you could afford it, just like he promised."

"What are you trying to say?" Michael's nostrils flared in anger.

"I met your housekeeper and her husband, a nice little live-in couple. Their only daughter, Ruby, is still in college. And your kids." He chuckled nastily. "Typical kids with messy rooms."

Fury almost choked Michael as he lunged at the man. "You bastard, you're threatening my family."

Charlie Madden was sufficiently far enough away that the lunge only glanced him.

"Men who do that don't usually live to tell the tale, Mr. Hennessey. Consider this your lucky day. You'd better think carefully on what you do; I checked out your lady with the art gallery, too. Rollie told me he thought she was loaded."

Michael was a swirl of wrong emotions as he tried to tamp back the baser ones that told him to strangle this evil man. He couldn't believe this was happening, and looked toward the window where he could see Carolyn and the children walking through the side gardens.

"What's to keep me from going to the police?" Michael said, bridled anger in his voice as he turned back to Charlie.

"Publicity, the fact that you'll never know when the danger to your family has passed, but mostly, the nuisance value of all this to you. Two hundred thousand is nothing to you."

"You said a hundred and fifty."

He fluttered his hand. "The price went up for my nuisance value."

"So, you're blackmailing me; it gives you the chance to do what Rollie couldn't do—come back to the till again and again." He turned away. "I won't pay off scum like you. I can protect my family and loved ones."

"Just like Rollie will protect his little girl and wife, too. What's her name? Glenda?" When Michael whirled around at his words, Charlie let out a hollow, low chuckle. "Of course, if you don't pay, he's the first one you'll find in a ditch sliced to ribbons." He stuck his hand in his coat pocket as he talked. "Let's hope his wife and daughter aren't around when he gets picked up."

Michael took a threatening step at him and pointed to the door, his voice loud. "You've left your message, now get the hell out of here."

"Three days. Deliver the money to this address." He handed a slip of paper to Michael as he stepped backward. When it wasn't taken, Charlie let it flutter to the floor before he tipped his head in parting. "If I don't see you in three days, the price goes up and you'll get a chance to start weighing your consequences." He turned and left the room.

Michael wiped the back of his hand across his mouth as he tried to take in all the man had said. The only other time he could remember dread of this magnitude seeping into his soul was upon learning of his mother's death. That news had been like icy fingers closed around his heart, crushing it. And that was close to what he felt now. His loved ones, all of them, were in danger. All because he had allowed a relationship to continue on way past its expected life.

He slammed his fist into the chair just as Carolyn came back in through the French doors. Michael looked up.

"Where are the kids?"

"They're still outside. I came in to—"

"Get them back inside," he ordered, and walked to the door and called them.

"Michael," Carolyn looked concerned. "What's going on? Do you know that man?"

He nodded. "Yeah, Rollie introduced us a while back."

"Oh," Carolyn said, "because I saw him at your house that week you were out of town."

Michael only nodded, remembering Charlie's words.

"And the strangest thing," Carolyn continued. "I was leaving the gallery one day, and as I got into an elevator, I could have sworn it was him on there with me."

Michael looked at her. "I want you to stay away from him, and if you ever see him again, either here or at the gallery, you let me know. Is that clear?"

"Michael—"

"Is that clear?" he asked.

"Yes, of course."

The kids were coming in through the door. "Are we still going to the park this afternoon?" Adam complained. "It's getting late."

"I've got to run an errand," Michael said, his thoughts both scattered and concentrated. "Carolyn, can you stay with the kids until I return?"

"Sure, Michael." She kept her voice low. "But what is going on with you?"

"I just need to check on some things, that's all." He tried to smile and bent his head to give her a kiss. "Thanks for staying a while longer." He straightened back up and watched as his children began to collect their things from the floor. "Adam, Halina, listen up. I'll be right back. Carolyn is going to hang around until I do. Best behavior, right?"

"Right," they chimed together.

Michael took off for the garage, and in no time, he had turned the convertible he'd chosen away from the house, and was driving it off toward downtown.

He chose the first downtown exit, and before long, he saw the sign for the Marriott Inn. A few days after their last conversation, Michael had called to see if Rollie had checked in, declining to speak with him, but simply making sure that he was all right. It seems old habits were hard to break.

Michael jumped from the car and went inside, where he soon found himself in front of Room 138. He knocked on the door and identified himself.

He heard the lock turn before the door slid the length of the security chain and positive identification was made.

And then the chain was quickly unfastened, and the door thrown open.

Rollie smiled. "Mi—"

Michael threw a hard punch at his old friend and it sent the unsuspecting man across the room, where he slammed into the opposite wall, knocking over the bedside lamp, before he slowly slumped to the floor.

"Michael," Rollie rolled over onto his stomach before he drew his legs up enough to crawl on all fours to the bed, where he pulled himself up. "Damn, man, why you want to do that?"

Michael shook his fist out before he rubbed his hand across soon-to-be-sore knuckles. But it had been worth the pain. "I figured you'd be laying low, and if you weren't dead already, you'd still be here."

"Oh, hell," Rollie muttered from the bed. "What's happened?"

"You should be damn glad I don't use a gun to settle things, you no good bag of—"

"—Wait a minute, man. What did I do?"

"You sold out our friendship, man, and big time. Your friend Charlie Madden came to my house and threatened my family, not to mention you, Glenda, and your daughter—"

"No, man—" he interrupted.

"For your gambling debts to the tune of two hundred thousand dollars."

Rollie's nose had begun to bleed, and he painfully made his way into the bathroom.

"You wanted to make it into a big game, and you just did," Michael called out to him. "Only, you may not live long enough to enjoy it."

Rollie came back with a wet towel that he dabbed at his nose. "I'm leaving town tonight," he said. "I'll keep out of sight until things die down."

"It's not going away, Rollie. You bit off a lot more than

you could chew this time." He looked at a man who had always seemed to be the life of the party; now it seemed as though the wind in his sails had disappeared.

"Not unless you pay him the money, Michael."

"Yeah, I know, Rollie. And I have to think about what I'm going to do. Either way, we're through." Michael could feel the emotion building in his head, and fought it. "You were like a brother to me, and cutting you loose is going to kill something in me, but I'll survive. I have before, and I will again. But I don't want you to try and see me, call me, nothing." Michael took one last look at his sorry former friend, and turned on his heel to leave.

"Are you gonna pay him?"

Michael didn't turn around, and continued to the stairs. Rollie had finally managed to sicken him. After all the threats that had come their way, he was still only interested in whether the money would be paid. We live and we learn.

Twenty-one

For the next three days, Michael lived a very personal nightmare made worse because he was responsible for it. That was due, in part, because he had not taken active control over the direction his life had flowed in those early years. He had been a willing pawn to others who had no concern, whatsoever, for his ultimate well-being.

So, while Charlie Madden and Rollie Anderson might be directing the show, he, Michael Hennessey, was responsible for signing them on.

And Carolyn. When they had parted on Saturday night, she had known something wasn't right, but he couldn't bring himself to tell her about it. For two days Michael had painfully avoided her calls, until she stopped trying. But, for his own peace of mind, he had called her office every morning to make sure she had arrived okay. He would then call Gerald, her night security guard, to make sure she arrived home safely each evening. He had picked a hell of a time to fall in love; in fact, he was turning out to be the very trash she'd scrupulously avoided, and after all he'd done to try and change her mind about him.

When Michael had made the decision the day before to make the pay-off, his banker had blinked at the strange request for such a large amount of cash; he had blinked even more when Michael teasingly suggested that he was being blackmailed. The banker didn't think it was funny. But he prepared the money for pickup just the same. Later on, Michael thought his banker might not have been so blasé after all; he suspected he had let Jeffrey, his agent, know about the large withdrawal because no sooner had Michael picked up the money, than Jeffrey began to call, calls which, again, Michael was able to circumvent.

And so, he had evaded calls from everyone who might have caused him to waiver or change his mind about the direction he'd set. He was not going to defer responsibility this time around, no matter how high-minded the effort. He would keep his loved ones from harm, and then, after this first test was met, he would consider his remaining options.

All this, and much more, flowed through Michael's mind as he now stood in the library at dusk on what had been a beautiful spring day and looked down at the two hundred thousand dollars neatly packaged and banded in the thin leather briefcase sitting open on top of the desk.

He lifted the glass of bourbon to his lips and allowed the burn which accompanied his swallow to acknowledge he was alive; because somewhere, deep down inside, Michael truly believed a kernel of his soul was crusted and dead, never to be revived. He set the tumbler down and looked at his watch. It was time.

Using the key from a ring in his pocket, Michael unlocked the bottom desk drawer, where he kept a cache of cash for emergencies. Underneath the stacks of banded bills, within a separate case, lay a small hand gun, the gray waffle-designed handle small and compact for self-protection. He pushed the gun into his coat pocket, and then relocked the drawer. These were crazy times.

He now closed the briefcase, locked it, and hefting the weight in his hand, left the library and the sanity of his house to go to a place which housed the insanity that was Charlie Madden's world.

* * *

Carolyn curled up on the window seat and looked down on the street as she talked on the phone with Stephanie. "I'm utterly confused about whether he cares. How do I explain I'm there for him if he's avoiding my calls?"

"He's avoiding you, too?"

"Well, I think so. Though the receptionist at the office told me someone calls each morning to see if I'm in. The caller never leaves a message, just an innocuous excuse for asking about me. And something else. Gerald, the downstairs guard, told me that Michael has been checking on me at night, but he doesn't want Gerald to tell me."

"Carolyn, I don't think that sounds like he doesn't care. In fact, it sounds like he cares very much. Give him time to deal with whatever is going on. He's obviously not ready to involve you, so don't second-guess his decision. He'll talk when he's ready."

"And then I can chew his head off if I think he should have shared it sooner."

"Right." Stephanie laughed. "Now you're sounding like a woman who's got it together."

"You know, he started acting odd the rest of the day after this man came to the house on Saturday." She nibbled her lip. "I'll bet all of this has to do with that man."

"Whatever it is, I don't think you should force it with Michael."

"But I want to be there for him, Steph; and I want to see him so badly that it actually hurts."

"Oh, you're in love, honey."

At Stephanie's diagnosis, Carolyn's breath caught in her throat. In love? She'd only known Michael for two months. But she'd also spent virtually every weekend with him. She groaned as she realized her sister was right.

"I knew there was a reason why I avoided this," Carolyn said. "I'm beginning to think that the workaholic life is much more fulfilling."

Stephanie's light chuckle came through the phone. "In the short run, maybe; but in the long run, love wins out every time."

Carolyn lay her head against the windowpane. "You sound like Davina. She thinks a few small frustrations are worth a good man."

"That's because in time, your man's going to have to deal with yours, too."

"I guess it would be a little vindictive to say I'm going to make sure Michael suffers for what I'm going through now."

"Oh, you don't mean that, and mark my words, honey. If he were to show up tonight, you two would be simpatico, and in a hurry to make up. That's what lovers do."

Lovers . . . she wished. Carolyn squeezed her eyes tight and tried to block him from her mind. But the vision stuck in her head wouldn't go away.

"Tell you what, Carolyn. Rather than worry over this, take a hot shower, go to bed early, and get some rest. I'll make a bet with you that by the end of the week, you'll have a different take on this. It's amazing how things can change if we let events take their course."

Carolyn promised her big sister she would. After they exchanged goodbyes, she sat in the window a while longer before she did as she had promised. She'd shower, call it a night and see how the rest of the week played out.

The deserted street was dark up ahead, and Michael pulled onto the side of the road, as he had been instructed, and flashed his headlights twice. He didn't wait long in his dark, quiet car before he saw another car slowly approach him from behind, and then pull alongside. The tinted passenger window slid down and a man Michael didn't recognize spoke.

"Follow us into the warehouse."

Michael started his car and pulled out behind them. Soon, he saw a dark building, and was waved ahead to enter the now-open door. When he reached the door, the lights came up and he drove inside and stopped behind another vehicle. A heavy metal overhead door dropped solidly behind him, trapping him and the car inside what looked to be an old warehouse. The lead door ahead opened and the car ahead of him was pulling out.

Well, I'll be damned. This looks like some sort of drive-through payoff drop point. Michael shook his head, some of the evening's stress relieved by this highly ridiculous scenario.

A knock at his window indicated he was to get out for a search. Michael stood from the car, and upon being frisked, one of the men secured Michael's gun, putting it into his own pocket.

Michael drew the briefcase from the backseat and followed the two men to an office along the wall. The inside of the warehouse was much cooler than the fresh air outside, and the few people he did see wore coats for the extra chill. He was ushered into the office and saw Charlie Madden sitting on the other side of the desk.

"I tell you, you were pretty convincing when I was out at your place," Maddden chuckled. "I didn't think you were gonna come. Have a seat."

Michael chewed on the inside of his jaw and worked to maintain his patience as he placed the briefcase on the table, but he didn't sit.

"He had a gun." One of the men who frisked Michael laid the gun on the table near the briefcase.

"That's nothing new for us around here," Charlie chuckled at Michael. "If everything's in order, you can have it back. So, can I count my money?"

Michael produced the key and unlocked the briefcase. Charlie opened it. After inspecting the bundles and doing some quick math, he announced the transaction was complete.

"You know, Mr. Hennessey, I don't know if Rollie understands how good a friend you are. He owes you his life, and you ought to tell him."

Michael held his hand out for his gun. At a nod from Charlie, one of the men placed it in Michael's hand. Michael, in turn, put it back into his pocket.

"Just so there's no misunderstanding," Michael said, "don't think this is the first of more payments. There will be no more—and under no circumstances." He turned on his heels and left the office.

Shortly thereafter, he was given the signal to pull ahead and out of the warehouse. As he left, he could see another car taking his place and awaiting its turn.

Michael didn't know how long he drove aimlessly around that evening; he needed to find cleansing for what had transpired, but a fast drive on a dark highway wasn't it. He continued to drive and search. And then, he found himself parked outside of Carolyn's loft.

Carolyn heard the doorbell and sleepily sat up in bed, wondering if it were her imagination. When the second doorbell sounded, followed by a knock, she crawled across the big bed and headed for the front door. She must have slept through Gerald's intercom call, she decided. What time was it, anyway.

She reached the door and, out of habit, peeked through the security fisheye. Michael. Carolyn's heart raced. Why was he here in the middle of the night? Something dreadful must have happened. She fumbled with the lock before she could throw open the door.

"Michael?" When she saw him, her immediate emotion

was relief. He stood there with one arm braced against the door opening, the other holding his coat. She didn't think he had ever looked better as his gaze slid from her face and downward to her unbound breasts.

She backed out of the doorway and he came through, his stride strong and his purpose clear. As he pushed the door closed with one arm, tossing the coat to a chair, he pulled Carolyn roughly, almost violently, to him, and pressed his lips to hers, slanting against her open mouth, again and again, in reckless abandon. It was a punishing kiss that hungrily devoured her soft mouth

"Michael?" Carolyn managed to pull away, shocked at her own eager response to passion she knew was out of control.

"Don't ask me to explain anything, Carolyn." The words were brusquely spoken against her parted lips. "I only know that I need to make love to you." He recaptured her lips greedily. "Right now."

He swept Carolyn, weightless, into his arms and carried her to the bedroom.

She broke from the kiss, and studied his lean, dark face. "I'm glad you found me tonight."

Michael eased her from his arms and onto the bed, where he eagerly followed. They feverishly stripped each other of clothing in their lusty rush to make contact with skin.

Naked for each other's pleasure, they became a mass of tangled limbs and mouths and tongues as Michael proceeded to devour Carolyn from her head to her feet while she, in turn, surrendered completely to his masterful seduction. And when she finally welcomed him into her, it was a raw act of possession that culminated in her cry of release. Only then did the tempo that had bound their bodies finally slow down.

Having found an exquisite harmony in their fierce passion, Michael and Carolyn were lulled into a peaceful sleep, exhausted and sated in each other's arms.

Twenty-two

Carolyn exhaled a long sigh of contentment, followed by a soft moan as she slowly awakened to the heady sensation of Michael's lips skimming along her neck.

It was still early morning and they lay in a lover's posture in the middle of the bed, her back intimately bound to his front as his hand continued to hold erotic reign over her senses.

"I don't know what's come over me, Michael." She sighed again as his hand slid across her belly. "I'm actually considering not going into the office this morning." She closed her eyes as she enjoyed the smooth coolness of his fingers as they now stroked their way along her side.

"Are you okay about last night?" he asked, and kissed her neck. "I came on a little strong."

"A little?" Carolyn teased him as she stroked his leg that was thrown possessively over hers.

He squeezed her. "You didn't seem to mind once we started," he taunted right back.

"At first, I was worried about you. You've been—I guess the word is preoccupied—these past few days."

Michael changed positions in the bed. He pulled up and sat against the pillows at the headboard, and then drew Carolyn close so that her head lay on his chest.

"I needed to be alone for a few days to take care of a problem."

She tensed against him. "What kind of problem, Michael? I could have helped."

"No, no," He smoothed his hand across her back. "This was Rollie's mess, and it really had to be handled by me. I didn't tell you about it because . . . well, you shouldn't have to deal with my old baggage; and I didn't want you involved in any way."

"It had something to do with that man who came to the house, didn't it?" When Michael didn't answer immediately, Carolyn lifted her head to glance at him. "Is he a friend of yours?"

"No." He chuckled. "Listen, don't worry about it. Rollie won't be bothering us anymore, okay?"

Carolyn raised up from his chest and gazed hard into his eyes. "If you won't tell me what happened, Michael, then you have to tell me if it had anything to do with drugs or women or I don't know, something from your past?"

"It wasn't about a woman. I think my last long-term girlfriend before I met you was before that Super Bowl when we first met."

"All right," she said with a grin.

"And it wasn't about drugs, Carolyn. I told you that before. I've always stayed away from them. Always."

Carolyn frowned at his intensity, and she asked the question that seemed right for now. "How did your sister die, Michael?"

He ran his hand over Carolyn's shoulder. "A drug overdose."

It embarrassed her that she had asked and she looked away.

"Don't," Michael said, and smiled as he tilted her chin back to him. "You shouldn't have had to ask. I should have told you, but I forget that there's a lot about me you don't know. She had been in and out of rehabs while my mother was alive and Adam was small. I was off playing football during the season, and just 'playing' off season. So, when my mom died, everything fell apart." He chuckled. "We were definitely not the American dream."

"Not many families are."

"We had money, though, and I gave Vivian, my sister, all the money she wanted, thinking that was the way to make her better. It didn't. She had another baby, Halina; same father as Adam's, the same deadbeat."

"Where is he?"

"Dead." Michael's tone was flat with no emotion.

Carolyn cringed at the tragedy the children had lived through.

"I was around twenty-five at the time, hitting a stride in the league, and wasn't paying any attention to her life— my mom had been the one who did that; but I gave her money. I had more money than I could ever spend, I figured, and I gave everybody money. But I wouldn't touch drugs because I was scared I would become the thing my sister had become." He looked at Carolyn.

"A few months after the Super Bowl, I was out partying and got one of those next-of-kin phone calls. Vivian had been found dead at a party, with her usual suspect friends. An overdose. Luckily, the children were with a babysitter."

Carolyn stroked his face and saw that his eyes were cloudy with the memory.

"They were also lucky that they had you."

"When my mother died, it was a shock, but my sister's death was like this wake-up call. The authorities told me that even though I was the only immediate family, I didn't have to be Adam and Halina's guardian. They realized I was young and didn't have a clue. But those kids clung to me, Carolyn. I mean, they were scared, confused, and I was the only person they knew as family."

"Oh, Michael, my heart is breaking for them."

"I love Adam and Halina like they were my own. And they will be, legally, and real soon."

"How could I have been so wrong about you? You did change."

"What about my impression of you?" he laughed. "I thought you were a tight—"

She hit him before he could finish. "Don't you even say that," she warned as she sat back. "But please, don't shut yourself off from me the way you did this week."

"I'm sorry. I thought I was doing the right thing by keeping you out of it."

"I'm not so naïve to think that we come to each other free of our pasts. But if we're going to have a future, we have to deal in the present."

It was then that she saw he made no attempt to hide the fact that he was staring at her bared breasts. "Michael, you're not listening, are you?"

He chuckled out loud. "There's nothing like making love to a beautiful, smart woman." He leaned forward and kissed the dusky peaks of her nipples.

Carolyn closed her eyes. "I thought we ran out of protection," she said.

"No way; I made sure we'd have extras." He raised his head. "And this time, you get to be in control."

Carolyn moved so that she now fitted astride his waist. "Mmm . . . I like this seat," she said as Michael's hands roamed. "With so much to choose from, let's see, where do I start?" A devilish twinkle lit her eyes as she leaned forward and kissed his chest.

And as Michael's head fell back to the pillows, Carolyn didn't think there was any chance she'd be getting to the office this morning after all.

If the beginning of that week had been extraordinarily trying for Michael, the latter half had been the antithesis.

Spending a warm morning-after in bed making love with Carolyn could only have been a plus; he had returned home in the afternoon to find everything in order and nothing any the worse for wear after having extricated Charlie Madden and Rollie from their lives. It was finished, and Michael was glad to put that final stamp on it.

Discovering there was much more privacy to be had at Carolyn's house, Michael spent the next two nights with her, slipping out early in the morning, though, so he wouldn't miss his breakfast opportunities with the children. He and Carolyn had agreed to spend the weekend doing some things the children enjoyed. And the time together seemed to have a great effect on them, as well.

With more than a week having passed now, Michael's main problem seemed to be preparing for the press conference at which the Wildcats would announce that he was joining the team. Jeffrey called to say it was all but a done deal at this point.

He sat in the kitchen at the breakfast table. The kids had already gone to school with Mr. Pitts, so when the chimes from the doorbell rang out, he figured Mrs. Pitts would get it, and returned to his reading.

She returned quite quickly, though, with her eyes stretched a bit wide.

"There're two federal men in the living room, Michael," she whispered conspiratorially, "and they want to see you."

Michael left the paper there and went out to see what was going on.

The two men were dressed in dark blue suits and identified themselves to him as federal agents, flashing shields as proof.

Michael glanced from the badges to the men. "So, what is this all about?" he asked.

"Mr. Hennessey," the first agent said, "we'd like to ask you a few questions, that's all. At a later time, if necessary, we may want you to come to our office if we have more questions or need further clarification on the answers you've already given."

Michael swallowed, and his mind went through a ton of events, dates, people, and places that these men could be interested in, but it kept hopping back to the one he'd hoped to forget forever.

"Ah, sure. Have a seat, please."

Before they sat down, the second agent stepped forward and read Michael his noncustodial rights, outlined the procedure they would follow, and then seemed to turn the show back over to the first agent. They all sat down in the living room.

The first agent began the questions. "Are you acquainted with a man named Roland Anderson?"

Michael looked from one agent to the other. "Yes," Michael replied. "I know Rollie . . . uh, Roland Anderson."

"You seem to be familiar with his alias, Rollie. Could you describe your relationship with him, please?"

"Sure, he's . . . well—" Suddenly, the question didn't seem so simple to Michael. "I grew up with him. He was a childhood friend."

"Go on."

"That's it. His friends know him as Rollie, so I guess he's what you call a friend." Michael could see that they were taking notes. "Is Rollie in some kind of trouble?"

"When was the last time you saw Mr. Anderson?"

Careful. Michael took in a deep breath and scratched his head. "I believe it was maybe a couple of weekends ago."

"Do you remember the circumstance?" The second agent now spoke up.

Be very careful. "He came by to see me, said he was leaving town in a few days. I had a dinner guest, so he didn't stay long."

"Are you acquainted with a man by the name of Charles Madden, Sr.?"

Michael frowned. "Are you going to tell me what this is about?" When neither man said anything, each patiently waiting for his answer, Michael gave in. "Yes; he was introduced to me by Rollie.

"Describe your relationship with Mr. Madden, please."

"There is no relationship. When I met him, I was told he was a fan, and that was it."

"And that was when you last saw him, at the time you were introduced?"

Michael nodded grimly, "That's right."

"And where did this introduction take place?"

"Why is that important?"

"Please, Mr. Hennessey," the first agent said. "Just answer the questions."

"We were introduced at a sports bar downtown, JT's Sports Bar and Restaurant."

"Is there anything else you'd like to change or add to your statements, Mr. Hennessey?"

"Ah, no, nothing I can think of."

"We may want to question you again. So, in the meantime, you may want to get in touch with a lawyer."

Michael drew in an unbelieving breath. "A lawyer? Am I in some kind of trouble?"

"It's just precautionary advice."

As the men stood up, Michael could say nothing, but watched them quietly exit the house through the door.

Alone, he paced from one end of the room to the other, recalling and then analyzing the responses he'd made to their questions. He had done nothing wrong, he'd simply not told them the whole truth, right? Michael closed his eyes tight, and what popped into his mind was his mother's comment that the color of truth was not gray.

Michael thought he should call Jeffrey. Right now.

Twenty-three

Carolyn was eating a late lunch in her office and browsing through the paper when she came across a news article in the local section.

"Oh, my goodness," she said. "That's him." It was the story of a local businessman who had been arrested for a host of racketcering charges, all federal crimes. But what caught her attention was the picture that accompanied the story. It was clearly the man who had come to both Michael's house and the gallery, a man Michael had warned her to stay clear of. The paper named him as Charlie Madden.

The article went on to say that other indictments were expected to be handed down based on a widespread investigation that had started over a year ago. Numerous subpoenas were also expected to be issued in order to enable the Grand Jury to sort through the evidence.

She couldn't remember if Michael had ever said what the man wanted when he came over. She closed the newspaper and called Michael.

When he answered she spoke quickly. "Michael, remember the man who came out to the house? Well, I saw something about him in today's paper."

"What did it say?" he asked.

"There's a picture of him, with his name, and it says

that he's been the subject of an investigation for over a year by the U.S. Attorney. He's been arrested for a list of Federal offenses."

When silence greeted her from the other end, she asked, "Did you know anything about this?"

He cleared his throat. "No. I'll read it later. Do you think you can come over here tonight?"

"Yes, if you'd like me to," she said, instinctively picking up on his mood. "Is something wrong?"

"I'll tell you about it when you get here."

Michael paced across the library with the phone. He was having a three-way conversation with Jeffrey, his agent, and a well-known local attorney, Donald Garland, whom Jeffrey had secured to act as Michael's legal representation if the need arose.

"Can we safely start out and agree that you are absolutely not involved in anything that is illegal?" Donald asked.

"Jeffrey knows me," Michael said, a little incensed at the necessary question. "Tell him I'm not involved in anything illegal, Jeffrey."

"Calm down, Michael," Jeffrey said. "These are things that have to be asked, and you know it."

"He's right, Michael," Donald added, "because I also know our federal government. It starts out with a few questions, and before you know it, they want to target you for something they've uncovered on one of their fishing expeditions. We know you've been no choirboy in your past; few of us are. But the key, Michael, is not to lie to them; don't give them an excuse to examine you any more than they already have."

Michael closed his eyes to the nightmare. "So, what's the next thing to expect from the feds at this point?" he asked Donald.

"Well, our problem is we don't know what they want

from you, and they won't show their hand, either. The news story would indicate they want information to use against this Madden character but from what you're saying, your interaction with the guy has been circumspect. So I'd say you have nothing to worry about."

"All right, then," Jeffrey chimed in. "What's a worst case scenario here?"

"Well, they could ask you, Michael, to come in for questioning because something in your answers didn't fit their information and evidence."

"Is that when you show up?"

"Yes, and if you clear up the problems, they could say fine, thanks for your help. But it's more likely that the information you give may be helpful with a case they're building against someone else, and you could be subpoenaed to testify before a grand jury or a live case on what you know."

"You're probably going to have to deal with the media, Michael, so get used to it if this goes any farther," Jeffrey warned. "You know this sort of stuff sells papers; celebrities and legal problems are grist for the mill. Depending on how you weigh in with public opinion, they'll use everything out there against you."

Michael sighed. "So, all I have to worry about is being maligned by the media no matter which way this goes, and whether the Feds will call me to testify in some case of theirs."

"Well, there is one more thing." Donald cleared his throat. "There's the off-chance that your testimony could contain something which might incriminate you." He paused a second. "And in that case, a grand jury could indict you."

It was late, the children had been put to bed, and Carolyn and Michael were stretched out spoon fashion on the long sofa in the library. Soft music flowed through the softly lit room.

After Carolyn had arrived earlier, Michael had closed them up in the library and told her about the visit from the agents and his subsequent discussion with Jeffrey and his Atlanta attorney, Donald Garland. He also insisted that nothing would come of the questioning by the agents; but he wanted her to be aware of what was going on.

"Michael," Carolyn asked, "how did they know to ask you about this man, anyway?"

"The only way I can figure is it had to be through Rollie. I met the guy at the sports bar the same night I ran into you, and it was Rollie who introduced us."

"Where is Rollie? Is he in trouble?"

"I don't know, and you know what, I don't care."

Carolyn turned on the sofa and looked at Michael's face. "You're not kidding, are you?" she asked, before she settled back down next to him. "What about reporters? Have any of them come around?"

"Jeffrey told me not to talk with anybody until my lawyer and I have a meeting. So I won't. But I didn't think about someone just showing up at the door, bothering the Pittses or disturbing the children."

"You've done nothing wrong, Michael, so you have to trust the system to see that. Maybe it'll all just blow over." She huddled under his arm. "You never did tell me why that man came to the house in the first place."

"Oh." His brow furrowed as he remembered. "It had to do with Rollie, that's all."

Michael didn't want her to feel the weight of these events, so he still chose not to tell her everything. It wouldn't be fair to her. If only it was all over; but it would be, soon. Michael squeezed his arms around Carolyn again, as if the act would draw her into him.

He pulled in a deep sigh. He wasn't worried, because when all was said and done, he'd done nothing wrong.

Surely the agents would see that in his answers to the questions and drop this. They had to see it, because he couldn't reveal that he'd given Madden money. There was no proof that Madden threatened his family, and Madden had nothing to lose by keeping quiet. Michael pulled Carolyn close again. It would all work out fine, just fine. Until the other shoe dropped.

Bruce Witherspoon scratched his head as he compared Michael's answers to the facts and the agent's questions.

"So, why is he lying?" the first agent asked. "Surely not to protect Madden."

Bruce shrugged. "Looks like he's telling us half-truths; he doesn't know that we already know the answers."

"Is he protecting his friend, Rollie?"

"Who seems to have disappeared from the Marriott Inn." Bruce made the comment as he searched for a sheet of paper in the file. He found it. "Nah, I don't think that's it."

"What about his culpability?" the Agent suggested.

"Only if he does something stupid, like lie under oath."

"So, what's next?" the Agent wanted to know.

"Go ahead, schedule a meeting in the next ten days. Leak a little info to our media sources, and let Mr. Hennessey sweat over the news stories for a few days. Maybe it'll work to loosen his lips up for us."

"You want him as a witness that bad, even though our circumstantial evidence makes it looks like he's dirty himself?"

"I want to throw everything I can on that low-life scum Charlie Madden. We'll have to gauge the hit Mr. Hennessey will take on cross-examination after he comes clean with us."

* * *

Over the next two weeks there was a scattering of news stories regarding tips and possible secret witnesses expected to testify in the trial of local businessman Charlie Madden, whose indictment had stemmed from another notorious local lawyer's case for money laundering. The grand jury remained impaneled to hear new testimony for the U.S. Attorney's wide-reaching case.

Michael tried to limit the newscasts so that Adam would not pick up on his interest; however, it was hard to sanitize an unexpected news story when you had no idea when it would present itself. So it was almost a relief when Michael got the word that the assistant U.S. attorney wanted to ask him questions in his downtown office. At least he'd find out where he stood.

"I want to go with you," Carolyn said the minute Michael told her about it.

"Absolutely not." Michael was firm. "Once I'm down there, that's it for me keeping this under wraps. I won't have the media camped out trying to get info out of you or your family." He pulled her into his arms. "Just be around when I leave their offices. That's all I need."

Michael and his attorney arrived at Bruce Witherspoon's office in the Federal Building early on the day of their meeting. They were escorted into a conference room by two stern-faced agents.

At this, their first encounter, Michael was surprised that the assistant U.S. attorney wasn't too much older than his own thirty years, and he was African-American, too. They shook hands.

"Mr. Hennessey, we need to revisit some questions you were asked a few weeks ago."

Michael braced himself for the questions, not quite sure what they were getting at, and provided the same answers as before.

"And that's your testimony, Mr. Hennessey?"

Michael looked back at Donald before he turned to the assistant U.S. attorney. "Yes."

"Then, we've got a problem," he said. "Maybe you should be arrested on obstruction charges right here on the spot—"

"Mr. Witherspoon," Donald stood from his chair in protest.

Witherspoon held up his hand. "Unless you want to back up that truck and give us another version."

"What do you mean?" Donald asked.

"We need information about Mr. Madden, his operation, and we think Mr. Hennessey can provide it."

"He's told you all he knows," Donald said.

"Not quite." Witherspoon looked at Michael. "We know that Madden has been to your house on at least two occasions, and you saw the man again three weeks after you met him at that sports bar.

"We also know that you visited your friend Rollie Anderson on the same day that Madden paid you a visit. Only you told us you hadn't seen him since the week before. So, you tell us, what's going on?"

"How—how do you know all that?" Michael looked at Witherspoon

"Consider yourself a part of our collection of pictures. If you've been anywhere in the vicinity of Mr. Madden during the last year, you're in there. That's why we want to talk with Mr. Anderson, too. Only we can't find him. He's disappeared."

Michael thought about the money, and now wondered if they were aware of that, too.

"Michael," Donald said from next to him. "Are we still agreed that you did nothing illegal?"

Michael looked at him. "I didn't break the law."

Donald looked at Witherspoon. "Give us ten minutes, please, and Michael will talk with you again."

When Witherspoon and the two agents left, Michael

looked Donald straight in the eye. "Madden threatened my family." He then told Donald the entire story.

Afterward, Donald sighed. "If you had proof, it would be great stuff for the U.S. attorney to use in his case. As it stands, I suspect they have pictures of you turning over quite a bit of cash, and it's on the record that you lied." He heaved another sigh. "Let's talk with them and see what happens."

When Witherspoon and the others returned, Michael told his story a second time, without pause, and this time the dates and occasions coincided with their record of events.

Witherspoon stood up. "Can I speak with you alone for a minute?" he asked Michael.

"Absolutely not," Donald said.

"We're not arresting Mr. Hennessey," Witherspoon said. "I just want to say some things off the record, and he can too. That's all."

"It's okay, Donald. I'll talk with him," Michael said.

When the others filed out, Witherspoon sat on the edge of the table, his arms folded, and looked at Michael.

"So, tell me, why should we believe anything you've said?"

"Simple. Because it's the truth."

"This time." He laughed. "You rich, spoiled sports celebrities are becoming a dime a dozen. Why should I believe you? I've got the money, the briefcase, and your picture handing it over to a known drug-dealing, pimping extortionist."

"Because I have everything to lose." Michael jumped angrily from the chair, knocking it over. "If this isn't cleared up soon, I stand to lose everything, and big time. I'm in the process of adopting my kids, I'm in the middle of negotiating a new long-term contract, and I've just got into a new relationship. Hell, I've got plenty to lose."

Witherspoon chuckled as he unfolded his arms and

stood up. "That's what I wanted to hear. I want some emotion. We agree, we didn't know what to think of you falling into our lap, but your version of events fits with what we know of Madden and how he operates. Unfortunately for you, the defense is probably going to tear you apart and make it look like you were just another cocky football player wanting to buy his own pipeline to his toot."

"Yeah, and they can get to the back of that line, too."

"All right, we'll go back in with your attorney, and we'll let him know that you're going to be subpoenaed as our witness, and you may testify before the grand jury if your information leads us somewhere else." With those final words, he shook Michael's hand. "Cheer up. It could have gone a lot worse, you know. I could have decided not to believe you."

Michael left the Federal Building and called Carolyn, asking her to meet him at his house.

Within the hour, they faced each other again in the library, and once again, he had to admit to a lie as he explained what had happened that night almost a month ago before he had come to her house. But this time it was hard to sell a broken promise.

When Michael saw the look in Carolyn's eyes upon being told the truth, his heart ached and he walked to the window.

"Carolyn," he began. "The man threatened my family, he threatened you, and I had no choice but to pay the money in the short term, until I could figure out what to do later."

"Why didn't you tell me everything? How many times did I ask you for the truth, and you supposedly gave it to me?"

"I was trying to fix things, hoping it would all go away.

I was afraid of losing you to the truth." Michael turned back to Carolyn. "And so, I kept the details to myself. I kept it from you, Jeffrey, my lawyer, the U.S. attorney, everyone. And I just paid the money."

"How could you?"

"I still didn't do anything illegal, Carolyn."

"You didn't? Tell me, did you or did you not give two hundred thousand dollars to that God-awful drug dealer who came to this very house?"

Michael clamped his teeth together, cooled by the anger he saw in Carolyn's beautiful eyes. "Yeah, I did do that."

"Then that should make it very clear to your children, to me, to everyone, that you did nothing wrong each time you have to explain it." She turned on her heel and left Michael standing at the window.

"Carolyn," Michael called to her.

She stopped at the door, but didn't turn around.

"I made a decision today to let things fall where they might. You need to make one, too, I guess. Either believe that, though misguided, I thought I was protecting my family by paying off a thug; or believe I have no values after all, and I was doing something far worse than I've ever done by dealing with that snake.

"Take your pick," Michael warned, "but don't straddle the fence so I have to guess which side you're on each time I look in your eyes." He returned to gaze out the window. Soon, he heard the library door close.

Michael didn't hear from Carolyn for the remainder of the weekend. And early in the next week, as expected, he was subpoenaed. What he didn't expect was Adam's reaction when he brought together Adam, little Halina, and the Pittses, to break the news and tell them what to expect outside of their house.

After the Pittses left with Halina—whose greatest concerns were that she didn't want to live with anybody else and that Carolyn had not been around for a few days—Adam, who had remained quiet and morose the entire time, stayed.

"You're older than your sister," Michael said to him. "Do you understand what I've been saying?"

"Yeah, I think so." He looked at Michael. "Does this mean you won't be adopting us anymore?"

"Of course not. Nothing will stop that." Michael frowned. "Why would you say that?"

"Well, what if they arrest you? What then?"

"That's not going to happen," he said gently. "I told you, I'm testifying for the good guys."

"That's not what they said on the news. I heard them last night. They said you were friends with the bad man and you gave him money, but everybody knows why you give money to a drug dealer."

Michael's heart was breaking as he stooped to get closer to his son. "Adam, you have to believe in our family. The news people don't—"

"You always want to know why I still call you Michael. It's because I'll never have a dad." Tears began to well in his eyes as he stood up. "You're going to go away, too, and leave us, just like everybody else."

"Adam," He watched as his son jumped up from the sofa. "I'll never do that." Adam ran from the room. "Adam—" Michael took off after him.

Twenty-four

"Justin, can I come in?" Carolyn asked as she peeked around her brother's office door. "Nora says you're leaving town tonight."

"Sure, I was expecting you," he said, and got up from his desk to meet her halfway. "I've been listening to the news. It's been kind of rough on you and Michael, huh?"

She nodded. "Worse on the relationship, though," she said. "I haven't seen him for a week. I don't know what to do, Justin." She looked up at her brother. "This whole thing is so tawdry, and I never expected anything like this to happen to someone I'm involved with. I don't know . . . I just don't want this in my life."

"Do you need him in your life, Carolyn?" He tilted his sister's face up so he could look into it. "That's what you have to ask yourself."

Carolyn didn't reply, but let Justin lead her to the chairs, where they sat down.

"You know, Michael called me yesterday."

She looked up. "He did?"

"Yeah. He knew you'd talk with me, and he wanted me to know that this is the last kind of shame he wanted to bring on you; but he only wants you to come to him if you believe in him. I have to respect him on that, and I agree. He even said if you showed me any doubt of your belief in his character, I should talk you into not seeing him again."

Carolyn looked away, still confused by the inability of her heart and her head to come to an agreement.

"He's pretty clear about this. Regardless of the evidence or the current opinion on television, he doesn't want you to come to him if you don't believe in him one hundred percent."

"But he lied to me; so how do I know he's telling the truth about what really happened? What do I believe?"

"What do you want to believe? If you need him in your life, Carolyn, you'll believe in him. Nothing else matters."

The Hardys, with the exception of Justin and Davina, who were out of town, were gathered at the table for dinner on Sunday afternoon. Carolyn sat in her chair, but poked at her plate—the food looked anything but appetizing.

"The papers don't know any more than citizen John Doe, so they're doing the worst kind of reporting. They're speculating too much about Michael's involvement in this," Stephanie said. "Let him testify first."

"Carolyn, Michael and the children didn't want to come over to dinner today?" Mrs. Hardy asked.

Carolyn looked up with lackluster enthusiasm. "Ah, no, he preferred they stay at home." She didn't explain that he didn't want her there, either.

Douglas looked across the table. "You should cheer up, Carolyn. When Michael gets his chance to testify, the news people will change their opinions, just watch."

"I can imagine how he feels, though," Roger, Stephanie's husband, said. "I hear the Wildcats are taking a wait-and-see approach about a contract."

Carolyn couldn't take any more of the comments and

pushed back from the table. "Excuse me, I have to leave."
As Carolyn headed for the salon, she could hear them
discussing her as she left.

"That was horrible dinner conversation for her to hear."

"Don't worry, Mom, we'll go see if she's all right."

"I'm sorry."

Carolyn entered the salon and dropped down on her
favorite couch. Not too long afterwards, Stephanie and
Alli joined her.

"Go ahead, girl," Alli urged her. "Let it out."

"I'm not angry with him anymore. I don't know what
came over me when we argued. I guess I was ticked off
because I had put him on this pedestal after having
thought he was lower than a floorboard, and—"

"And now you're learning he's like all the rest of us . . .
somewhere in between," Stephanie finished.

Carolyn looked up at her sister, her eyes moist from
unspent tears. "Right. But he shouldn't have kept what
he did from me, right, Steph?"

"Everybody handles things differently," her sister replied.

"We share the same values. I think I know that. And
he couldn't have faked his caring for his children or jeop-
ardize that adoption. Both of us want big families. Why,
I was walking around thinking how I wanted to have his
babies."

"And at the rate you two were hitting the sack for a
while there—"

"Alli—" Both sisters threw her warning glances.

"Well, every night I'd call you, he was there, and you
always acted like I was interrupting something."

"You're incorrigible," Carolyn said, "but I love you."
And her tears turned into infectious laughter as all three
of the women hugged.

* * *

It took most of the day for Carolyn to clear her schedule for some time off. She wanted to talk with Michael, and then she wanted to be free for however long it took to clear the air. When she arrived at his house that afternoon, the children had not yet returned home from school. Mrs. Pitts was glad to see her, and told her she would find Michael in the library. That's where she found him.

"Hi," she said as she looked around the door. He sat at the massive desk, looking like a man alone in the world.

When he saw Carolyn, Michael straightened in the chair. "I didn't expect you."

"I know," Carolyn said. "Can I come in?"

He stood. "Yes, please. What's on your mind?"

"I understand you've been subpoenaed, and you're expected to testify toward the end of the month?" She took a few more careful steps into the room.

He nodded. "That's what they tell me."

"Then, good luck. I know the jury will believe you because I believe you, too." She slowly moved across the room until she was at the desk. "I'm with you all the way on this, Michael, and I want to be by your side when you testify."

He had remained stoically behind the desk. Only his eyes gave Carolyn a glimpse of what he was feeling. She could see the longing, it mirrored her own; but she could see the pain, too.

"There'll be news cameras. The eyes at Geary & Geary might be on you."

"I don't care. Maybe it's time that I test the waters to go out on my own."

"You're sure?"

"As sure as my love is for you, Michael."

He wouldn't move. "Don't say it if you don't mean it. Don't say it."

"I love you, Michael Hennessey."

And then, he did move. In one motion, he was out from behind the desk and, gathering Carolyn in his arms, he held her snugly.

"I love you, Carolyn." His voice cracked with emotion. "I always have. I just didn't know it was returned, so I held back, and I'm sorry."

"No, it's all right. What's important is that we're in the same place now." She stepped back from him. "I've missed the children. How are they taking all this?"

He grabbed Carolyn's hand and drew her to the sofa where they both sat. "Actually Halina is the trooper. It's Adam I'm worried about. I never realized how fearful he was that the adoption wouldn't happen. It's the reason he never calls me anything other than my given name."

"That does explain a lot," she said. "They must wonder if I abandoned them, too. I shouldn't have stayed away."

"No, you had to do what was necessary, as you said, to get us both in the same place," Michael said. "We're a family, and we'll heal."

"We were a little fractured for a while. Do you think we could all do something together, maybe this afternoon, even? It's beautiful outside, and I'd like to see the children."

"Piedmont Park. Halina loves the place. I'll have Mrs. Pitts put together a picnic basket, and when the kids get in with Mr. Pitts, we'll all go to the park and celebrate— we'll celebrate our family being whole again."

Michael and Carolyn kissed to seal the deal.

Everyone had been busy since their arrival at Piedmont Park for the picnic. Halina was preparing her cassettes, and Adam was busy sketching everything that caught his eye. The Pitts were also there, and mostly everyone just enjoyed one another's company.

"Last call for food before I start closing it up," Mrs.

Pitts announced. With no offers, she started to pack up the leftovers.

"Can we get a dog, maybe?" Adam asked. He was busy sketching a dog whose owner tossed a Frisbee back and forth.

"If you need one to sketch, we can always get some stuffed ones," Michael joked. He was reclined on a blanket near Carolyn, who had chosen to sit on the cement bench.

"Dogs are a lot of responsibility," Mr. Pitts said, "but if Michael agrees to let you have one, I can help you train it," he offered.

"That'll be great," Adam said.

"In that case, we'll bring this up for discussion later on," Michael said.

"We haven't had a recital in a long time," Halina announced as she loaded her cassette into her player. As Adam groaned, the adults agreed that she could play something for them.

As Halina pressed the play button, her voice, singing "I Believe I Can Fly," floated through the spring air. It seemed to lift the spirits of them all. Smiles stretched on all of their faces. Even Adam stopped his sketching, and turned his ear to the cassette player as Halina's tiny voice, sharp and clear, flowed over them all.

As the last strains of the song were heard, they were all struck silent for the span of a few seconds before they gave her spontaneous applause. Even the passers-by clapped.

"Michael, she does have an incredible little voice," Carolyn said as he got up to go to Halina.

Halina beamed under the attention that she was receiving from everyone. Even Adam had walked over, and was now looking at the player.

"You're in trouble, Halina."

Halina turned on her brother. "I am not."

"You've been taping other people's conversations," he accused and pointed to the player. "Listen."

Carolyn turned and saw that Michael was already listening. He had his hand raised for quiet and words, as clear and sharp as Halina's voice had been, came flowing from the recorder.

They heard Michael and Carolyn comment on who would be visiting unexpectedly, and shortly after that, Michael's curt command that she take the children from the room. It was then that Charlie Madden's nasal baritone was heard and Michael's suggestion that if he didn't leave, he'd call the police.

"That's my conversation with Charlie Madden," Michael shouted to no in particular. "Listen."

Carolyn, like the others, was mesmerized by what she heard, and she and the Pittses, along with Adam, hugged one another in uninhibited joy and anticipation.

Little Halina was not sure what to make of everything, and Michael picked her up in his arms as he allowed the tape to play for another minute before he carefully shut it off.

"Did I do something wrong, Daddy," Halina asked from her perch in his arms.

"Oh no, sweetheart," he said with a wide grin. He looked over her shoulders to Carolyn and the others. "Everything is just right."

Carolyn gleefully shoved her cell phone into his hands. "Here, I think you should be making a call to your lawyer, and then things can be set right with the entire world."

And as he made the call, she snatched up the recorder and held it in her arms as though it were a brick of gold.

It was early June, two weeks to the day after Michael testified successfully, that he received a personal visit from Bruce Witherspoon at the house.

"You've really helped our case, and while it's not over with, I think Madden's going to do time on most of the charges."

"That's good to hear," Michael said as he stood with Bruce in the living room.

"Another thing," he said. "Your friend, Rollie. He surfaced out in L.A."

"Well, I'll be damned," Michael said. "Are you charging him with anything?"

"Stupidity isn't a crime, but he might make a good witness since he may have seen some of Madden's dealings."

Michael shook his head. It was true, Rollie did have nine lives. But it made Michael feel better to know that the man he used to call friend wasn't somewhere dead in a ditch.

"And your little girl. Everyone who listens to that tape thinks she's the bomb. If she's not doing it now, she ought to be getting some professional training."

"Yeah, that's what I'm hearing," Michael said with a grin. "I'm also hearing she wants her tape back. She says it's her best recording."

"You got that right." Bruce reached behind him and pulled something out of his back pocket. It was a white envelope, and he opened it up. "We dubbed her song onto another tape since the original is precious evidence." He handed it to Michael.

"Thanks," Michael said as he turned it over in his hand. She and her brother are on a little trip with my housekeeper's family; but she'll be happy to see this when she gets back."

"Your extorted money, the two hundred thousand—it'll be returned, too; though, as yet I don't know how soon."

"As long as it's in the mail," Michael said.

"Ah, listen," Bruce started. "While I'm here, I just want

to say you really are a hero to a lot of people around here now that the truth is out."

Michael frowned at the man he knew to be tough as nails in court.

"I know, I know, you don't even think I believed you at first," he continued. "Well, let's put it this way, I wanted to believe you because I get so much stuff coming my way that's not in the least credible. It was good to get a touchdown for a change." He patted Michael's shoulder. "Be seeing you," he said, as he turned for the door. "Or, maybe not," he called back over his shoulder.

Michael smiled as he bade him goodbye and closed the door.

"Who was that?" Carolyn asked, as she peeked from behind the library door down the hall.

Michael turned at her voice. God, he loved her, and it seemed to grow by leaps and bounds each day. He quickly strode to her down the hall until he reached the library door where she stood.

"I swear, Carolyn, if we get interrupted one more time—"

"You'll what?" she asked, and stepped from behind the door, her naked form glowing under his watchful eyes.

He smiled as he once again peeled his shirt over his head, unzipped his pants and slipped out of them, now as naked as she was. He closed the library door. Again.

"Never mind," he said, as he came to her. "We just won't answer the damn thing next time it rings. Now, where were we?" He lifted her up and set her down on the edge of the huge desk.

"That's what I wanted to hear," Carolyn said, and leaned into the circle of his arms where she felt safe, protected and, most of all, loved. It was a sensation, an emotion, that awakened her senses to all the possibilities that lay ahead for them and their family.

Epilogue

It was the last week of August, and the first game of the Wildcats' pre-season was about to start in the All-Star Dome. Carolyn and her sisters were in attendance for Michael's big debut as the city's newest and most celebrated player in some time.

But so were the friends who had stood tall next to him during the hellish turmoil he'd faced this past spring before the season had begun: the Pittses, Jeffrey Kingston, and even Bruce Witherspoon, who had been so willing to believe in him. In fact, Michael had secured about fifty tickets that Carolyn had judiciously distributed. And they were all seated in one general area, with Stephanie's two children sitting with Halina and Adam down in front of the adults.

Carolyn saw the green-and-black Wildcats uniforms crowding onto the field, and she anxiously searched for Michael's number. She had not seen him since the day before, and more than likely wouldn't see him again until much later that night, when they would all celebrate his introduction to the Atlanta fans.

She turned to speak with Jeffrey, and only then did she realize that his seat was empty. She looked around, curious as to where he had disappeared to.

"Look," Adam said to Carolyn, and pointed to the home

end of the field. "The team is stretching, but I don't see Dad."

Carolyn's heart warmed every time Adam referred to Michael as his dad. She knew Michael was both proud and relieved that the adoption was now official. He had waited so long for Adam to accept him as his dad, keeping his wish for acceptance a private torment. Adam, too, had waited a long time before he felt he could believe in Michael enough to say it. It had all turned out well for both of them.

"Maybe he's still in the tunnel," Mr. Pitts offered. "They'll step back inside anyway when the announcer gets ready to make the introductions," he explained. The tunnel was the underground walkway that connected the players directly to the field from a whole network of rooms, including the team locker rooms, located under the dome.

More and more people were packing into the domed enclosure now as it neared kick-off time. Alli, Mrs. Pitts, and the children now stood with the crowd, and getting into the spirit of the day, yelled cheers to the rollicking music that helped set the mood.

Alli turned to Carolyn. "Look," she said. "Jeffrey is trying to get your attention."

Carolyn saw him in the aisle of their section, and true to Alli's words, he was motioning for her to come with him.

"I'll be right back," she said to Alli.

"Go on," Alli said, as she bobbed up and down. "I'll tell Adam and Halina."

When Carolyn made it to Jeffrey's side, he caught her hand in his and pulled her with him.

"Where are we going?" she asked.

"We have to hurry. Michael asked me to bring you down to the tunnel. He wants to see you before the game starts."

Her curiosity raised, Carolyn went with him. They

joined up with a stadium events guard who, after a nod to Jeffrey, led them through a side door in the cavernous cement loge and down another flight of stairs until they found themselves in the severely lighted tunnel, with the opening to the field not far away.

A few players walked through, as did trainers and other personnel, all going in and out of doors, or onto the field. The open end of the tunnel led directly onto the deep green artificial turf of the playing field.

The click of Carolyn's heels echoed as she followed Jeffrey to the end of the tunnel where she saw Michael dressed in full football gear, his helmet in his hand. He was talking with the Wildcats' head coach, a friendly man she had met this past summer.

"Oh, there's Michael," she said to Jeffrey. She turned only to realize that Jeffrey had gone. She turned back as Michael stepped away from his coach and called to her.

When she reached him, he drew her to him with one arm and gave her a great kiss before he smiled down at her.

"It's almost time for the game," she said with a smile, and stepped back to study him. "Jeffrey said you needed me down here."

"Yeah. Come on, walk with me." They did, arm in arm until they reached the end of the tunnel. "I wanted you to see how the field looks from this level, with the people and the noise going on," he said. "It's a different feeling down here on game day."

"You love this, don't you?" she asked.

"For a long time, it was the only thing that made me feel alive . . . and one day the kids showed up and gave me a new perspective." He led her from the tunnel and into the dome until they were on the edge of the turf grass.

He looked into her eyes. "And now, you've settled into my life and showed me what being alive really means.

Nothing touches me the way you do, Carolyn, and nothing makes me more complete."

To her genuine surprise, Michael dropped to the grass on one bended knee, right in front of her.

"Michael, what are you doing?" Carolyn looked on in astonishment as he pulled something from under his jersey.

It was an exquisite little square box—a deep blue velvet, with a platinum bow affixed to the top. And that's when Carolyn realized what he was about to do in this very public way. Her eyes stretched wide as Michael drew her hand into his.

"I've loved you for a long time, and we've been through so much together—"

"Oh my goodness, Michael." Carolyn's hand flew up to her mouth.

"I want us to always be together, and propositions have played a big part in our life. So I'm offering you yet another proposition, but this one will be as man and wife."

She gasped as she anticipated his next words.

"Carolyn, will you marry me?"

Her heart sang with love as she shared the elation that spilled from Michael's eyes.

"Yes, yes, I'll marry you, Michael."

He opened the box and she saw the ring, a beautifully shaped diamond that sparkled from its perch with as much pride and joy as she felt. When a loud cheer went up around her, she was overcome by the fact that the entire stadium had witnessed their betrothal and with overwhelming approval.

He slipped the ring from the box and slid it onto her finger before he stood.

A steady roar picked up all around them until it was deafening. Michael smiled down at her and spoke the only words that mattered.

"I love you."

"I love you, Michael."

When he slipped his hands to either side of her face and kissed her hard and long, the crowd's noise became riotous.

"Michael," Carolyn whispered against his mouth, "shouldn't we have talked with Adam and Halina first before we let the entire dome know?"

Michael smiled down at her. "When I told them I wanted to ask you to marry me, it was their idea that I do it here with the whole family present."

And while Carolyn savored this exquisite happiness, and as the team began to surround them with congratulations, she could hear loudspeakers trumpet all around her:

"Ladies and Gentlemen and fans of all ages, you just witnessed it! Her answer was a resounding yes! And if you'll keep your attention on the MonsterTron screens, we will now present to you Mr. Michael Hennessey and his soon-to-be bride, Miss Carolyn Hardy."

ABOUT THE AUTHOR

Shirley Harrison grew up in south Florida, where she always nurtured a passion for writing and art when she wasn't at the beach. After receiving her Bachelor of Science degree, she moved to the metro Atlanta area where she currently resides with her family. She is employed full time in a demanding job in the tax law field. And if that's not enough to keep her busy, Shirley is an accomplished oil painter, gardener, and a regular Peachtree Road Racer.

The birth of Shirley's career as a writer started around 1996, when she decided to combine her love of art and mystery and include it in a romantic setting. The effort resulted in her first romantic suspense novel, PICTURE PERFECT, which debuted in February 1999 to great reviews. Since that debut, Shirley has had three other romantic suspense novels published: UNDER A BLUE MOON, DANGEROUS FORTUNE, and THE PROPOSITION. This most recent story reunites members of the Hardy family who were first introduced in PICTURE PERFECT.

If you would like to contact Shirley with questions or comments, feel free to write her at P.O. Box 373411, Decatur, GA 30037-3411 (self-addressed, stamped envelope is needed for a reply) or send her an E-mail at sdh108@aol.com.